BORDERLAND

ANSON SCOTT

To my grandfather, Paul, for showing me the way

(...and to Blu--I miss our days in the park)

Prologue

I only have twenty minutes to get back before bad things happen to Paul, but it will take thirty minutes to get there.

It's a beautiful day, and from my perch on a big bag of *narco* cash outside an old mineshaft cut high in the side of a steep precipice, I can see three states in two nations. "Big Sky" is an understatement and white billowy clouds building over mountain peaks more than a hundred miles away threaten rain, but not today.

An airliner cuts a stark white trail of ice crystals across the unblemished blue like a scar, and I think about the passengers: a cross section of humanity packed in a metal tube hurtling through space at three-quarters the speed of sound. Business-men—sorry, businesspeople, grandmas, students and trailer-park queens sit together in the seventy-eight degree comfort of chairs thirty-thousand feet above the earth; most, except the white-knuckler in seat 18C, completely unaware that about a soda can's worth of aluminum separate them from a horrific death. Instead of marveling at "breaking the surly bonds of earth," they're listening to their iPods, miffed that they aren't getting free peanuts.

Just a few days ago, I might very well have been their pilot, but a phone call changed all of that. Thanks to my dad, I'm sitting in the desert trying to figure out how to outsmart a man who kills people for a living. I have a plan, but since this is my first day fighting international crime, it may not work.

"Whaddaya think, will it work?" My friend raises his eyebrows and doesn't respond, but I'll take his weakly wagging tail as an endorsement.

I stand and lift the heavy bag, my wounded arm screaming in protest. There's a mile or so of rocks, sand and every spine-bearing species of plant you can imagine between the bad guy and me, but at least it's downhill.

"Ready, boy?" My exhausted dog struggles to his feet.

Nineteen minutes now and I'm not a foot closer.

Better get going.

Chapter 1

Officer Ignacio Reyes sat in the Juarez briefing room and daydreamed about his wife, hundreds of kilometers away in Cancun. When he had joined the *Policia Federal* he had known there would be sacrifices, but had never realized what his desire to make a difference would cost him in the end.

After President Felipe Calderon declared war on Mexico's drug cartels, Reyes saw it as his call to arms and had resigned his commission in the Air Force to join the *PF*. He had never expected to be ripped away from his beloved family and the beautiful Cancun. The only consolation was that he had been accepted as a probationary recruit into the prestigious *Grupo de Operaciones Especiales,* Special Operations Group.

To Reyes, Northern Mexico was a hellhole, an oceanless desert with cold winters, choking smog, unpalatable food and stupid *Norteños.* The "people of the north" were a bunch of backwards hicks whose close proximity to their English-speaking neighbors had bastardized their language to the point he could hardly understand them. Worst of all, his wife and child were still back home in Cancun. He could not afford to move them so they were staying with her mother until he could save enough cash to bring them to Juarez. It had been six months since he'd made love to his wife.

He sat in the briefing room, daydreaming about teasing her supple breasts through the nearly sheer fabric of his favorite old Air Force t-shirt while she moaned his name...

"REYES!"

He was startled out of the dream by the booming voice of Sergeant Jorge Montoya, and dropped his empty metal coffee cup to the floor. His colleagues laughed.

"Welcome back, *pendejo*. You're driving lead. De la Rosa, Villareal and Santos will ride with you. Cordona's team will be in the trail SUV. Any questions?"

"Why can't de la Rosa ride with us?" Ramon Cordona asked. He winked and pursed his lips in the direction of the only female officer in the room.

"Because she likes men with IQ's bigger than their dicks, Cordona," the sergeant replied. The room filled with laughter. Cordona smirked and Alejandra de la Rosa blushed. "Sexual harassment" was a term alien to the *Policia Federal*.

Despite the ribbing from his sergeant, Ramon Cordona was a rising star in the *PF* and a team leader in the Special Operations Group.

GOPE, as they were known colloquially, were the tip of the spear in the offensive against the cartels, and they knew their trade. They were selective to the extreme, and trained to the highest standards. Many in their ranks were sent to America to learn the latest tactics from the FBI, DEA and U.S. military Special Forces.

Cordona and his team were the best the *Policia Federal* had to offer, chosen for their loyalty, intelligence, marksmanship and physical conditioning. With the exception of the new members, the team carried themselves with a swagger that could only be earned under fire. Reyes and the three officers assigned to the lead vehicle were probationary inductees of this elite fraternity and their performance on the mission would be closely scrutinized. Any lapse could be grounds for elimination and being caught in a daydream didn't help Reyes.

The day's mission was routine, simply a reconnaissance patrol to *Colonia Puerto de Anapra*, one of Juarez's poorest neighborhoods situated to the west along the desert border with New Mexico. Miles of dirt roads, corrugated metal shacks, and its proximity to the arid mountains made Anapra an ideal staging point for millions of dollars' worth of marijuana, heroin, cocaine and crystal methamphetamine that the cartels shipped with FedEx efficiency across the border every day.

The majority of *Anapra's* residents worked in the large *maquilas*, or factories, for an average of thirty-five dollars a week and turned a self-preserving blind eye to activities of the *narcos*.

A rare anonymous tip relaying the whereabouts of two large meth labs was the impetus for the recon mission. No arrests or confrontations, just a quick foray into the mostly lawless *colonia* to verify the tip. Cordona knew exactly where to find the labs, and would avoid them.

***

The team filed out of the briefing room, each of them dressed like a futuristic storm trooper in long-sleeved black Nomex flightsuits, combat boots, utility belts, skateboard-style knee and elbow pads, leather palmed shooting gloves, helmets and black Kevlar body armor that could stop all but a high-caliber rifle round.

Every officer carried a tazer, pepper gas and Glock .40 caliber semi-automatic pistol, but Cordona's team also carried the H&K MP-5 submachine guns favored by the U.S. Navy Seals. Each vehicle was equipped with a twelve-gauge tactical shotgun, and Morales, Cordona's number three, had a rotary-fed 40mm grenade launcher capable of launching its high explosive rounds up to four hundred meters.

Sergeant Montoya nodded to each of them as they filed past, watching Reyes, de la Rosa and two other candidates mount up in a modified Ford extended-cab pickup, and Cordona's team get into the *Grupo Especiale's* newest Chevy Suburban. Both vehicles were painted jet black, with LED light bars on the roof, push bars on the front end and the seven pointed star logo flanked by "POLICIA FEDERAL" in large, white block letters across the doors.

As the recon team rolled out of the lot, Sergeant Montoya walked back to his desk, fished out his cell phone and sent a short text message. His betrayal complete, he slumped into his chair, lowered his head, and with drooped shoulders crossed himself and wept.

***

Ricardo "Tuco" Medrano deleted the text message, closed the pre-paid flip phone and slipped it into the pocket of his khaki jacket. He then walked slowly to the curb and deliberately flicked his cigarette butt into the *Bulevar Ignacio Bernardo Norzagaray*. The signal made, he looked up, down and across the wide street, pursed his lips and nodded to himself fully satisfied that everything was in place. Five minutes.

***

Things were looking up for Reyes. This would be a relatively easy mission, a thirty-minute drive to Anapra on the *Bulevar Ignacio Bernardo Norzagaray* for a quick check of the properties that the informant had fingered as meth labs. They would look for the telltale signs--blacked out windows, trash piles with antifreeze, lye, drain opener and acetone bottles, portable generators and a dead giveaway, the strong smell of ammonia.

The air was crisp, and a northerly overnight wind had blown out the thick brown inversion layer of cooking fire smoke and vehicle exhaust that blanketed the Rio Grande Valley on most days, revealing the cerulean desert sky. He could see the gleaming crucifix on Mount Cristo Rey, miles away in New Mexico.

And then there was de la Rosa. She was the most beautiful woman Reyes had ever seen. He glanced sideways at her as often as he could, and checked his passenger side mirror considerably more than necessary.

Her hair was pulled into a ponytail that gleamed in the morning light and framed her perfectly sculpted face. When she smiled, her full lips revealed straight white teeth, and dimples formed in her smooth cheeks, but most striking of all were her light green eyes. Their effect, combined with her light brown skin and silky, jet-black hair, was mesmerizing--he felt that she could look right through him.

She was tall for a Latina and had the body of an athlete. Station legend had it that she had kept up stride for stride with Cordona on a five kilometer fitness test, dropping behind only when he sprinted the last hundred meters.

Probably most impressive was that she had the brains to go with her looks. Reyes had heard that she had a law degree from the University of Texas, and was only in the PF to prove a point to her rich, chauvinistic father and boost her already bright future in politics.

As he was driving down *Avenida Juarez,* past the *Plaza de Toros* bullring towards the *Bulevar Norzagaray,* Reyes was daydreaming about his threadbare Air Force t-shirt again, this time imagining how it would look on de la Rosa, her nipples firm in the cool morning air, leaving enough, but not too much, to the imagination.

She saw but ignored Reyes' surreptitious attempts to ogle her. "Sorry they laughed at you back at the brief."

"Oh, it's okay," he replied, "I was thinking about my family in Cancun. At least Cordona drew the spotlight off of me pretty quickly."

"Yeah, he has to be the center of attention." She blushed for the second time that morning.

Villareal chimed in from the back seat, "Watch out for that *maricon*, he has more girlfriends than Tiger Woods."

"Hmph," she looked out the window and smiled to herself.

Reyes' heart dropped a little as he realized she'd never be interested in him, not that he wasn't good looking in his own right. His strong Mayan features were handsome, but he was no Cordona, tall and built like a professional athlete. He was also a little ashamed at himself for his mental disloyalty to his pretty little wife, dutifully taking care of their child in Cancun.

With his mind back on the road, Reyes checked his rear-view mirror. The Suburban driven by Cordona's number two, Lerma, was too close. Procedure called for a generous spacing between the elements in the caravan, generally four to six car lengths to allow for maneuverability in an ambush. The lapse irritated Reyes, but he reminded himself that Lerma had done this before and knew what he was doing. Besides, this was a cakewalk and nobody knew they were coming.

***

It was approaching eight o'clock, still fairly early in Juarez, but the usually bustling downtown was starting to show signs of life. Businesses up and down *Avenida Juarez* were rolling up steel security doors and unlocking wrought iron gates in preparation for the day. Street vendors were pushing their carts, laden with fruits, vegetables, pastries, homemade candies and large glass jars of lemonade and *horchata.*

And of course there were the beggars.

The *Americanos* had built their "Great Fence," a rust colored monstrosity that didn't completely stop the flow of humanity northward, but did slow it down. Many of the people who had come from the interior of Mexico hoping to cross into the United States looking for jobs that would pay them the unheard of sum of five dollars per hour were stuck in Juarez, unable to get over (or under) the fence.

Without the resources to go home, they simply stayed and slept in the parks, under overpasses, and in the dark alleyways of *el centro,* the downtown. They begged to get by. Many just put on sad eyes and held out their hands to passersby, but the industrious among them either stole or spent their last pesos on small boxes of chewing gum, *chiclés*, that they would sell to tourists at a generous markup. Each box contained fifty packages of four small, flat candy-coated pieces of chewing gum in assorted "fruit" flavors that lasted until the candy melted away: usually ten or twelve good chews.

Shortly after Reyes turned left onto IBN, followed closely by Cordona in the Suburban, a large man stepped into the street, smiling and holding out a box of *chiclés*. Reyes slammed on the brakes and yelled, "What the fuck?!" stopping just short of the large, grinning man.

The beggar was huge, but had the look of a child. He had chubby cheeks, his eyes sat too close together, and his thick, open lips revealed a crooked mess of teeth. The inexperienced officers in the truck had their eyes trained on the man-child standing in front of them, absurdly smiling and holding out his box of gum, and they didn't notice the gunmen pouring out of the shops on both sides of the street.

Tuco Medrano, wearing a black ski mask, walked quickly across the busy street, calmly drew his .45 caliber semiautomatic and put two rounds through the driver side window of the lead truck. The bullets struck Officer Ignacio Reyes in the head, killing him instantly, and sprayed bloody bits of brain matter and bone all over his wide-eyed female partner.

***

Ramon Cordona, unable to see what had caused the lead to stop, muttered under his breath, "Reyes, what the hell are you doing?"

Then he saw the gunman.

"Ambush! Go, Lerma, GO, GO, GO!"

Because he had been following too close, Lerma could not move forward. He threw the powerful Chevy into reverse and gunned it, but the heavy morning traffic was choking the street, and all he managed to do was ride up over the hood of the car behind him. The four experienced *federales* opened the doors and tried to take cover.

Eight shooters with AR rifles and AK-47 machine guns had taken position slightly behind the two police trucks, four on each side, using parked or stopped vehicles for cover. It was perfect positioning to give clear fields of fire and avoid hitting each other in the crossfire. As soon as the officers opened the doors of the SUV on the driver's side, they were cut down in a hail of bullets, the open doors providing a perfect channel of fire for the shooters. Lerma and Morales were dead before they hit the ground, their body armor ineffective against the high-velocity rifle rounds.

Cordona and Garza, closer to the sidewalk on the passenger side and slightly protected by the now panicking civilians and a small vendor cart, were both able to get out of the vehicle and return fire at the men crouched behind the parked cars. Using the open, armored doors for cover they followed their training. One peeked out quickly to acquire a target, then called it to the other who popped up and engaged. The technique was effective; they managed to kill two of the shooters with clean headshots but they couldn't risk leaving the cover of the vehicle to try to help their comrades still stuck in the lead truck.

With the driver dead, and the woman in the front seat immobilized and in shock, Tuco turned his attention to the back seat. Both young officers were struggling to get their weapons out of their holsters; they were obviously not full-fledged members of the Special Operations Group or they would have had the MP-5 submachine guns, but Tuco already knew that.

Before he could raise his weapon, the street-side gunmen, their mission accomplished on the second vehicle, approached from the rear and sprayed the truck with their AK-47's. Villareal and Santos, two young fathers, died with their seatbelts on. Alejandra de la Rosa, mostly shielded by the dying men behind her, was struck in the left shoulder.

***

In his last act on earth, Raul "el Raton" Garza, a low level *La Linea* enforcer and no relation to officer Juan Garza, fighting for his life on the other side of the Suburban, pulled the pin on a Vietnam era grenade and rolled it under the police vehicle.

"NO!" Tuco screamed.

The grenade detonated almost directly under officer Garza, in a bright flash of smoke, fire and pink mist.

Fucking pendejo, thought Tuco. *I told them he was mine.*

He turned to vent his fury at El Raton, but it was wasted effort. As the high explosive detonated and released its energy into the truck and unfortunate policeman, it blasted a piece of steel flooring from the truck and sent it out of the open door directly at "The Rat." The dinner-plate-sized piece of metal spun like a Frisbee and hit him at an angle that took half of his face and the top of his head clean off, like he had been run through a meat slicer. His body twitched in the street.

Tuco cursed the dead man and checked the urge to unload on his corpse.

***

The ambush took less than a minute.

Two black Cadillac Escalades pulled up, the gunmen piled into them, and their three dead comrades were loaded into the back of the second SUV. The top of el Raton's head lay forgotten in the gutter across the street.

Tuco watched to make sure that his brother, Guero, still smiling and clutching his box of gum, was safely in the lead Cadillac. Still masked and expecting the worst, he walked around the burning Chevy and looked down at Cordona. The *federale* was sprawled on the sidewalk, weaponless, clearly in a great deal of pain, and to Tuco's relief still very much alive. His legs were a mess; Tuco could see the mangled flesh through the torn black flight suit, and his left foot was twisted at an impossible angle.

Cordona looked up at his masked face, then to the gun in Tuco's hand. His eyes were filled with pain and hatred. "Go on, you fuck!"

Tuco lifted the mask and Cordona's eyes opened wide with recognition. "Tuco."

Tuco replied matter-of-factly, "You chose poorly, old friend."

Cordona glanced over at the Ford where Officer de la Rosa was struggling weakly with her seatbelt and brought his gaze back to the man standing near his shredded legs. Tuco shook his head slowly. "She wasn't worth it."

"Fu…" Ramon Cordona's last words of defiance were cut short by a bullet to the forehead. His eyes, still open, rolled back in his head as if searching for the brain that lay on the sidewalk behind him.

This left only one.

Tuco made his way to the passenger side door of the Ford pickup. The window had been blown out in the fusillade that killed the officers in the back seat. She was still alive, struggling in a futile effort to get to her gun.

Her left arm was useless from the wound in her shoulder and her partner's body lay across her lap. She had lost a lot of blood, and Tuco could see she didn't have the strength to get to her weapon from under the dead man's weight. As he approached, she stopped struggling and kept her eyes on him.

Tuco stopped a few feet from the passenger door, raised his gun and pointed it at the center of her forehead. She was as beautiful as he remembered, even with the gore from her partner's head splattered across her face.

And those eyes…

They were electric, like nothing he had ever seen. She was calm, looking straight through him and he felt a chill as though she was tickling his soul. A single tear rolled out of the corner of her eye and down her right cheek.

Tuco lowered the gun and thought, *have I really become this monster?* He looked once more into those haunting eyes, raised the gun, and pulled the trigger.

Chapter 2

Besides the broad painted dash of the centerline and a few of the bright white runway edge lights, there was not a whole lot to see out of the cockpit windows.

As Edgar Allen Poe might have said, "It was a dark and shitty night." Ok, Edgar probably wouldn't have said that, but you get my point. It was the kind of night you would rather be curled up with your favorite girl and a nice glass of really old scotch, watching a romantic comedy, and hoping you were earning enough points to get lucky. Not the kind of night you wanted to be flying a sixty-ton airplane into the scary black yonder.

But hey, this is the Big Leagues, and as a crusty old airline captain once told me, "It's hard flying jets."

The control tower cleared us for takeoff, and after turning on the landing lights to give anyone else dumb enough to be out in this weather a chance to see us, the First Officer advanced the throttles, released the brakes, and over forty thousand pounds of thrust started us on our way into the inky night.

It's not quite like an Italian sports car or a crotch rocket, but I am always a little awestruck by the power and acceleration it takes to get a big hunk of steel and aluminum moving fast enough to break the hold of gravity. Like an ungainly albatross running across a beach, an airliner isn't so sexy on the runway, but when it breaks into flight, pure grace.

Takeoff is the most exhilarating part of flight, and also the most deadly. When an airplane starts the takeoff roll it is at its heaviest. It is sluggish and loaded with fuel, the engines are at full power and giving all they've got to force the bird into the air; there is little room for error.

The cockpit shuddered as the Boeing started rolling down the runway, the three foot wide centerline stripes disappearing beneath the nose of the jet, the edge lights nothing but blurry streaks in my peripheral vision.

"Eighty knots," I called out.

"Check."

Faster still, the nose wheel thumping loudly over the reflectors set into the concrete surface…irritating, but a good indicator that the First Officer was keeping it straight down the center of the runway. I could feel the airplane wanting to fly.

"V-one," I said. It was the speed at which the airplane was going flying, no matter what. If we tried to abort the takeoff now, the 737 would careen off the end of the runway, killing us, and our precious cargo, in a spectacular fireball that would boost the ratings of the morning news shows.

"Rotate."

The First Officer eased back on the yoke, willing the bird skyward. As he paused to let the wings vault us into the air, all hell broke loose. A bright red light with the word "FIRE" printed on it flashed briefly in our faces, followed by the amber "Master Caution" light and several others indicating something was seriously messed up. The engine instruments of the right engine were quickly spooling down, which in layman's terms is B-A-D, bad, but Chet, the First Officer, didn't notice any of that.

He was looking outside, and in the immortal words of Goose in *Top Gun*, "doing some of that pilot shit."

An engine failure on takeoff, or V-one cut in pilot-speak, is a big deal, but if handled correctly, using the Pavlovian response that is hammered into us by practice, practice and more practice, the loss of an engine is a very survivable event. Apparently Chet missed that day at practice.

He panicked a bit and pulled hard on the yoke, forcing the 737 into the air when it wasn't quite ready to fly. He effectively removed any visual references that might have helped him gain control, particularly, the runway lights and markings.

We were screwed.

The jet began a rapidly accelerating roll onto its back. Chet, with a bovine expression of resignation on his face said simply, "Oh, shit."

The famous last words of almost all gooned-up pilots.

The big airplane smashed upside down into the ground in what would have undoubtedly been fodder for a week's worth of talking heads' in-depth analysis and uninformed speculation.

***

Luckily, we were sitting in a flight simulator in Austin, Texas. The "sim" is a $40 million computerized box on hydraulic stilts that lets airline pilots practice and be tested on emergency procedures that are too dangerous and way too expensive to practice in a real-live airplane.

Chet was having a bit of trouble with the dreaded V-one cut, it had gotten into his head, and someone had the bright idea I could snap him out of it. My name is Douglas Jacob Martin, pilot extraordinaire, barroom scholar, example to lesser men and charmer of the fairer sex. Well, ok, I'm a pretty good pilot. My friends call me Jake. My mother calls me Douglas.

Ten years ago if you had asked me where I would be today, I certainly wouldn't have believed it would be at this backwater, cut-rate little excuse for an airline trying to help this kid pull his head out of his ass, but fate and the airlines work in mysterious ways.

Like a lot of guys in the flying business, I had started as a military pilot, but the world of Naval Aviation is a far cry from its glory days of yore. Gone is the hard flying, hard drinking, skirt chasing world that my forbears knew, and in its place is a politically correct bureaucracy that puts more weight on administrative skills and ass kissing than leadership and flying. But I guess that's just a reflection of our society as a whole.

I'd had enough, and faced with the prospect of two years on "the boat," I got out of the Navy, but like a hostage with Stockholm Syndrome, I couldn't cut the ties completely and stayed in as a Reserve Officer. A weekend a month and two weeks out of the year…yeah, right.

I hit the big time and was hired straight off active duty by an unnamed major airline that rhymes with "American Airlines." Jake's future was bright. The airlines were kicking some ass, and pilots were reaping the rewards. I was looking forward to a six-figure income, international flying, a juicy retirement and all of the flight attendants I could want, but the fairy tale ended on September 11, 2001.

I held on through the first few rounds of layoffs, but when fuel prices surged after it became apparent the Iraqis were not going to cooperate as planned after the invasion, I found myself on the street. It was too late to grab up any of the few good flying jobs that remained, but at least there was the Navy Reserve. In a cosmic confluence of luck, timing and irony, Uncle Sam sent me to the Great Nation of Afghanistan to drink sour tea and talk progress with the village elders.

While I was playing around in the poppy fields, an old Navy buddy sent me an email and asked if I'd like to sign on to fly with a very small regional outfit that served Texas and Mexico. It was cleverly named Texas International Air, and flew Boeing 737s in mostly charter operations serving "businessmen" with a need for discreet and expeditious travel to and from Mexico.

Faced with a choice between flying for "Tex-Mex Air" or selling pencils on the street corner, I took the job. Sometimes luck in life is about whom you know, and since my buddy was the Chief Pilot of this sketchy little operation, I returned from my tour in Afghanistan to a job as a Captain and Instructor at Texas International.

In all fairness it wasn't a bad gig--we did fill the gap in business travel by flying rich kids from Texas college towns to the sunny beaches of the Mexican Riviera. Even though I was making little more than half the pay I was earning at American, it beat standing in line for government cheese.

***

So there I was with Chet, a more-than-capable kid with a huge confidence problem. Some people are just not cut out for flying large airplanes, but Chet had enough time and training, and had proved himself capable of the task. He had simply allowed a training event similar to the one we just experienced wrap itself around his brain and insert the seed of doubt, much like a man experiencing impotence for the first time. If he didn't work through the doubt and get a handle on it soon, he'd never get it up again, so to speak. It was my job to give him the handle.

When I was a young lad just starting my Navy flight training, a grizzled old Master Chief Petty Officer welcomed my class to his survival lecture with a short speech about his take on pilots. He was a Combat Search and Rescue Swimmer with a hard physique and a pair of golden Air Crew wings perched above the huge collection of ribbons on his chest.

"Given enough time, and enough bananas, the Navy could teach a monkey to fly," he boomed. "Unfortunately, the Navy doesn't have enough time, or bananas, to teach a monkey to fly, so that, gentlemen, is why you are here!"

What he didn't say, but we all knew, is that 20,000 monkeys had applied for flight training that year, and only 342 had the academic aptitude, physical characteristics, and personality to be selected to the Navy flight program. Similarly, Chet had been selected to fly for the National Guard, so I knew he had the same aptitude.

"Well, that was fun. What happened?" I asked.

"We got an intermittent fire warning on the right engine, then the engine failed and caused an adverse yaw to the right and…"

"Whoa, hold on a minute there," I interrupted, "you saw all of that going on as you were trying to fly the airplane?"

"Well, yeah…"

"And what did you see *outside*, on the runway?"

He thought about it for a second, "Uh…"

"Exactly. You're thinking about this way too hard, you should be concentrating on what's going on outside of the airplane. Be the monkey, don't crowd your head with left, right, fire, whatever. See what the airplane is doing that you don't want it to and correct it! I'm not a smart man," I lied, "so I don't think about anything other than making sure the aircraft is rolling straight down the runway and that I've got it under control before I get it in the air. Your co-pilot can tell you what's going on, *comprende*?"

My phone vibrated in my pocket, so I missed his answer, but I could see his head bobbing up and down in the epiphany of understanding. Who the hell was calling me?

"Okay, let's try it again."

I reset the simulator to the takeoff position, and this time Chet handled the emergency like the pro I knew he was.

"What engine did you lose this time?" I asked.

"Uhhh…I don't know."

"Perfect."

My phone buzzed again as we prepared for another takeoff, and this time I pulled it out and looked at the caller ID. It was a number I didn't recognize, but the area code was one I knew very well, 915, my hometown. I had no idea who would be calling me from El Paso. My Mom had left years ago, and I hadn't seen the place from less than 30,000 feet for over ten years. If it were important, they'd leave a message.

Chet was a rock star, I put him through the ringer on four or five more V-1 cuts and he handled them all without a hitch. I even gave him a nasty crosswind on the last one, and he didn't flinch. Sometimes you just have to go back to the basics--fly like a monkey.

As we finished up his debrief, I remembered the phone call and wondered if they had left a message. I congratulated Chet on getting his groove back, signed his paperwork, sent him on his virile way, and then my hand went straight for the phone.

There was a voicemail.

***

"This is Ronald Mitchell from Sampson, Mitchell and Mitchell, and I'm calling Douglas Martin in regards to his father, Daniel Martin. Please return my call at…"

An attorney, they were my favorite. I wondered if he'd heard the one about a cruise ship full of attorneys hitting an iceberg…never mind. Then there was my father, another one of my favorites.

I hadn't heard from him in over ten years, and it wasn't that I didn't want to hear from him, I just didn't care. Then out of nowhere, about a week ago he left a message, nothing specific, just, "Hi Jake, this is your dad. Call me." Like we talked every day. When I finally got around to calling him back, his line went straight to voicemail, but I didn't leave a message or give him a second thought.

What kind of trouble was he in now? If he thought I was about to bail him out of something, he was as wrong as a football bat.

I dialed Mitchell's number and after a short conversation with a very sexy sounding receptionist, I found myself on the line with Ronald Mitchell, esquire.

"Mr. Martin, I'm afraid I have some very bad news. Your father, Daniel Martin, has passed away. I'm very sorry.

"He named me the executor of his Last Will and Testament, and as his only stated heir, you are the sole inheritor of his property. Is it possible for you to come to El Paso to read the will and handle the affairs of his estate?"

"Well, Mr. Mitchell, I'm sure I can work something out, but I'd like to know a couple of things. First and foremost, how did he die, and secondly, what kind of estate did he have, a bottle of tequila and a couple of cartons of cigarettes? The man wasn't exactly a model citizen, I can't imagine he left behind much of value."

"I'm sorry Mr. Martin…" His voice could put a hypnotist to sleep, and I pictured a tall skinny man with coke bottle spectacles. "…I am not at liberty to discuss the nature of your father's death, nor the value of his estate over the telephone, however, I think it would be in your best interest to come to El Paso and attend his affairs."

Was this guy for real?

"It would be well worth your while," he continued.

He had my interest.

After some quick mental gymnastics I replied, "All right, I can be there next Wednesday around noon, and if I have to stay to wrap things up, I can spend the night and tie up any loose ends on Thursday morning."

"Hmmmm…" This guy must be a real hit in the courtroom. "I think it would be better if you could get here on Monday and stay the week."

"A week? Mr. Mitchell, I have a job."

"It would be worth your while, Mr. Martin."

My mind was racing.

"Okay, I'll see what I can do. Can I call you tomorrow?"

"That will be fine, Mr. Martin, I look forward to your call. Again, I'm very sorry about your father." I doubted he really gave a shit. He was polite, but had all of the energy of a hooker on her last trick of the night. The line went dead.

I should have been thinking about the fact that my father was dead, but his loss was no great blow to the world, and dead or alive, the best I could muster for him was apathy. El Paso, on the other hand, was a different story. I'd always said that El Paso was a great place to grow up, but I wouldn't want to live there.

It held a lot of memories for me, mostly good, some bad, and the idea of going back for the first time in years was more than a little intriguing. Equally intriguing was the cryptic lawyer's reference to an estate that would be "worth my while." It looked like I was heading to El Paso.

Chapter 3

It had been nearly a week since the ambush on *Bulevar Norzagaray* and though he would never admit it, about that long since Tuco had managed more than a few hours of troubled sleep.

He stared absentmindedly out of the window of the black SUV as it rolled through the dilapidated neighborhood where he spent his teen years. It was known to the people who lived there as *Francisco Villa*, and to some of the more cynical neighbors across the border, Hollywood Heights. Named for Mexico's most famous bandit and revolutionary, *Francisco Villa* was a third world collection of ramshackle houses, huts and lean-tos perched in the northern foothills of the Juarez Mountains overlooking the inappropriately named Rio Grande.

Unpaved streets lined with trash and open sewers wound haphazardly through the rough desert topography, with tin and cinderblock structures hanging precariously on rocky hillsides and painted in the Mexican favorites, pink, turquoise, and baby-shit yellow. Electricity had not found its way to the entire neighborhood and the streets were dark, choked with the smoke of cooking fires that settled into stratified bands as the night air cooled.

Guero sat in the back seat, his face lit by the glow from his portable Playstation, eyes glittering and rapt by whatever electronic world danced across the screen. Tuco watched his older brother for several minutes, always amazed at the irony of a big man with a child's wit, playing his game with a small puppy curled up in his lap.

The poor little mutt would probably share the fate of countless others, literally loved to death. It would be an accident, of course, but the puppy would die; smothered under the weight of the large man when he rolled over in his sleep, crushed in a loving embrace, or, in a brief but brutal flash of temper, flung across the room after a playful nip. Tuco caught a glimpse of himself in those short, violent outbursts that were invariably followed by inconsolable sobbing over the broken corpse. Guero would mope until they found him a new victim with a wiggly tail and all was forgotten. He would never comprehend nor learn from the consequences of his actions and could only live in the moment.

Tuco had come to understand that his brother would never change. Fortunately, puppies were not hard to come by in the slums of Juarez.

***

Tuco and Guero started out as Ricardo and Juan. But Manny changed that. Manny was different.

Looking back on it, Tuco saw what his mother, Marcela, had been, but as a child he only knew not to bother his mamá *when her friends came over. That was fine by him.*

Some of her friends just came to the door and handed her a small package in exchange for some money. Then she went to her room and wouldn't come out for the rest of the night.

Others would stay awhile. They went to her room while the boys watched TV. Ricardo thought they were wrestling, or maybe jumping on the bed with his mamá.

Most would leave, handing her money on the way out and taking no notice of the boys. Some would say "Hi". One put his cigarette out in the palm of Juan's hand. Then there was Manny.

He was their friend. After he finished wrestling with their mother, Manny stayed and watched movies with them. He told them he was going to buy them a house with a yard where they could play.

The early memories of Manny and Juan were the best of Ricardo's life, and the best of all were nights watching the Spanish-dubbed The Good, The Bad and The Ugly. *They watched the Sergio Leone classic over and over, acting out the showdowns with cocked finger pistols.*

It was Manny who gave them their nicknames, Juan, as the oldest, got Clint Eastwood's character's name, Blondie, or Guero in the dubbed version. Ricardo became Tuco. The names stuck.

Until the kittens came.

***

Tuco turned to consider his driver, an emaciated, hook-nosed *mestizo* with a sloping forehead, weak chin and a prominent Adam's apple that bobbed every time he swallowed.

That this inbred peón *had ever been a cop is fucking crazy*, Tuco thought. *But then again the same could be said of me.*

Known as "El Cuchillo", the Knife, the driver was a paid assassin or *sicario*, and one of *La Linea's* best interrogators. He was an artist with a blade who could cut into a man and withdraw his darkest secrets with shiny, razor sharp tools.

Tuco once watched him remove a living man's face. He took one tiny patch of flesh at a time until the faceless, blubbering man was staring through lidless eyes at a bloody mosaic of his own skin pasted on a mirror that had been set so he could watch every cut of the operation. The poor bastard had given up everything he knew by the time his right cheek was skinned, but Cuchillo finished the job anyway.

Just for the fun of it.

Tuco was looking at the man's hands on the steering wheel, wondering what other horrors resided with the dirt and grease under his long, ragged fingernails, and didn't notice that he had said something.

"Huh?" Tuco asked.

"I said, I hear there's three of them. Goin' to be a good night!" He finished the statement with a chronic sniff, a side effect of regular cocaine use.

"We'll see."

"My blades will be dull by the last one. Always sucks to be last."

El Cuchillo's laugh was a high-pitched cackle that grated his nerves. The puppy whimpered from the back seat and Tuco tried to remember when they had last let it do its business. It wasn't that he cared about soiling the car's leather upholstery; he just wasn't particularly thrilled about the prospect of riding around in a vehicle that smelled of dog crap.

"Pull over, the dog has to go."

"But, Boss, we're almost..." a sideways glance from Tuco cut off the protest in mid sentence, "...*si, patron.*"

Few men could challenge Cuchillo and live, but he had seen Tuco in action and was smart enough to know when to shut up. He pulled over to the side of the sandy, rutted street, next to a small vacant lot...careful to make sure his boss was clear of the filth flowing in the open gutter.

Tuco stepped out and opened the rear passenger door to let his brother tend to the dog. Guero was still enthralled in the game he was playing and hadn't even noticed that they had stopped and that cold night air was filling the Caddy.

"C'mon, Guero, your puppy has to potty."

Guero looked up questioningly, remembered the dog, and comprehension dawned on his chubby face. He grabbed the puppy gently, stepped out of the truck and placed it on the sand, where it immediately assumed a splayed leg stance and voided its bladder in the dirt.

"Puppy's peein'!"

Guero smiled and looked from the dog to Tuco and back again.

"See Tuco, puppy did good! Good puppy."

"Yes, *'mano,* good job, now let's go."

Guero lumbered back to the truck and climbed in, forgetting the puppy, which was squatting for act two. Tuco chuckled to himself as he picked up the empty pup and was struck with an odd feeling of déjà vu. He shook it off and got into the truck. They were only a few blocks from their destination and already running behind.

He looked back at the vacant lot but this time couldn't shake the memories away.

**

Manny drove Marcela and the boys to Tuco's first day in kindergarten. Tuco couldn't remember ever being separated from Juan, so he figured it was his first day of school, too.

While his mother whisked Guero off to a special class, Manny took Tuco to his.

"Let's go find your seat." Manny guided him around the short little tables. "Here it is...'Ricardo.'" He took a pen out of his pocket and scrawled "Tuco" next to the boy's neatly lettered name. "There, that's better."

Tuco watched his teacher approach. She smiled and he was fascinated with her lipstick and straight, white teeth. "Hi, I'm Miss Van Valkenburg, and what is your name?"

He started to say "Tuco" but the memory of a mangled kitten flashed through his young mind. "My name is Ricardo."

"But we call him Tuco," Manny blurted, flustered by the pretty young woman.

"Ok, Tuco it is."

"No, Miss, my name is Ricardo."

Manny gawked at him, but remained silent.

She smiled at Tuco, "You can go pick out a toy and go make friends in the play area, Ricardo." It was Manny's cue to leave.

"Alright, buddy, I'm leaving now, you have fun and be good."

Tuco turned wordlessly and went to look for a toy.

"Thank you Miss." Manny would never be able to say "Van Valkenburg." He started for the door.

"Thank you, Mr. Medrano." He didn't bother to correct her.

***

As years passed and Tuco's exposure to the world outside of the projects, his mother, Manny and especially Guero widened, so did his desire to extricate himself from them.

He made friends at will and grades came easily. Ricardo became Richie and he tried to stay away from the apartment in the Jackie Robinson Federal Housing Project as much as possible. He resented having to make dinner on the nights his mother was too high, taking care of his brother and getting him ready for school when she was too hung-over.

On the playground at school he learned the terms "crack whore" and "retard" and knew that he was double cursed.

Manny still came, but things were different. Tuco insisted they call him Ricardo, and an infraction by Guero would elicit a violent response. His forgetful brother often ended up crying in Manny's arms after an unintentional slip.

Tuco eventually stopped taking part in the evenings with Manny and Guero, spending more time studying alone in his room or talking on the telephone. His resentment for the brother who couldn't take care of himself grew day by day and the chasm between them widened.

***

The weight of the water balloon felt good in his lap. He was thirteen and riding around with a friend in his older brother's car.

"Check it out, here's one on the sidewalk! Nail him, Richie!"

A tall, familiar form shuffled along the sidewalk, his shoulders hunched and back to the boys in the car. He walked with a pigeon-toed gait that Tuco recognized all too well, and he carried a single book that Tuco knew as his favorite, but that he would never be able to read.

A few days earlier Marcela had told Tuco he could go to a movie with his friends, but reneged at the last minute when one of her "dates" wanted a companion for a party. She made him stay home to watch Guero.

He later heard that a girl he liked ended up making-out with another boy in the theater. Tuco ignored logic and put the blame squarely on his brother.

As the car pulled even with Guero, Tuco cocked his arm, took aim and threw the heavy balloon as hard as he could.

"Fucking-A! You nailed him!"

"And look… he's a 'TARD! Awesome, man!"

The boys hooted and hollered while Tuco watched his brother recede in the mirror. At sixteen, Guero was bigger than most men, and anyone passing by would have found it odd to see a large, blubbering boy with a torn and muddy copy of Dr. Seuss' The Cat in the Hat. *Tuco knew it was Guero's favorite because it reminded him of a time before school.*

Before the kittens.

Tuco joined his friends' celebration.

***

The Escalade pulled up to the house that once belonged to his grandparents. They both had died years before and left the home to Tuco. He sold it to *La Linea*, who used for interrogations.

The neighbors called it a death house.

El Cuchillo had some work to do. There were three of them: a Sinaloa accountant with his whore and a bodyguard.

Tuco sighed and got out of the SUV, steeling himself to a long night of other people's pain and suffering.

***

Tuco, Richie, *watched TV. His brother's book--ruined by a water balloon--lay on the coffee table, an indictment of Tuco's cruelty. Guero sat on the floor and played with a toy truck. Manny entered the front door wearing a threadbare sport coat with his hair combed and smelling faintly of Old Spice. He held a wilted bunch of cut flowers.*

"Oyé, muchachos, I bought us a house today, with a backyard! Where's your mama?"

Tuco, puzzled, pointed with his thumb towards his mother's bedroom. Manny smiled at the boys, took a deep breath and started down the hall.

Then Tuco remembered that it wasn't Manny's usual night and his mother had company. He thought about stopping Manny, but it was too late.

The door creaked when Manny opened it, and Tuco heard an unfamiliar voice. "Shut the fucking door, esé!"

His mother slurred, "Iss' okay, baby, he don' mean nothin'."

Manny, crushed by his shattered delusion, sulked back through the living room. He dropped the flowers on the coffee table and walked out of the front door. Moments later he returned, and without acknowledging the boys, staggered slowly down the hallway as if he were drunk, tears streaming down his face.

At the sound of the first gunshot, Tuco ran back to his mother's bedroom. A shout was cut short by the second report. When he got there the room smelled of sex, Old Spice and spent gunpowder.

Tuco saw a hairy, naked stranger hit the floor, arterial spray pulsing in a crimson plume as he fell. His mother was sprawled on the worn shag carpet, a dark hole in her temple and her blood bright against the dingy sheets of the bed. She stared with unseeing eyes at the dying man in front of her.

Manny turned to Tuco, a grimace on his tear-streaked face. Through sobs he said, "I'm so sorry, Tuco."

Tuco would never forget the string of saliva spanning Manny's open, quivering lips before he put the gun in his mouth and pulled the trigger.

Someone screamed, "NOOOO!"

It was Tuco.

Too late.

He loved Manny, hated his mother. She had ruined it all.

Something in Tuco snapped, and he felt… nothing.

The mortally wounded john lived for a few minutes more, his eyes wild and pleading, with one hand on the gaping wound in his neck and the other reaching out to Tuco. Tuco stood and did not move, watching the man die with morbid curiosity, like he had watch the kitten die years before.

A few days later, Tuco and Guero were living in Juarez with grandparents they had never known.

Chapter 4

A week is usually a lot of time to ask off on short notice, but there were plenty of pilots at Tex-Mex Air willing to pick up my hours, so in the end it wasn't that hard to get a leave of absence. Besides, I was grieving for my dear, departed father, and who knows, if it was worth my while like the slow talking lawyer had implied, my days of flying snotty-drunk rich kids to Cancun might be over.

I like to dream about winning the lottery, too.

There were lots of little details of everyday living that a normal person would need to address, but fortunately I already lived a pretty mobile lifestyle, and leaving for a week was not a huge deal. Then there was Andrea.

***

Andrea was a pretentious half-wit nymphomaniac flight attendant with a smokin' body and an ecstasy habit. She was also, for lack of a better term, my girlfriend. Who said being a pilot didn't come with benefits?

Andrea worked for Texas International and was out to prove to her daddy that she could make it on her own before she inherited the millions he had earned chasing and catching ambulances. Have I mentioned how much I like attorneys? It's amazing how much a brain-dead jury will award a high school dropout with a sprained ankle for missed wages and "pain and suffering."

Andrea was doing a bang-up job of proving her worth as a self-sufficient proletarian, living in a condominium with a stunning view of Austin's skyscrapers and driving a car I wouldn't be able to afford, well, ever. Nothing boosts your independence like a monthly allowance, but who was I to complain? Hanging out in her upscale, albeit messy, glass-walled palace beat the heck out of watching TV in my cracker-box apartment. Besides, I was the primary beneficiary of her exceptional skills in the sack, and how often do you get to exact a little revenge on a blood-sucking lawyer by banging his daughter in the condo, car, hot tub, ski chalet and private jet that he paid for? If you can't screw the attorney, might as well screw his pride-and-joy.

We met at work on a trip to Cancun, and despite my strict personal code against messing around with flight attendants, I have two brains that are often in conflict. Fresh out of another in a long line of toxic relationships, I was vulnerable, and by vulnerable I mean looking to get laid.

Normally, on the first night of a layover, the crew checks into the hotel and meets in the lobby to decide on the best place to get tacos and beer. Andrea, citing the need to "freshen up" from the "grueling" three hours of schlepping cokes to college kids, skipped out on dinner but whispered through cranberry red lips, "I'll be up late."

She leaned in so close that I could feel her erect nipples on my back as she slid her room key in my pocket.

I don't remember much about the tacos or where we ate them, but I do remember downing a few shots of tequila and nearly crawling out of my skin wanting dinner to end. When we finally made our way back to the hotel after two hours of listening to the older flight attendants talk about their cats, I hightailed it to my room, took the world's fastest shower and headed to Andrea's room. I was not ready for what I found.

One of the perks of flying is that on layovers we get to stay in some pretty nice hotels. In this case it was the Cancun *Palacio Royal de la Playa*, which in English means the Nice-as-shit-hotel-on-the-beach. Our rooms are first rate--usually an ocean view, Jacuzzi tub, and one of those beds with all the fancy linens and feather pillows that make you want to sleep for days. Andrea's "accommodations" however, made mine look like a room at an hourly-rate flophouse, and my first thought was that there must be a mistake. I was the captain and this was the room that I was supposed to get! Then I remembered hearing something about her being some rich lawyer's kid and things started to clear up. It was a huge suite, complete with a wet bar, three enormous flat screen televisions, and two naked girls in a giant hot tub.

Andrea was seated on the edge of the tub, with her back arched, head thrown back, and her breasts pointed skyward. A tanned blonde was kneeling in the bubbling water doing something that I think is still illegal in some southern states. A bottle of tequila sat next to the Jacuzzi with shot glasses lined up like a firing squad.

Andrea heard the door shut behind me and looked up startled. Realizing that she was no longer getting much of a response, the blonde turned to see who had interrupted her--I think I recognized her as one of the passengers on our flight.

"Where have you been?" I detected the hint of a slur in Andrea's sultry voice. "You're late, get your clothes off and get in here!"

***

If it hadn't been for the tequila shots at the taco stand, I'd like to think that I would have turned and walked away in a state of moral indignation. But the reality was that a platoon of Marines couldn't have kept me out of that hot tub. It was an auspicious start to an otherwise doomed relationship.

I should have just enjoyed the first night of debauchery and walked away, but never one to let good sense get in the way of good sex, I stuck around for the ride. Hot tub antics notwithstanding, it was a normal enough relationship for the first few months--we ate dinner in normal restaurants, had drinks at normal bars, and danced in normal nightclubs. Life was good, but like a frog in a slowly heated pot, I didn't notice that normal was slowly devolving to absurdity, and the water was beginning to boil while I sat enjoying the bubbles.

When a man lets his penis do the thinking he tends to ignore the larger, logical brain screaming things like, "Women who initiate threesomes with virtual strangers are usually insane!" Therefore, it came as a complete surprise to me when she wanted to start hanging out in swingers' clubs and became obsessed by the idea of another threesome with the gender odds in her favor. Now I'm less than inclined to be in the same room with another naked man, much less be close enough to cross swords with him, so I gently declined with a "No friggin' way!" Call me a hypocrite, but no… friggin'… way.

She took my refusal in stride and pretty much dropped the subject. Confident that my articulate rebuke saved her from an encounter she would later regret, I went back to thinking with my pecker.

The day before Chet's Flying Circus and the mysterious call about my father, I was doing the preflight for the homebound leg of a trip when I got a text from Andrea. It said something about whipped cream, a blindfold and her tongue in my--well let's just say the flight got in ahead of schedule and the night lived up to my expectations.

As I rummaged around the next morning, looking for my clothes, I found three men's socks--a pair and one lone ranger--none of them mine. Apparently their owners, in a rush to get out of there, had written off the socks as the cost of doing business.

I thought about waking her up and having at it, but since I was already late, I tied the socks in a knot and laid them on my pillow.

I hadn't talked to her in the two days since the great sock discovery and ignored the thirty some-odd texts and voice messages, but I needed to deal with her before I left for El Paso.

By deal with her, I meant dump her. All in all, I think it went pretty well.

In an epic display of poor planning, I called and asked her to meet me at a quiet little wine bar just around the corner from my place, hoping the snooty jazz, subdued lighting and soothing colors would prevent a scene. She showed up after I'd already downed a couple of glasses of shiraz, late as usual, acting like everything was peachy and wondering if something was wrong with my cell phone.

"Hi, You."

I hated that.

"Sorry I'm a little late, traffic just sucked." She lived less than a mile away. "Oooo... is that a merlot? We should try that new Spanish place tonight, I hear the tapas are awesome."

That did sound good...

"I like that shirt, is it new?"

It had been a gift from her. I took a sip of the wine. Where was good ol' J. Cuervo when you needed him? The way she bounced around subjects reminded me of a dog chasing a laser pointer.

"Did you see the socks?"

She shrugged. "Yeah, sorry. Hey, I dropped my trip tomorrow, you wanna go to Dallas?"

"No, I don't want to go to Dallas! I thought it was pretty clear that when I said 'no friggin' way' to joining in a double-team fantasy, I meant that I thought it would be bad for our relationship. How did you get, 'No thanks Hon, I'm gonna sit this one out, but go ahead and book your own threesome' from that?"

It was a little louder than I intended. The couple at the next table shot us a glance, and the man gave Andrea a quick once-over that settled on her chest. It made me want to pop him in the face, but it was hard to blame him. I took a deep breath and continued a little more quietly. "Listen, I have to leave town for a while. My father died and I have to go to El Paso to straighten out his estate. I think it'd be a good idea if we just use this to kinda' go our separate ways, know what I mean?"

"WHAT? You're dumping me?" The guy with wandering eyes and his date openly gawked at us now, along with the rest of the bar. I know I wasn't all that close to the dearly departed, but thanks for the condolences, bitch.

"Let's just say I'm setting you free to pursue other interests." *Like a five-way with the Dallas Mavericks*, I thought. "I just can't get used to the idea of you screwing around with other guys." Thank God I'd used condoms.

"That didn't seem to bother you when you got to fuck me and another girl!" She had me there, and I was sure I heard Wandering Eyes Guy choke on a piece of goat cheese.

"That was totally different." Lame, I know. "And that was before we started getting serious." I actually pulled it off with a straight face. "I just don't think I can go on with the image of you... you know... like that, with them... I just can't do it. I'm sorry."

"This is such bullshit!" she shrilled before throwing what was left of my wine in my face and storming towards the door. At least tequila wouldn't have stained. "This isn't over," she yelled before stopping and turning back towards me. "Jake, you're such an asshole." I could barely hear it, and it was hard to see through the wine, but I think she was actually crying.

She'd get over it.

***

After I paid for the wine and slithered out of the restaurant, I walked the couple of blocks back to my apartment. The fall air was crisp and despite my wine-soaked shirt, I enjoyed the clean coolness compared to the stuffiness of the wine bar. I opened the door to my apartment and was greeted by my dog, Blu. Always glad to see me, he was the best thing to come out of another doomed relationship--a gift from a girl in a desperate attempt to tie us together with the common bond of pet ownership. It didn't work.

I went into the kitchen and threw my shirt in the trash; there was no point in trying to get the wine stains out of it. Besides, it was a style more suited to a flight attendant anyway. A couple of bottles of beer hid behind a forgotten science experiment in the fridge, so I grabbed one, turned on the late news and plopped down on the couch. Blu hopped up and put his head in my lap. He was smart enough to know he wasn't supposed to be on the couch, but also smart enough to know I'd let it slide this time.

Andrea was just one more heap in a junkyard of broken relationships, but I was nothing if not consistent. Most of the women I dated were basket cases, like Andrea, who had a few traits in common--they were great in bed, they were crazy, and they were great in bed.

My mother had pretty much decided that I was a lost cause, afraid of a strong and balanced woman, and not interested in a girl unless she was a looker with big tits and a low IQ. While I have to admit a pretty smile and a nice rack go a long way to break the ice, looks aren't everything, and I was looking for an intelligent, independent and preferably sane woman. I had found the woman who I thought would last for the long haul, but timing and circumstance would force me to wait. So in the mean time I was entertained by the shiny, substance-free distractions like Little Miss Multiple Partners.

***

As I sat on the couch scratching behind Blu's ears, ignoring the news and sipping my beer, I thought about how my romantic life had changed on an autumn day nearly four years before at a park across the street from my downtown Austin apartment.

It was early October and the large oaks and Texas ash were just starting to turn--their vibrant reds, yellows and oranges set against a severe blue sky. The fall air had a rare clean quality that made everything stand out in high definition. Perfect Frisbee weather.

Blu lived for one thing and one thing alone--the Frisbee. Aussie Cattle Dogs are cow herders, but I don't think anyone ever bothered to tell my dog that catching a disc in mid-air was not part of his job description. For Blu, there was nothing better than making an impossible grab and strutting like an NBA rookie who jammed one over Shaquille O'Neal. If I so much as whispered the word "Frisbee," he'd start to drool like, well, one of Pavlov's dogs, use his nose to open the cabinet under the kitchen sink, grab his soft flying disc, and drop the slobbery mess in my lap. If that weren't enough, he'd bark to ensure he had my attention while bouncing like a hyperactive kid.

The park was the perfect spot for our daily game of fetch. An expansive, grassy field ringed with large trees and a meandering jogging trail, it was mostly used for kids' soccer on Saturdays and the occasional touch football game. Even with a couple of games in progress, there was plenty of room for me to throw my arm out and let Blu run until he had his fill. When Blu decided the game was over, he'd make the last catch and trot past me heading for home. Of course he always looked both ways before crossing the street.

Unlike most of his breed, Blu was everyone's friend, and often offered complete strangers the opportunity to join in his fun and throw the disc for him. If they weren't squeamish about a little slimy drool and had a reasonable arm, he'd let them toss it a few times before bringing it back to me. But if they couldn't spin a Frisbee properly, he wasn't shy about giving them a disdainful look and ignoring them. That's how Blu introduced me to Alex.

We were several throws into our session when Blu made his catch and trotted past me with the spitty disc hanging like a dead squirrel from his lower jaw. I mistook it for his signal that he was done for the day, and it seemed a little early, but instead of heading toward the apartment and looking back to see if I was coming, he stopped and dropped his gooey Frisbee in the lap of a rather attractive woman sitting on the grass with her feet together and knees splayed in a groin stretch. *Great timing bud*, I thought, as I gave a sheepish shrug of apology. I had seen her running around the park, just another jogger with great legs and a ponytail.

Despite Blu's unsolicited advance, she didn't seem too put off and stood to throw the Frisbee. I could tell she was not too happy about touching the spit and grass-covered dog toy, but she was a sport and threw the Frisbee like a wet fish. He cocked his head as if to say, "really?" and loped after the disc as it rolled on edge like a quarter across a floor. This was usually the point that he would bring the Frisbee back to me, but in a magnanimous display of good sportsmanship, he took it back to her and laid it at her feet for a second try.

There were a couple of reasons for me to intervene. Of course I wanted to prevent my dog from bugging the pretty woman when she obviously had more important things to do, but more than that, I wanted to get a better look. Her second throw, while not perfect, was head and shoulders above the first, and Blu actually caught it mid-air. We got there at the same time, and he dropped it at her feet for another throw.

"I'm sorry, he can be a real pest."

"Oh that's okay, he's cute," she said with a slight Spanish accent. "How did you teach him to do that?"

"Well, we started when he was a pup, he was good at fetching things so I started using the Frisbee to…"

"No, I mean how did you get him to single out the girls in the park?"

That kind of caught me off guard, and since my intentions were pure, I wasn't using my best material from Jake's School of Charm and Witty Repartee.

"Uhhh…"

"Just kidding. He doesn't miss very often, does he?"

"No, he's pretty good."

Blu squirmed like a kid who has to pee, so she picked up his disc and threw a nice spinner for him.

"I'm Alex."

Her handshake was firm and self-assured, and coated with the drool and dead grass from Blu's Frisbee. She grinned mischievously, knowing full well she had just slimed my hand.

"I'm Jake, and that's Blu. Thanks for being a good sport."

"No problem, I don't mind a little slime now and then," she said as I wiped the goo off of my hand and onto my pant leg. "It's nice to meet you, but I really should get going. I want to finish my run before it gets dark."

Sunset was at least an hour and a half away, so she was lying or way too serious about running; either way, it felt like a polite dismissal.

"Nice to meet you, too."

She started off and after a few paces turned back and said, "I need to practice with that Frisbee... hopefully I'll see you guys again." Then she set out at a pace that I couldn't have matched on my best day.

Blu and I gawked after her as she ran into the distance, her tan legs pumping and sable ponytail bouncing to the rhythm of her stride. Maybe I'd start jogging again.

I threw a few more for Blu before he called it a day and trotted off towards the apartment. Later, as I sat on my balcony, watching the last rays of a nice sunset fading over the park, I saw her run through the light of a street lamp on the running path. Her stride long and graceful and her pace blistering. At least she hadn't been lying.

***

Lost in the memory of Alex, I had missed the sports, weather and Leno's monologue, only to come back and find Jay on the streets of LA, interviewing some moron who knew which celebrity the fattest Kardashian was screwing and was positive that the Gettysburg Address is where the President lives. What a country.

It was getting late, and my four-legged buddy and I needed to get an early start for a long day of driving, so I really should have headed for bed. Instead, I cracked the seal on the remaining beer and watched some young star who looked like he just got out of bed tell Leno how sad he was about the plight of some third world country that he couldn't point out on a map. I sipped my beer and slowly drifted towards sleep, my last conscious thoughts of Alex and her piercing green eyes.

Chapter 5

The house where Tuco had spent his teen years bore little resemblance to the shell he stood in now. It was the same shabby, run-down concrete and cinderblock structure that it had always been, but since he inherited it upon his grandmother's death three years before, it underwent interior changes that rendered it unrecognizable.

Gone were the original interior walls and the meager furnishings that his grandparents collected over the years; in their place was a small room separated from the rest of the house by a thick security door, which led to the rest of the house. The kitchen and bedrooms had been converted into a detainment and interrogation facility.

Guero sat in the anteroom on a threadbare cloth sofa, watched a small color television set and absentmindedly stroked his sleeping puppy. A bare bulb hanging from the ceiling provided more than enough light for the tight space. All of the windows were covered from the inside by thick sheets of plywood secured to the cinderblock walls with masonry screws. High-strength steel grates, disguised to look like cheap decorative wrought iron, covered the exterior windows, and the inexpensive wood laminate exterior door had been replaced with a heavy security door, also made of high-strength steel. Two heavy-duty deadbolt locks secured it. One lock required a key from both sides and it would be very difficult for anyone to get into, or out of, the house unless Tuco allowed it.

Satisfied that Guero was enthralled with Sponge Bob and unaware of what was going on in the adjacent rooms, Tuco grabbed his blazer from the back of the sofa, unlocked the door and stepped onto the brick patio overlooking the trash-strewn courtyard and neighborhood outside its low walls. Beyond the hills and ramshackle houses, less than half a mile north, Tuco could see the lights of El Paso reflected in the muddy Rio Grande. The house was perched on a hillside in the *Colonia Francisco Villa*, and had a good view of the low hills to the north where the neighborhood's namesake garrisoned his rag-tag troops prior to their rout of the *federales* in the spring of 1911.

Tuco pulled a short, thin cigarillo from the interior pocket of his tailored sport coat. In the chill of the early morning, he lit the hand-rolled Cuban and thought about Doroteo Arango, the simple *peón*-turned-*bandido*-turned-revolutionary hero, and better known to history as Pancho Villa. Shortly after Tuco arrived in Juarez following his mother's death, he had sat with his grandfather on this same patio as the old man recounted the story of Pancho's victory at the Battle of Juarez, as seen through the eyes of an eight-year-old boy.

His grandfather told him that during the battle, the *gringos* lined the rooftops north of the border dressed in their Sunday best. The women carried parasols against the desert sun.

They ate picnic lunches and jostled to get a view of the battle, oblivious to the pain and suffering caused by the tons of lead tearing through human flesh. An occasional stray round would find a target on the north side of the border, but even that did little to quell the bloodlust of the spectators. Villa's army played to the Americans, knowing they loved an underdog, and that a victory in Juarez ensured an increased flow of arms and supplies to the rebels from benefactors in the United States.

In Tuco's eyes, Pancho Villa personified the struggle of the common man against the corruption of the Mexican government. It is a view that he used to justify his own actions, but something had gone horribly wrong. The idealism of youth had capitulated to the pragmatism of life in Mexico, but even pragmatism could not explain the depraved brutality that had swept him up like a leaf in a dust devil.

He took a long drag on the bitter cigarillo and thought, *It's all bullshit, the* narcos *claim they are cut from the same cloth as the famous bandido, hiding behind the same veil of a great struggle against a corrupt government. But just as Pancho was a cold-blooded, indiscriminate killer, so are the* narcos.

So am I.

I am a narco.

It's all bullshit.

Killing was always part of the business, mostly turf violators, sticky-fingered mules, snitches or the very occasional trouble-some judge or politician who didn't respect how the system worked, but the violence had escalated into a horrific frenzy of carnage and one-upsmanship. As cartel leaders knocked each other off, their successors had to find more and more outlandish ways to show they would stop at nothing to hold power. Machismo ran deep and the gruesome violence had become spectacular and absurd.

Severed heads were rolled across dance floors, crowded house parties were sprayed with bullets to get at a single informant, and most egregious of all in Tuco's estimation, they had involved children.

One of Sinaloa's most feared *sicario's* calling card was a slashed throat cut so deeply the head remained attached by only a stringy sinew--the assassin was a twelve-year-old boy. He was effective because his victims were oblivious to the threat posed by a mere child. An orphan recruited from the streets, he was desensitized by cocaine and systematic exposure to increasingly shocking acts of brutality.

Reprisal came within days of the ambush on Ramon Cor-dona's convoy. A Sinaloa death squad killed an off-duty *Policia Federal* sergeant who they knew was on the Juarez Cartel payroll. As he returned home from a trip to the grocery store with his oldest child, the assailants riddled the policeman with bullets while he sat strapped in the front seat. His son made it out of their small Toyota and managed to take three running steps before he was gunned down in the glow of the car's headlights. Tuco watched the news footage that showed the boy's mother wailing over the bloody body of her seven-year-old little boy.

It's all bullshit.

Tuco dropped the spent butt into the dirt and crushed it with a twist of his toe.

Is it too late for me?

He gazed across the river at the bright lights of the Sun Bowl Stadium. As a youth in a world that seemed so far away from him now, he had dreamed of playing football there.

Looking down at his pants, the blood, some of it still wet, appeared black in the weak fluorescent light of a lonely streetlamp. It reminded him of liquid chocolate.

Tuco took another look at the lights of El Paso across the river shining through the smoky haze. He held his breath for several seconds, then let it out in a moment of decision and opened the door.

Chapter 6

Blu and I had been on the road for just over five hours, and I was loving every minute of it. Miles and miles of rolling hills, giving way to vast flat expanses, wide open blue skies and fellow travelers headed to destinations unknown. Life on the road is the stuff that artists have lauded and songwriters romanticized for generations—probably even before C.W. McCall's venerable *Convoy*.

It is a symbol of America—freedom in its purest form—the promise of opportunity laid out before you with a dashed white line on black asphalt to show you the way.

What a load of crap.

Driving sucks. Period.

I'll take sitting in coach with a kid kicking the back of my seat any day over mile upon mile of tumbleweeds, telephone poles, truckers on amphetamines and brain dead rednecks in the fast lane doing ten under the limit.

It's nine hours from Austin to El Paso. Nine glorious hours of treeless waste, and if you're dumb enough to let your satellite radio subscription lapse, nothing but Mexican radio to keep you company. Well, Mexican radio and a dog whose farts will melt the hair out of your nose.

My gaseous little friend was the reason I was still on the road instead of elbow deep in a plate of *chile rellenos* and beer. I couldn't leave him behind for a week and I needed some wheels in El Paso, so there we were, somewhere east of Ft. Stockton listening to Spanglish play-by-play of a Cowboys vs. Giants nail-biter. New York was up by twenty-one late in the fourth quarter.

There aren't many better ways to enjoy good ol' American football than to listen to it relayed by Mexican commentators in flowing Spanish. It's not called a romance language for nothing, and even if you don't speak it, you still get the point.

"*Ahora lanza la pelota* TONY ROMO, *y es agarrado por una* TOUCHDOWN! TOUCHDOWN, DALLAS COWBOYS! *Hay, hay, hay!*" Okay, maybe I embellished the last part a little.

Thanks to my alcohol-assisted walk down memory lane the night before, Blu and I didn't get started until close to noon. I had hit the snooze button at least twenty times, and my dog has never been much help when it comes to packing. So we were a little behind schedule, about six hours. Stopping every hour to pay the rent on all of the coffee I was drinking didn't help us catch up.

We were looking at pulling into El Paso around ten p.m. and I hoped to hell that Ronald Mitchell, Esq., Mr. Excitement-in-a-Bottle, had followed my instructions and left a key under my Dearly Departed Dad's welcome mat. When I called to ask him about staying at my father's place, he started to hem and haw with a bunch of legal jargon about "probate" and "highly irregular" and such.

"Listen," I cut him off. "I don't want to hear any of your legal mumbo bullshit. Just leave the key under the goddamn mat!" Okay, maybe those weren't my exact words, but I think he got the point.

Guess I'd know for sure in a few hours.

The Cowboys dropped another heartbreaker by twenty-eight points, and all that was left on the radio were a bunch of yelping *mariachis* picking on Spanish guitars, blowing on trumpets and singing about dark-eyed Mexican maidens on high-fidelity AM airwaves. A distant thunderstorm announced itself with intermittent bursts of loud static, and Blu announced himself silently with an eye-waterer.

Mexican radio notwithstanding, hours on the road give you time to think.

My father was dead.

I really didn't know the details, only that no services were planned, and that the good Mr. Mitchell, Esq., would fill me in first thing in the morning. My dad hadn't crossed my mind for what seems like years, but the white lines whizzing by brought the memories back.

Loaded up in the family cruiser, an Oldsmobile station wagon, at four in the morning, still in my PJs and crammed in the back with the dog. Digging through the ice chest for a Schlitz, at what couldn't have been much later than ten a.m.— "It's noon on the east coast"—and handing it forward.

DUI wasn't illegal *back then*, in fact it was a prerequisite for manhood, and the kid whose mom started MADD was still in the crib.

Camping in a pop-up trailer near a lake somewhere in the mountains of New Mexico, the tall pines a nice change from hot, dry El Paso. Fishing for rainbows with a push-button combo, my hook loaded with salmon eggs that glowed an eerie, neon pink. Running back to the pop-up for more beer. Playing with my toy truck in the dirt, "Goddamn it, you're tangled up again," only to discover it was the biggest trout of the weekend, biggest of the year.

The drive home, Dad, one hand holding a beer and the steering wheel, the other, middle finger extended, pointing at the suped-up Chevy Nova that just whizzed by doing ninety. It would be a few more years before I knew what he meant by that gesture.

I had used the gesture to salute a fellow driver just hours before.

A desert tortoise, plodding across the shimmering asphalt and about to disappear in the parched yellow grass of the median. "Look Jake, a turtle."

"Can we stop and catch him?"

"Those things have diseases."

I knew better than to argue.

"Maybe we can get one at a pet store when we get home," added Mom the Moderator, but I knew that *"maybe"* meant that the subject was closed.

I still wonder if that tortoise made it to the other side.

A little kid with wet hair and wearing one of his dad's old t-shirts, holding up a silvery fish nearly as long as the kid is tall. His father stands next to him holding up a pathetic little trout, both of them smiling.

I think I still have that Polaroid somewhere.

He coached my little league team, took me to work with him on the occasional Saturday, and taught me to "chew with my fucking mouth shut."

Then, one day when I was fourteen, he was asked to leave.

Late nights at the bar were standard procedure, but when my mom acted the sleuth and discovered him in bed with another woman, his gig was up. He took her at her word and got the hell out, way out.

Mom moved on with her life, but I never forgave him. Teenage logic told me that he valued alcohol and bar tramps more than my mom and me, so I rejected him in turn.

After a three-month hiatus, he tried to come around again, but I didn't want anything to do with him. Without a family to keep him grounded, he fell deeper into the cycle of addiction, which only reinforced my anger and set the stage for what turned out to be a doomed relationship.

Mom did a great job of filling both roles, using a crappy Helen Reddy song as her anthem, and eventually my feelings of anger and abandonment turned to apathy. My teenage years were filled with happiness and great memories—Mom's version might differ a bit, but who's splitting hairs?

A blurry grey flash through the beams of my headlights startled me out of the walk down memory lane. Probably a coyote, I couldn't tell as it bounded off into the darkness. Whatever it was, it was lucky, I had seen dozens of furry corpses littering the interstate since I left Austin. Cars seemed to win most of the contests, however some of the deer I saw spread in pieces across the side of the road were undoubtedly the cause of many a body shop owner's delight.

A faint glow in the distance heralded the end of my journey. The black void of the desert gave way to the bright twinkling lights of El Paso and her more populated sister to the south. A desert city at night looked like a cosmic hand had scattered a giant fistful of diamonds on black velvet, and the dry desert air made them shimmer and sparkle. The lights ended abruptly where the Franklin Mountains, southern tip of the Rockies, cut through the heart of the city like a ragged wall, separating east from west. A break in the wall is the city's namesake, *El Paso del Norte*, the Pass of the North, christened by Sixteenth-Century conquistadors based far to the south in Mexico City. The Rio Grande flows through the gap as it winds its way to the southeast, forming the boundary between Texas and the state of Chihuahua. Pinched into the narrow pass is downtown El Paso, an unimpressive collection of tall buildings that hasn't been augmented since the late seventies.

Interstate-10 winds through the city that was a great place to grow up, but a place I am glad to have left. It was too small for me. The town had changed in the fifteen years or so that I'd been gone; big box retailers added to the mix and some of the old standbys gone for posterity, but for the most part it had the familiar feel of a broken-in pair of jeans.

I rolled on through the east side, where most of the population lives. It is mostly flat and covered by urban sprawl spreading eastward towards the Hueco Mountains like a fast-growing fungus. The peaks of the Franklins, marked by the flashing red beacons atop 50,000-watt radio towers, loomed as I drove west.

Nestled up to their craggy east face are some of El Paso's older neighborhoods. Built during the economic boom before WWI to accommodate a growing population, they fill the space between downtown and the Army base.

Our long drive behind us, Blu and I stood in front of one of those old houses. Well, I stood. Blu ran around pissing on every shrub, wall and vertical surface he could find. It looked like my dad had kept the place pretty well maintained. Wish I could say the same for the neighborhood.

The house once belonged to my great-grandparents and standing out front brought back more childhood memories. The home had smelled of old dust and Ben-gay, and my great-grandfather had hair growing out of his freakishly large ears. I never liked the visits; frankly the place scared me. But it seemed much smaller now than when I was a kid.

It was a modest, craftsman-style home with a large front patio, surrounded by a low brick wall and thick brick columns that held up a low, gently sloped roof. It even had a basement, which must have been a bitch to dig in the rocky soil. As a kid I used to poke around down there, happy to be free of the musty old people. I imagined it was an Egyptian tomb; the darkness, dust and black widow cobwebs lent an air of authenticity to my adventures. Basements like this one fell out of style in El Paso about the time of Henry Ford's Model T. In Austin, the small property would have fetched a pretty penny, but El Paso had yet to be bitten by the gentrification bug, so it was just another old house in a declining neighborhood.

I climbed the stairs of the raised concrete porch and held my breath as I bent over and lifted the mat that said "Only Knock if You Have Beer." To my relief, there was a small manila envelope containing a single key.

"The peckerwood came through for us, Blu."

He raised his ears and cocked his head at me, but otherwise continued to pee on a juniper bush.

I guess it wasn't reasonable to expect the house to be like it was when my great grandparents lived there, but what I found was a huge surprise. The only thing that I would peg as my dad's, besides the redneck doormat, was a stuffed trout over the stone fireplace. He must have hired someone from *Queer Eye* to decorate the place. I was impressed. The original wood floors had been impeccably refinished, and the walls painted in bold but earthy tones.

His furniture was neoclassical craftsman in warm oak and rich, buttery-soft leather—ok, I made that up, but you get the point--the stuff was pretty nice.

The whole place was classy--not an adjective oft associated with my father--totally out of place in this neighborhood, and way beyond the means of a small time dreamer who was as good at business as a chimp doing calculus.

The *piéce de résistance* was the basement. It had been converted into a state-of-the-art media room, complete with calfskin recliners and an electronics suite that rivaled an IMAX theater-- even had a wet bar with beer on tap. Maybe it was all the stuff, but it seemed much smaller than the crypt I explored as a kid, more so than the rest of the house—but I guess it *had* been over twenty years, and a long drive with a hangover.

At the end of my tour, I went back to the truck to get my bags and fetch the dog. He had wandered two doors down and was watering my new neighbor's plants. Blu was nothing if not thoughtful.

I knew before looking that there was beer in the refrigerator, and with the exception of a lonely olive floating in its jar, I was right. He had progressed beyond the old standby Schlitz-in-a-can and moved up to Schlitz-in-a-bottle. I grabbed one of the three six-packs, contemplated but passed on the olive, went downstairs, and plopped down in a fine Corinthian leather media chair to catch the football highlights on ESPN—English version. Halfway through the third bottle of Milwaukee swill, I cursed myself for forgetting about the tap in the wet bar. It was late and I was ready for bed, but I checked the keg anyway—more Schlitz. I made a mental note to buy some decent beer, drug my tired body up the stairs, and forgot to investigate why the basement was half of what it used to be.

I opted out of the master bedroom, and chose instead the one furnished in 1930s little-old-lady style. It seemed like nostalgia at the time, but in hindsight I probably just didn't want to sleep in a dead man's bed.

Chapter 7

Guero slept in the fetal position with his head resting on the shabby arm of the sofa, Sponge Bob prattling on in the background. His puppy lay curled up in a towel, safe for the time being at least from the prospect of accidental suffocation. Tuco grabbed a threadbare blanket off of the back of the couch and spread it over his older brother; the thin cotton throw was the only thing left in the house that had belonged to their grandparents.

He stood for a moment and watched his brother sleep and smiled to himself, because he knew that the soft snoring, barely audible over the television, would soon give way to the sound of a braying mule.

Tuco always did his best to keep Guero insulated from the horrors that went on in the next room. It made his job a little more difficult, but he managed. Exposing his brother to the reality of life in the cartel would be no different than exposing a child, but he would never entertain the thought of leaving Guero in the care of others.

Occasionally he would let Guero take some minor role in their operations, but only if he could ensure his brother's safety. When the gunplay started in the Cordona ambush, Guero was rushed clear from the line of fire and into an armored SUV where he could watch the shootout unfold. Like a young kid watching a movie, his challenged mind could not process the reality of people dying in front of him and he cheered at the spectacle. Tuco wondered at himself for taking that kind of risk with his brother's life, but justified it by Guero's reaction. While he would never admit it, in the dark corners of his mind he knew that if the unspeakable were to happen, it might not be such a bad thing.

Tuco turned from his sleeping brother, opened the door to the back room and nearly gagged on the overpowering odor. His time outside and the cheap cigar had cleared the smell from his nose and the fresh assault on his senses made him regret taking the break. He could tolerate the stench of sweat, urine and blood, but the sickly sweet aroma of singed hair and burnt flesh was hard for him to stomach. Two bare-bulb light fixtures cast an eerie glow on the layer of smoke that collected near the ceiling.

They had been at it for nearly twenty-four hours. Shortly after they arrived, a van pulled to the back of the house and three prisoners, two men and a woman--bound with zip ties, gagged, and hooded--were transferred into the interrogation room through a back entrance. El Cuchillo was ready for them.

With the help of a cattle prod, Cuchillo forced the unfortunate bodyguard to strip naked and tied him face down to a perforated metal examination table. Once satisfied that his powerfully-built victim could not struggle free from the thick plastic restraints, Cuchillo prepared for what he jokingly called the *La Linea* Spa Treatment.

His massage implements were an electric belt sander, reciprocating saw, propane torch and common table salt. If anyone outside of the house ever heard the screams within, they wisely kept it to themselves.

Just before Tuco had stepped out to smoke the last of his cigarillos, the bodyguard finally died. The man was strong and accounted for himself well, but bravery didn't count for much in this game. He was only the bodyguard for the older, weaker man, and they knew he had little, if anything, to offer. His slow torture was calculated to induce fear in the accountant and loosen his tongue.

The girl was next.

Tuco had no idea who the woman was—a girlfriend, a hooker, or just some poor wretch with horrible luck who picked a bad time to dance with the accountant. It really didn't matter, either way she was an innocent, but also a means to an end.

The vermin Cuchillo couldn't wait to go to work on her. Tuco's stomach turned at the thought of the sexual pleasure that the greasy bastard would derive from hurting the girl.

The sight of the pretty young girl curled up next to the old man scratched at a familiar wound.

***

Alejandra de la Rosa was the first woman accepted into the demanding Grupo Especial *training program, and the formerly all-male team was not very happy about it. According to prevailing but groundless rumors, her rich and influential father paid for her spot on the team, and the chauvinistic cops would do everything in their power to hinder her success.*

If she had been the stereotypic tough girl, Tuco would have been right there with the rest of the federales, *but de la Rosa was beautiful and he was smitten.*

Despite her good looks and stellar performance on the team, her presence was an affront to Mexican virility, and any unpleasant job at the police barracks was hers by default. The other recruits never cleaned a toilet, and none of the veterans seemed to be able to aim their urine half as well as they aimed their pistols.

Passing was good enough for most recruits, but de la Rosa was held to a higher standard. Only when she exceeded the standards by a wide margin was she allowed to progress.

Tuco wanted to step in and correct the injustice, but he didn't dare let his squad mates see his weakness for her.

The incessant hazing stopped just short of sexual assault. One day, when she made her way to the barracks, her bed had been laid out with a Grupo Especial *flight suit, fuzzy handcuffs, pink plastic gun and a large, strap-on rubber penis.*

When she showed up the following morning dressed in the ensemble, dildo strapped prominently between her legs, the team got the message—she wasn't going to quit. The hazing eventually stopped and she was held to the same standard as her classmates, even though she continued to outshine them. Her strength and confidence got her through the ordeal.

And Tuco Medrano wasn't the only team leader smitten by Alejandra de la Rosa.

***

Is it necessary to bring the girl into this? he thought.

Yes.

Sleep deprivation and the bodyguard's grisly torture had not achieved the desired effect--a loud "boo" should have caused the trembling, wheezing accountant to spill his guts, but so far, he wasn't talking.

They had to use the girl.

While Tuco was outside, Cuchillo had tidied up the body-guard's remains and drained what was left of his blood into an orange Home Depot paint bucket. For dramatic effect, he had dismembered the mutilated body with the reciprocating saw and stuffed the parts into clear plastic bags that would be distributed later as warnings in very public places. His head, sans eyelids and tongue, sat on the floor under the exam table, the one intact eyeball staring accusingly at the accountant whom its owner had failed to protect.

"Anything?" Tuco nodded towards the frail looking man sitting against the wall.

"No, *patron*, but he tried to go to sleep again," said Cuchillo with an evil grin that revealed his yellowed teeth, "I dint let him."

The accountant sat upright against the wall on the bare concrete floor, his arms zip-tied to an anchor in the cinder block wall above his head, his legs similarly affixed to the floor and dressed in a pair of dirty boxers. The thick plastic zip ties severely chaffed his wrists, and blood flowed down his arms in long, thin rivulets.

A thick copper wire looped around each of his big toes ran to threaded posts on an aged wooden box with a knurled plastic selector knob on top and a hand crank on the side. The knob could be twisted to select a range from one to ten on a worn copper dial--the midrange numbers had nearly worn away with use.

Tuco's grandfather had used the box to make money from stupid Americans on Juarez Avenue. He wore it suspended from a strap around his neck. Two polished metal cylinders about the length of a man's finger and twice as thick were wired to the box. Walking through the bars and discothèques, clicking the cylinders together to get the attention of drunken soldiers and college students, he charged them a few pesos to test their manhood.

Suckers with more money than sense eagerly paid to grip the handles and hold on as long as they could while he cranked the handle and shocked the crap out of them. Only the strongest, or dumbest, held on for more than a second or two with six selected on the dial, and none held beyond seven.

Tuco looked at the dial and saw that it was set at nine.

"*Pendejo*! I need him alive!" he barked.

"But Boss, it's just a little…"

Tuco turned and grabbed Cuchillo by the shirt, "It could stop his fucking heart… look at him!" he hissed through clinched teeth.

He let go of the *sicario's* shirt, relieved to be clear of his body odor and rancid breath. Normally any man who dared to speak to Cuchillo that way would have been opened from his crotch to sternum, disemboweled by the cruel, curved-blade karambit that he always carried in his front pocket—but he knew better than to mess with Tuco. It would be a death sentence, so he checked the impulse to spill his boss' guts onto the concrete floor.

"Lay off the juice, he's about to tell us everything we want to know."

"Si, *patron*," he said with look of contempt that Tuco caught as he turned away.

Tuco knew that the narcotics trade was a cash business, and the Mexican cartels generated nearly one hundred billion dollars a year in revenue. They didn't accept Mastercard, Visa or even American Express, so the fives, tens and twenties tended to pile up, creating a problem for the people on the south side of the border who wanted to spend them. As drugs flowed north across the border, guns and money flowed south. Law enforcement and rival cartels knew that if they could stop the drugs OR the money, they would win the game, so the money routes were every bit as important as the drug routes.

Tuco also knew that the best way to transfer large amounts of money was electronically, so turning large piles of illicit cash into legitimate assets that could be transferred via the banking system, versus the back of an exhaust-spewing tractor trailer was a high priority for the savvy cartel boss. The accountant tied to Tuco's late Abuelita's kitchen floor was the brain behind one of the Sinaloa Cartel's most successful money laundering operations.

If Cuchillo could torture some secrets out of the old man, Tuco knew his boss would be very pleased.

As he watched the proceedings, Tuco realized he had miscalculated the girl's importance. The old man was trying his best to act as if she meant nothing to him. He had watched with horror as the bodyguard's skin was removed with the belt sander and his fingers and toes roasted slowly with a blowtorch, but was passively looking on with feigned indifference at the girl tied face up to Cuchillo's table.

The girl wasn't older than twenty-one or so, and it was now clear that she was not one of the cheap whores preferred by cartel underlings. Her black cocktail dress was high quality, and probably came from one of the exclusive boutiques across the border in El Paso. The jewelry, which had long since made its way into Cuchillo's pockets, was set with genuine diamonds and not the cheap glass that most of the street girls wore. Even her hair, skin and nails were clearly more meticulously cared for than a Hollywood starlet's.

She lay on her back with arms extended over her head and legs slightly spread. Cuchillo zip-tied her slender wrists and ankles to each corner of the long metal exam table and stuffed a washrag in her mouth to prevent her from crying out, but Tuco doubted she would make much noise. She was bearing up to the ordeal with a quiet dignity that impressed him. Only her rapidly-moving eyes betrayed her distress; they darted from her captors to the wiry man tied to the wall. She watched Cuchillo's every move, knowing he was the most immediate threat, but even through the fear, Tuco could see the hate in her eyes.

The interrogator stood close to the table, carelessly wielding a lovingly sharpened straight razor and licking his lips, while he ogled the helpless girl. Tuco felt his stomach turn when Cuchillo ran his dirty hand up the inside of her smooth leg and under the hem of her short dress. It was the first time she struggled against her restraints.

"Quit your squirming, *puta*, or I will drain one of your fucking eyeballs," he hissed while holding the glistening blade millimeters from her rolling eyes.

She immediately stopped struggling and a tear flowed down the side of her face as he thrust a filthy finger past her lacy panties and as deep as he could inside of her. The pleading look she gave Tuco was hard for him to ignore, but he knew that now was the time--he had to turn all of his attention to the accountant.

Tuco had heard all of the arguments in the American press that torture doesn't work, and that put under enough stress a person will tell you anything you want to hear. He doubted the Americans had ever sanded the skin off of a terrorist and rubbed salt in the wounds, or cut pieces off of a living person while their loved ones watched, but one thing he was sure of was that they always talked.

Always.

If you don't lead them with stupid questions, they always tell the truth.

Always.

The accountant was near his breaking point. Tuco could see the fear and indecision in his eyes. Gone was the feigned indifference, replaced by sheer terror as Cuchillo molested the girl. Tuco watched his captive's resolve evaporate—his eyes never left the number-man's face, but the sounds coming from the table told him exactly what was happening. He heard the whisper of the blade as it cut away the cloth of the clinging dress, and her soft whimper at the soft snap of her bra and panties falling to the razor. Three soft slaps and, "Look, *patron*, she shaved it for me already," followed by a fourth, firmer slap and, "perhaps I shave it closer for you later, eh, *puta*?"

Then the familiar metallic click-clack of the shiny metal electrodes, reattached to grandfather's box.

Tuco saw it—the moment of decision where love out-weighed duty and the accountant broke. It happened as the old man watched Cuchillo roughly insert the thick electrodes into the struggling girl's vagina and rectum.

"She likes it, boss, I really think she likes it!" punctuated by his high-pitched, nasal cackle.

Tuco was puzzled for a moment by the relief he felt when the accountant said, "Stop, I'll tell you everything."

He looked back at the naked girl and the wires running from her privates to the box sitting between her feet. Normally he would set the hook deep and allow Cuchillo a few turns on the handle, but something that he couldn't explain made Tuco raise his hand and call off his dog. Cuchillo's disappointment was clear.

He leaned into the defeated accountant who repeated in a quiet whisper. "Don't hurt my little girl, I'll tell you everything"

And he did.

***

It took nearly an hour to get all of the information out of the accountant. Tuco gave him water, the first he had had in twenty-four hours, to lubricate his lips and tongue. He even resorted to smelling salts a few times to keep him awake, but he kept the information flowing.

Tuco did his best to stay positioned between the accountant and Cuchillo, who seemed content to ogle the nude girl and sneak the occasional grope. He didn't trust the slimy ex-cop beyond the length of his short blade and didn't want him to hear anything the accountant was saying. Tuco hoped that if he did hear anything at all, it wasn't enough to put together the bigger picture. Tuco's life depended on it.

When the accountant had finished his tale, Tuco asked several questions to verify details and probe him for inconsistencies, but his story didn't falter and Tuco believed he was truthful. He stood and stretched, a decision made on his next move.

"Get her some clothes," Tuco ordered.

Cuchillo moved to the wires attached to the electrodes still inside the girl.

"No," Tuco snapped, "let her do that, just find her something to wear."

Cuchillo sulked off like a whipped dog while Tuco used wire snips to cut the thick plastic ties that held the girl to the table. She pulled away from him and curled into a ball on the table. Cuchillo returned with a worn flannel button-down.

"It's all I could find, *patron*."

"That's fine." Tuco covered her with the shirt and moved to cut the ties that restrained her father. The plastic had cut deep, cruel furrows around his wrists and ankles, and as they were removed, fresh blood seeped from the wounds. The accountant cried out in pain as the blood flowed back into his arms. He tried to make his way to the exam table, but only moved a couple of feet before curling into a position similar to his daughter's.

She moved under the flannel and Tuco saw her wince as he heard the successive metallic clinks of the electrodes falling onto the table. After a few moments, she sat up, put on the shirt and gingerly stepped down to attend to her father.

Tuco allowed the reunion, and he and Cuchillo watched as father and daughter offered each other solace in hell.

"Come here, please, *señorita*," Tuco said softly as he held his hand out to her. "You will be safe."

The frail man nodded to her and she went to Tuco, tears streaming down her face. He led her out of the room and sat her on one of two old but plush recliners next to the couch where Guero still slept. He picked up the sleeping puppy and set it in her lap.

Tuco couldn't help but notice how the front of the girl's flannel shirt had opened slightly and teased him with the creamy smoothness of her skin and pleasing swell of her firm breasts.

He thought again of Alejandra.

Tuco stirred from the memory and a thought crossed his mind: *What harm could an old man do?*

He pushed it aside before returning to the interrogation room.

"Kill him and clean up the mess," he ordered Cuchillo. "Then get some rest, we're going to El Paso in the morning."

Chapter 8

This is about as exciting as it gets for a money chaser, thought Special Agent Christa Adams.

Most of her time on the job at the Drug Enforcement Agency was spent sifting through financial records--paper and electronic--looking for the little inconsistencies known to be primary indicators of money laundering. Then there was the wrangling with lawyers and accountants, two of the most amorphous professions on the planet. She found all of it exceptionally mundane.

But this morning, Adams stood on the Yandell Drive overpass near the University of Texas at El Paso, bundled against the chilly air in a borrowed DEA windbreaker and mesmerized by the blinking hazards of a tractor-trailer parked in the center lane of Interstate-10 East.

"Man, look at that traffic!" Her partner had returned from a conference with the El Paso police officers huddled near the semi and broke her trance.

She looked away from the carnage under the truck to see carnage of a different sort. The EPPD had shut down the eastbound lanes of I-10 and the traffic was being diverted through the university. It was rush hour and four lanes of traffic were backed up as far as she could see, well beyond the Sun Bowl Stadium and tall smokestack of the abandoned copper smelter.

There's no way out for them, she thought. The section of highway was built through a natural choke point, with mountains on one side and the Rio Grande on the other. They were dead center in the Pass of the North.

"Yep, they're screwed."

Christa turned back to the action below and leaned out over the guardrail to get a better view. A police officer with a measuring wheel was pacing off the broken red streak that started on the pavement directly beneath her and ended somewhere under the cab of the parked big-rig a few hundred feet away. As the cop passed a shoe that she was pretty sure still held a foot, he dropped a numbered, tent-shaped plastic marker and continued pacing. Less recognizable clumps of bloody matter lay scattered along the course of the red streak.

"Is it our guy?" she asked.

"Well there's not much left of him, but the cops say the tattoos are consistent with Acosta."

"Damn it."

***

Christa had started out as a star in the DEA, destined for the kind of choice undercover assignments that spawned shining careers. Recruited out of Penn State, she had graduated at the top of her class and within a year was sent to Cartagena, Colombia, which despite the common perception after the death of Pablo Escobar, was still the heart of cocaine production.

Her short-lived star peaked at a ceremony in which the visiting National Drug Control Policy Director presented her with an Award of Excellence. His Deputy Director expressed his appreciation for Christa's excellence in a more personal way.

When the director saw her leaving his deputy's hotel room the next morning, she was on the next plane stateside. Her paramour was politely asked to end his stint at the White House Office of National Drug Control Policy.

The only thing that saved her job was the fact that she genuinely did not know that the man was married. Well, that and the breaking of the Hooker-gate scandal in which a bunch of Secret Service agents hired some Colombian prostitutes and had the temerity to welch on the bill. The penalty for screwing the Drug Czar's (married) right-hand man was assignment to the "laundry detail."

Her rookie partner John Reynolds' story wasn't nearly as tragic. The former Army Ranger earned his way into money chasing by finishing last in his class at Quantico.

***

After a year in El Paso, Christa was starting to feel close to something big--and she really needed something big if she hoped to do anything more with her career than comb through spreadsheets and ledger books--but the mangled corpse wedged between the Peterbuilt's undercarriage and highway concrete was the second setback in less than a week. The first was the execution-style murder of a coin-operated car wash owner, presumably carried out by the young gentleman spread thinly down the center lane of I-10 East.

"Was it Mitchell?"

"Yep."

"Can we prove it?"

She nodded toward the truck. "It would have been tough enough to tie young Beto there to Mitchell before the lawyer got a hold of him. So what are the odds whoever helped him off the bridge turns themselves in and rolls on Mitchell?"

Less than a week before, a man who identified himself as Daniel Martin had called into the El Paso field office offering up some important information about "a large sum of money and his sleazy lawyer, Ron Mitchell." His case was referred to Adams' desk. She had long suspected that the lawyer was the conduit for over a hundred million dollars a year of laundered Sinaloa Cartel funds, but before she could make contact with the potential informant, he was killed during an apparent robbery at his carwash.

Alberto "Beto" Acosta was the prime suspect in Martin's murder and Christa's best shot at getting to Ronald Mitchell, attorney-at-law. Three days after the killing, Acosta was stopped on suspicion of DUI. A search of his car turned up a bank bag full of quarters and a .38 revolver, the same caliber weapon used against Martin. Facing a long stay in state-provided accommodations and a potentially lethal injection, Acosta offered up a tale of murder for hire in exchange for a plea bargain. Unfortunately his story changed and he clammed up tightly when his lawyer, none other than Ronald Mitchell, swooped in to rescue him from the clutches of his own confession.

"Why would the judge give him bail?"

"Mitchell played up some booking errors, and I'm sure he never expected our boy Beto to come up with a million dollar bond."

Mitchell had beaten her to the punch. Again. It had become a recurring theme.

A friend at EPPD had tipped her off about Acosta, and she and Reynolds were on their way to the jailhouse to interview the killer when they got the call that led them to Yandell Drive and I-10.

His bond had been posted less than an hour before his assisted suicide.

"What now?"

She shrugged and tried to hide the dejection in her voice, "Martin's son is meeting with Mitchell this morning. I think we should go visit him this afternoon."

"What if he doesn't cooperate?"

She took one last look at the remains of Beto Acosta and started towards their car.

"We can threaten RICO, but you read his file, he seems like a real boy scout. He'll cooperate."

But if he doesn't, she thought, *there's always the secretary.*

Chapter 9

"Mr. Mitchell will see you now," announced Katy, my new lawyer's receptionist.

She exceeded all of the expectations created by her sexy telephone voice--her silky brown hair, full lips and ample lung capacity formed a prettier picture than the girl I conjured out of our phone conversations. Ronald Mitchell, Esq., however, was not what I had envisioned at all.

I imagined a gaunt, birdlike Ichabod Crane, but what sat behind the large oak desk was more akin to Jabba the Hut. At any moment, Carrie Fisher would pop out in a metal bikini to offer us some freshly squeezed space-bug juice. The guy was the size of a small hot air balloon.

His office was decorated with the kind of cheap southwestern crap you'd find at a swap meet, clearly something out of one of those room-in-a-box furniture superstores. Apparently Ronald Mitchell, Esq. didn't run in the same *Queer Eye* decorating circles as my father. His office lacked any personal expression. Of course if the bald, corpulent lawyer sitting behind the desk had chosen Katy out front, his taste couldn't be all bad.

He lumbered out of his chair, leaned across his desk knocking aside a cardboard box and offered a pillowy hand.

"Hello Mr. Martin," in a droning monotone, incongruent with his big body. "Glad to finally meet you. Your father spoke well of you." His first lie. "I take it you found the key?"

"Yes, thank you," I shook his hand, trying my hardest not to cringe at the clammy wetness of it. The watch on his right wrist told me he was a lefty. Since it cost more than my truck, it also told me he was good at screwing people out of their money. Or maybe he was just compensating for a small penis. I was going to tell him he could call me Jake, but changed my mind. I really didn't like this man.

"Glad to meet you too." *My* first lie.

"I am sorry for your loss, and I am sorry that I haven't given you many details surrounding your father's death, but hopefully I can clear some things up for you today. Your father was shot and killed in an apparent robbery at one of his places of business." He spoke in his slow monotone, and I almost missed it because of the part about my dad being murdered. Plus, the white, pasty residue at the corner of his mouth distracted me.

"Did you say *places?*"

"Yes. Your father owned several coin-operated self-serve carwashes here in El Paso. You might be familiar with the type I'm talking about--you pay for time on a high pressure spray nozzle to wash your car and use a large canister vacuum to clean out the interior."

I nodded and probably rolled my eyes a little—a bad habit that I have when someone assumes I'm an idiot and overstates the obvious.

"He had ten locations around town, and they were quite lucrative. A week ago Sunday he was collecting the cash from one of the locations on the West Side--" He had a hard time keeping eye contact at this part. "--when he was shot three times during the course of a robbery. I was told he died instantly." I was pretty sure I know what that meant: execution style. "The police are still investigating but don't have any leads. It could have been a planned robbery or just a target of opportunity too good to pass up. The assailants made off with over ten thousand dollars."

My father was brutally murdered, but oddly, I focused on the minor details and not the bombshell he just dropped. Maybe it was shock, or maybe I really just didn't care.

There were several things in the story that didn't sound right. Ending his days as a bullet catcher seemed appropriate, but running a successful--much less lucrative--business didn't sound like something Dad could pull off.

"How did a man who could screw up a winning lottery ticket manage to scrounge enough cash to open a squirt-em-off carwash, much less ten of them?"

"Well, um, please be patient, I will get to that, but however he got there, he was quite successful." He pushed a legal folder across the desk and let out a soft grunt with the effort.

"This is his Last Will and Testament."

That the old man had a will was one of the biggest surprises of the day—I came by my distaste for lawyers genetically.

"You can read it at your leisure, but in summary, he leaves the house on Louisville Avenue with all of its contents, a 2008 BMW sedan, and cash and securities worth three-hundred, seventy-two thousand dollars to his son, Douglas Jacob Martin of Austin, Texas." He paused for effect.

My day just got a little brighter. Did my apathy know no bounds?

"As for Spic-N-Span, the carwashes, he is... uh... was the principal owner, however, there is a small group of investors who share an interest in the business."

He pushed a second folder across the desk, no grunt.

"As the executor of his will and legal counsel for his estate, I recommend that you sell his share of the business to his partners. I have taken the liberty of consulting with them, and they have agreed to buy out your father's interest for the sum of six hundred thousand dollars, payable immediately. It is more than market value for his share, but they are willing to pay a premium to ensure a quick resolution."

"So, as legal counsel for his estate, in your opinion what are my other options?"

My question took him by surprise and the top of his balding head flushed ever so slightly, a bad trait for a poker player...or lawyer.

"Uh...well, I guess you could stay here in El Paso and run the business, but it would be... well... a lot of work... and, uh... this is really a very generous offer, and it's all laid out in this agreement here in this folder." Despite the stumbles, it was the fastest I had ever heard the man talk, and sweat broke out in dewy beads on top of his freckled melon.

"Okay, I will take a look at this and think it over...at my leisure. What about the funeral arrangements?"

"Yes, the funeral. Well, uh, your father wished to be cremated."

That jarred his memory and he reached over to the plain cardboard box and pushed it across the desk just like the folders. The grunt was back.

"This contains your father's remains. The body was released by the Coroner's Office on Friday, and the instructions in his will were very clear, so I arranged the cremation."

Nice box.

"He didn't want any formal services, but his final wish was to be scattered in Florida, at a place he told me you know well--a place you visited together often when you were young. If it is alright with you, I would like to be there when you, um, place him at rest. To pay my respects."

I thought about that for a second and nodded.

The meeting lasted for another thirty minutes or so, with Quaalude Ron, Esq., droning on about this and that, and me signing some documents that took my net worth from zero-to-sixty in three seconds flat. I was the proud new owner of my great grandparents' old house, a modest BMW currently residing at the El Paso Police impound lot and a fairly hefty bank account, less of course the cost of Mr. Mitchell's legal services. I couldn't wait for the reckoning with the Internal Revenue Service.

As I left, he encouraged me for the thirtieth time to take the buyout. I told him I would give it some serious consideration and we agreed to meet again on Wednesday after I had a chance to look over the documents. It slipped my mind to tell him that I was planning some pretty heavy research into the value of Spic-N-Span Carwashes, LLC.

He closed with, "Please let me know when you plan to attend to his remains; I'd really like to be there."

I found that a bit weird, but didn't give it much thought.

"Have a great day Mr. Martin." It was the receptionist.

Feeling bold with a fat bank account, a carwash business and a box full of Dad under my arm, I decided to push my luck.

"Thanks Katy, and please call me 'Jake.' Hey, how would you like to have dinner with the richest guy in El Paso?"

"Love to, is he a friend of yours?"

Ouch, but the smile told me I had a chance.

"See you Wednesday."

"Bye, Mr. Martin," she smiled again and turned back to her computer, fiddling with a lock of her silky brown hair.

I was so in.

***

I sat in my truck with Dad on the seat and the engine running. The reality of what I just heard hit me like a snowball full of rocks. My father was dead, murdered, and the chance of reconciliation gone forever. I didn't want to acknowledge the emotions swirling around in my head, so I set them aside for later. Compartmentalization is an old pilot mind trick, where you keep everything in its own neat little box to deal with on your own time. People really don't want their pilots thinking about a knocked-up daughter or overdue mortgage while trying to land in a snowstorm.

I set aside the emotion and concentrated on the facts. Dad was dead because he was mixed up in something bigger than he could handle, and clearly the lawyer was involved. Getting me to sell out was a high priority for Ronnie Mitchell, Attorney at Law.

I needed to think about the carwash business. Nearly a million bucks and a house were beyond my father's capabilities, so where, or more accurately, whom did the money come from?

The other issue that stood out was the whole Florida thing, and Mitchell's eagerness to attend the funeral. I had no idea what it was all about, but of one thing I was sure: my father and I had never set foot in the Sunshine State.

Chapter 10

It was still early when Tuco left his grandparents' old house to pick up something to eat. Guero and the girl were sleeping; Cuchillo had disposed of the accountant and his bodyguard, and brewed a pot of substandard coffee.

Tuco stood at the counter of the small neighborhood grocery and paid for the pastries, orange juice and pack of cigarillos.

While he waited for the change, he noticed the front page of *El Mundo*, the sensationalist Juarez newspaper, and felt like someone doused him with a bucket of ice water. Under the headline "*Cara de la Muerte*" was a grainy picture of him pointing his pistol at the face of Ramon Cordona.

"*Mierda.*"

As Tuco bolted out the door, the clerk wordlessly waved the pesos in his direction, shrugged, and slipped them into his own pocket.

***

Tuco had the same feeling once before, on his last night as a federale.

His sixth sense had nagged at him that there was something not quite right about the raid. They had received tips from informants all the time, but never with the kind of specifics and level of detail that came with this one. It all seemed too neat, so Tuco voiced his concern to the leader of the raid team, a senior sergeant who was also on the cartel payroll. The sergeant told him to be quiet, keep his paranoia in check, and stay with the vehicles to keep any interested bystanders away from the scene.

The sergeant gave the signal and they shattered the door with a portable battering ram. Dressed in civilian clothes, they entered the dark house with weapons drawn and met no resistance until the sergeant stepped in behind the last man. A single blast from a tactical shotgun obliterated his face. It was the only shot fired by the Sinaloa-aligned Policia Federal special ops team hidden behind strategically placed sofas. Taken completely by surprise, the crooked cops dropped their weapons immediately.

Tuco heard the federales' shout to surrender but simply drove away.

He traded one career for another, abandoned any pretense of propriety and went to work full time for the Juarez Cartel. It was not long before he earned a spot as one of the top jefes in La Linea. Tuco answered only to Jose Luis Fratello, the leader of La Linea and right hand man to Don Vicente Carillo. He made more in a week than he had in a year as a federale, and was able to provide more than Guero would ever need.

Then out of the blue, during an interrogation of a Sinaloa soldier, he heard a name from his past. The narco explained how Cordona had betrayed him. The revelation stunned Tuco, but disbelief and disappointment soon gave way to seething anger.

An old friend in the Grupo de Operaciones Especiales, Sergeant Jorge Montoya, owed him a favor and eventually helped set up the operation that would deliver Cordona on a silver platter.

And seal Tuco's fate with the cartel.

***

Guero woke on the couch, sat up and yawned loudly while rubbing his eyes with his oversized fists. He stood and shuffled over to the small television, turned it on and considered the cartoon dogs on its screen like an art critic at a Warhol exhibit. Satisfied with what he saw, he turned and noticed the girl for the first time.

"Hi." No response.

"HI." A little louder, but with the same result.

"Hi." The third time with a gentle poke to her hip.

She opened her eyes to Guero's round smiling face just inches from her own. He was oblivious to the fear and disorientation in her face as she pulled away and tried to cover more of herself with the thin blanket.

"I'm Guero, what's your-name-that's-my-puppy."

"*No hablas Español?*"

"I'm Guero. That's my puppy, you can pet him."

"I, I am Graciela."

"Grass-la. You like my puppy?"

He reached down and stroked the squirming puppy nestled in her lap. She realized that Guero wasn't much of a threat, unlike the men from last night, and she relaxed a little.

"Where is the other man?" she asked.

"I dunno, working maybe, yeah, working," he scooped up the dog. "Puppy needs to potty, Tuco gets mad if he shits on the chair."

"Tuco?"

"Tuco's my brother, I'm Guero. You like 'Two Stupid Dogs'?"

Confused by his rapid-fire questions, she started to answer but was cut short by the sound of a key in the door.

"Tuco!"

Graciela curled back into a ball on the recliner and tried to make herself small under the blanket as Tuco opened the door and stepped in carrying a grocery bag.

"Tuco! This is Grass-la, she's pretty. She likes 'Stupid Dogs.' Can we eat pancakes? I'm hungry."

The girl thought he seemed distracted, and hurried, but his demeanor changed when he spoke to the childish giant of a man.

"Good morning, Guero. I brought you some donuts and juice. You can share them with your friend." He looked at the girl. "Graciela?"

She nodded meekly.

Tuco set the pastries and juice on the small end table and turned to her. "You can use the bathroom to freshen up. I'm going to get some cups, do you want coffee?"

"Coffee tastes yucky." Not Guero's favorite drink.

The girl just nodded.

He found Cuchillo smoking the last of a cigarette and drinking a cup of his nasty brew. Tuco knew from experience that his coffee tasted like it was strained through a greasy rag. Maybe so, but it would have to do. He lit one of the cheroots and inhaled the acrid smoke.

Cuchillo had removed all traces of the previous few days' evil. There was nothing left to indicate that two men had been brutally murdered in this very room.

"Morning, *patron*."

"Good morning. We need to be ready to leave in fifteen minutes. We're going to El Paso and I want to use the warehouse tunnel."

"But *Patron*, I have my green card, we could just drive."

"No, traffic is heavy, and we need to get there as soon as possible." It was thin, but like the coffee, it would have to do.

Once they figure out he's missing, if they don't know already, then I'm screwed, Tuco thought. "What did you do with the bodies?"

"They are waiting to be picked up," he nodded towards two large blue barrels. "Shouldn't we string the bags on the bridge?"

"Not our call," Tuco lied.

Standard cartel procedure called for one group to kidnap, another to interrogate, another to kill and yet another to bury and dispose of the bodies. The system ensured a broken chain, so if one element were caught it wouldn't bring the whole system crashing down. In certain cases, high-ranking *narcos* like Tuco were given the honor of torturing, killing and publicly displaying the remains of important adversaries. Those were precisely his orders for the accountant, but if the murder were made public, it might shut down his plans. So the dismembered bodies of the accountant and his bodyguard waited in barrels that wouldn't be retrieved.

"Be ready to go in fifteen minutes."

He poured a cup of coffee for the girl and Tuco felt like he was walking a tightrope in a windstorm. Since the downtown ambush, he had found himself questioning his own character and motivation, and wondered where along the path his ideals had been corrupted. He once had seen himself as one of Villa's revolutionaries, fighting the good fight for the dispossessed, but now that foundation had crumbled. The business had lost its honor, and the information he pulled from the accountant only confirmed the fact. Greed prevailed and honor was dead, but the accountant had also given him a key to redemption, and more importantly, a way out.

With his face all over the front page of *El Mundo*, he could see the door to escape slamming shut. He was one of the most trusted and effective operators within *La Linea*, but a low quality surveillance camera captured his image when his vanity overcame judgment and he showed himself to Cordona.

The last time a *La Linea* lieutenant's photograph appeared in print, it didn't go well. The boss of bosses, *Don* Vincente Carillo, whose own picture appeared in many papers, allowed no such indulgences for his operators and ordered the man's disassociation from the cartel. It was Tuco who put a bullet in the back of his own predecessor's head. The man, like Cordona, had also been his friend.

He entertained no doubt that Cuchillo would do the same for him, and they were not friends.

Compounding the severity of his transgression was the fact that the Cordona ambush was not sanctioned. He might be able to talk his way out of trouble for the photo, but such an operation without the blessing of the *Don* was unforgivable. The only reason he wasn't dead already was that the cartel leaders were sleeping off the weekend parties and wouldn't see the paper for another few hours.

None of it mattered. His decision was made, the front-page photo just accelerated the timeline a bit—and eliminated any other options. If he got across the border before the article made its way to *Don* Vicente, Tuco stood a good chance of success. Cuchillo was the wild card standing between Tuco, ten million dollars in cash, and a new life.

"How was the girl?"

"What?" the question startled Tuco out of his thoughts.

"The accountant's *puta*. How was she? I was hoping you'd leave her to me; she looked so fine." He stretched the last word out. "But it's okay, I understand, *Patron*."

Tuco just shook his head.

"I hope you fucked her good, that little bitch. What do you want me to do with her?"

"I will handle it, she is my problem."

"Si, *Patron*. I'd like to have that kind of problem, for jus' fifteen minutes." His grin was filled with crooked, yellow teeth.

Fucking animal, thought Tuco, *I should put him down.*

The idea of the *sicario* writhing in a spreading pool of blood and piss brought a slight smile to Tuco's face, but it would have to wait. He needed Cuchillo for the time being.

In El Paso, the Juarez Cartel used a Mexican-American gang, *Barrio Azteca,* to run their operations. Tuco questioned the wisdom of using a volatile and unpredictable street gang to administer the bulk of the cartel's business, but he couldn't argue with the results.

Cuchillo was a liaison between the *Aztecas* and the upper echelons of cartel leadership. With his help, Tuco could use the gang's safe houses and muscle if he needed it, with no questions asked—a feat he couldn't pull off alone. Once he'd served his purpose, Tuco would deal with "The Knife."

"Ten minutes."

He returned to the front room to find the young woman sitting on the couch next to Guero eating one of the fruit-filled pastries. Guero was talking around a mouthful of half-chewed turnover, explaining the complex relationship between the animated dogs prancing across the screen.

"The coffee is bad, really bad, but it packs a punch."

She looked up at him with dark eyes, still tinged with sleep and something else, and mumbled, "Thank you."

Fear and contempt.

He felt a twinge of regret for her father but pushed it aside. If he had let the man live, there would be no chance his plan could work.

Tuco once again found himself attracted to the girl, but instantly realized the absurdity of the thought. *I kidnapped, tortured and killed her father, and for all she knows, the same may still be in store for her. Hell, if this had been two weeks ago, she would have been violated by that* maricon *in the other room then killed and thrown in a barrel just like her father, but fate smiled on this one. She was in the hands of the new-and-improved--how did that old American President say it--a kinder, gentler Tuco Medrano, a real Renaissance man.*

He snorted to himself and the girl shot him a startled and puzzled look.

Back to business: "In a few minutes, we are going to leave. Once you hear us drive away, wait ten minutes and you can do whatever you want. The front door is unlocked. If I see you step out of this house before we are out of sight, I will come back and cut your throat."

It was brutal, but it was the only way she had a chance to make it out of this alive. And preserve Tuco's chance of success. Cuchillo had to believe that the girl was neutralized, if he saw weakness he would pounce.

"Are we clear?"

She nodded her head, hope creeping in with the fear and contempt.

"C'mon, Guero, it's time to go." He took the big man's hand and led him to the door.

"My puppy!"

"Graciela will take care of him." He turned to her. "Won't you?" She nodded again.

Guero started to protest, but Tuco's look stopped him cold.

"Graciela and the puppy are *going away*, understand?"

"Going away, Grassssss-la and puppy."

"Good." He used the euphemism anytime Guero accidentally killed a hapless pet, and he hoped Guero would repeat it for Cuchillo's benefit.

Tuco ushered his brother through the door to the back room, using his bulk to shield any view of Graciela. When he shut the door behind him, an apology hadn't even crossed his mind.

Chapter 11

The tunnel had taken three years and nearly 100 million dollars to complete and was the first of its kind. Underground smuggling routes were nothing new--in fact U.S. authorities have discovered at least a dozen tunnels linking the U.S. and Mexico. However, those were dug under the border in Arizona and California that is little more than an imaginary line marked by a fence. This one crossed under a river.

Tuco, Guero and Cuchillo entered the Juarez warehouse, nodded to the guard who recognized his boss, and entered the tunnel through a cleverly disguised entrance hidden in a bathroom stall. They walked towards El Paso in a concrete-walled, ventilated passage that stretched over three quarters of a mile under the Rio Grande and two border highways that flanked it. It was tall enough for Guero to walk upright and wide enough to allow passage of an electric-powered utility tram--similar to a golf cart--that was used to haul product. The paved tunnel even had a drainage system to pump out seeping ground water. Small, low-voltage fixtures spaced at twenty-foot intervals cast just enough light to prevent the men from running into each other. Well, almost.

"Sorry." Punctuated by Guero's deep jovial giggle. He liked the way it echoed down the long chamber.

Limited only by the supply of narcotics, the tunnel could transport over fifty million dollars' worth of baled drugs in less than eight hours. With the entrances concealed by legitimate freight companies, the movement of trucks at all hours raised no suspicion on either side of the border. The route was worth over ten billion dollars per year to the Juarez Cartel, and its location one of the organization's most closely guarded secrets. Just the rumor of its existence helped precipitate the war with the Sinaloas that bloodied the streets of Juarez with an average of ten bodies a day.

They had made it to the Juarez entrance without incident, and Tuco didn't bother looking back for the girl. By now he was sure Graciela had made it back to the safety of her family, where they could mourn another victim of the trade.

Tuco considered his predicament as they walked. He needed two or three hours alone to call on the accountant's U.S. contact, a lawyer who arranged business for the Sinaloas. There was no choice but to leave Guero with Cuchillo at the safe house, because the lawyer was expecting just one visitor. With any luck he would be back before Cuchillo made contact with the cartel and learned of Tuco's new status. Tuco hated to rely on luck, but unfortunately, he didn't have any other option. He cursed himself for the ego-driven indulgence he took with Cordona, who might just end up with the last laugh after all.

As they approached the end of the tunnel, it struck Tuco how odd they must look; he was dressed in chinos and a ridiculously expensive tailored sport coat, his hulking brother Guero in jeans and a red flannel baseball jacket with grey sleeves, and Cuchillo in stained khakis and t-shirt with a long leather coat more suited to a slaughterhouse.

The three men exited the tunnel in El Paso through a freight-truck maintenance pit. If the men working in the garage were surprised by their sudden appearance, none of them showed it. Generous cash bonuses and the implied threat to life and limb ensured their discretion. A black Escalade, gassed and ready, waited for them in a shed behind the maintenance bays.

Cuchillo drove them to a dilapidated house buried in El Paso's Magoffin neighborhood. Tuco had heard that it was a historic district, but it just looked old and worn out to him. It was the type of neighborhood once inhabited by the cream of El Paso society, but was left behind as the old guard died off and subsequent generations moved to the more fashionable heights overlooking the city.

Some of the old homes must have been magnificent in their day, but were now just crumbling shells converted into substandard apartment buildings surrounded by low chain link fences. The rusty and dented old beaters parked around the once stately houses belonged to the tenants doing their best to scrape by, while the shiny new cars and lowriders sporting visible-from-space chrome rims belonged to the movers and shakers. Mostly gangsters and drug dealers, they were the retailers in the cartel supply chain.

As they pulled up to the two-story adobe Tuco got out and opened the back door for his brother. "Guero, I want you to stay here with Cuchillo for a little while, I have to go talk to a man."

"Okay. Are you going to talk to him about a new puppy?"

"We'll see."

"I didn't hurted that last one."

"I know, *'mano*. You did well."

Tuco grabbed his brother's bag from the back of the SUV, wrapped his free arm around the big man and pulled him close. "Be good, big brother."

"Okay. I don't like Cuchillo, he smells like onions and farts," Guero whispered. He laughed at his own use of the word "farts."

"Yes, he does--" *and much worse,* Tuco thought, "--but you'll be okay. Now get in the house and Cuchillo will find some cartoons for you." He said the last part a little louder for the *sicario's* benefit.

The odiferous Cuchillo nodded his assent.

"Okay. Bye, Tuco." He took the gym bag handle in both hands, tucked his chin to his chest and ambled up the narrow concrete walkway leading to the front door.

"I'll take good care of him, *Patron*. How long will you be at the lawyer's?" Both men caught the slip immediately, but neither acknowledged it.

"I should be back very soon," Tuco replied, and wondered how much Cuchillo had overheard.

The accountant had mentioned the lawyer several times, but the details about the money were barely whispered--and only once. Had Cuchillo tortured the old man for an encore before ending his life? At this point it was academic. Without the lawyer, Cuchillo had nothing and could only hope to get a cut. Tuco and Guero would be long gone before he knew what had happened.

Still, sitting in the leather driver's seat, a cold dead hand tickled his spine as he pulled away from the safe house and watched his brother disappear into the black, gaping mouth of the doorway.

Chapter 12

After my meeting with Ronald Mitchell, Esq., I felt a little drained, so I took Dad to lunch. Well, he waited in the car while I enjoyed some of Chico's best work.

Once upon a time someone named Joe, not Chico, decided to drown three rolled tacos in a cardboard french-fry boat full of spiced up, watery tomato sauce. Then he covered the whole mess with grated, government-quality cheese, called it a "number one", and an El Paso staple was born. The brave-at-heart could get a dollop of finely minced, scorching-hot jalapeño added to the mix for an especially heartburn-laden experience.

I worked my way through a couple of orders of "number one--extra indigestion, please" while I mulled over the week's odd developments.

There was a lot that just didn't add up: why didn't the cops notify me that my father had been murdered, why was someone so eager to drop $600K on some insignificant carwashes, and how the hell did my inept dad, who made an Amway salesman look like Steve Jobs, manage to ferret away nearly four hundred thousand U.S. dollars?

While I savored the last of the tasty deep-fried treats, I pondered the Florida reference. It was a code, and a code from our past that my dad assumed that only I would understand.

I was fairly sure my father had never been to the state of Florida, and 100 percent sure that we had never been there together.   On the other hand, the Florida Mountains, pronounced flo-REE-da, were a rocky island of desert peaks about a hundred miles west of El Paso. Most El Pasoans didn't even know they existed, a fact my dad was counting on to keep his code a secret. We used to camp there when I was a kid, setting up a pup tent near an abandoned stone prospector's cabin nestled at the mouth of a narrow, rocky *arroyo*. He loved the peace and solitude, but I absolutely despised it.

But why not just say, "Scatter what's left of my sorry ass in those godforsaken mountains you hated so much as a kid"?   It was clear he wanted me to go out there, but didn't want anyone else to know. Not even his buddy Ronald Mitchell, Esq.

The whole affair was fishier than a hooker's crotch on Sunday morning. It smelled like narcotics trafficking.

My dad? Involved with drug dealers? I'd bet my left testicle on it.

Chapter 13

"I'm sorry, but you have to make an appointment." Tuco stood across the desk from a middle-aged, slightly overweight woman with bright red lipstick, burnt-orange rouge and 1970s surplus blue eye shadow.

Tuco had stood in front of her desk in the lawyer's office for five minutes, trying to convince her to let him see the attorney. He took a deep breath instead.

"Listen carefully. You will call him on your interphone and tell him that Mr. Mendoza from Mazatlan Imports is here to speak with him. Now. If you do not, I will put a bullet between your pretty blue eyes." As he finished the statement, he eased his coat open just enough that she could see the butt of the Sig Sauer slung under his left armpit.

She picked up the phone and dialed with trembling fingers. "Uh, a, M-Mr. Mazatlan is here to see you and it seems very important... yes, yes right away."

Her first attempt to hang up missed the cradle and the receiver clattered noisily to the desk. "I'm s-s-sorry for the misunderstanding, sir, Mr. Mitchell will see you now."

She flinched as he walked past and let himself into the lawyer's office. The attorney stood before his desk and offered a pudgy hand. "Mr. Mendoza, I presume. I'm Ronald Mitchell. I must apologize for Ms. Rooney, she is filling in for my regular receptionist." His hand felt like raw hamburger stuffed in a rubber glove.

"Please, have a seat," the lawyer said timidly. "Do you have something for me?"

Tuco pulled a pen and small notepad out of his coat pocket and wrote out a sixteen-digit alphanumeric code. He tore out the sheet and handed it to the lawyer.

Mitchell waddled his way around the desk to a cringing chair that creaked in protest when he rolled himself into it. He pulled a writing platform from under the desktop, compared something written on its top to Tuco's code, looked up and smiled.

"It is a pleasure to meet you Mr. Mendoza, but I must admit that based on the instructions from Mr. Martinez, I wasn't expecting you so soon." A twitching eye punctuated the statement.

"Yes, well, my associates are anxious to conclude this unusual piece of business. The package is now ready for delivery and frankly, we would like very much to be rid of it." He hoped the fabrication seemed credible. "I understand you have made arrangements for the exchange of funds?"

"Yes, of course, but I wasn't planning on the exchange until later this week, if not early next. I'll have to confirm this with Mr. Martinez." The twitch returned, accompanied by fine beads of sweat on his forehead.

Tuco knew from the accountant that flexibility was built into the plan and there was something the man in the overtaxed chair wasn't telling him---but of course Tuco had secrets of his own. There was the unpleasant little fact that pieces of Mr. Martinez were stuffed in a fifty-gallon plastic drum and that the real Mr. Mendoza, whoever he was, would be dropping by later this week. Both men were lying--Tuco was just better at it.

"Please feel free to call him, I'm sure he won't mind being bothered when his instructions were so clear."

Mitchell did his best to stay calm, cool and collected, but the cold stare from across the desk caused his testicles to retreat deep into his abdomen. "No, no, you're right, that won't be necessary."

Relieved that his bluff worked, Tuco wrote a few lines in his notebook, tore out the sheet and slid it across the desk. "Here is an address and instructions for completing the transaction. Please understand that my organization's leadership is beginning to have second thoughts about this business agreement and Mr. Martinez and I feel like we should move forward quickly or they may back out."

"Yes, I understand." Mitchell could see the deal unraveling before his eyes. Who knew the cartel had a conscience? He vacillated for a moment between coming clean and one more attempt to find the ten million dollars that had vanished into thin air, two million of which were destined for his Cayman account.

"I will make the drop before midnight on Wednesday." Decision made. "I will convince my client that it is in their best interest." *And if I can't find the money*, he didn't add, *I'll just say they backed out. No harm done.*

Then he remembered the people who had already given him and the dead chickenshit alcoholic ten million dollars cash money. He didn't figure the Arabs were any more forgiving than the Mexicans.

"Are you alright?" asked Tuco. The sweaty man had turned white.

"Yes, yes. Thank you--just a bit of indigestion. I should stay away from the *huevos rancheros*. Everything is fine, Wednesday at midnight."

"Wednesday *before* midnight," Tuco corrected.

"Yes."

When Tuco opened the door to Mitchell's office, Ms. Rooney dropped her full cup of five-dollar caramel cappuccino all over the desk.

***

Tuco drove around south El Paso under the pretense of looking for a pet store or a sign on a telephone pole advertising puppies for sale, but he was really thinking about his visit with the lawyer. His gambit seemed to work, but it was clear that the attorney was hiding something important.

The cartels often used American lawyers to facilitate their laundering operations and sometimes the counselors got greedy, but this was a sweet deal. It was the easiest commission he would ever make, so it didn't make sense that he would risk his own life to cross the Sinaloas.

Maybe the third party had cold feet, promised more than they could deliver, or ran out of money. However that was a thin supposition. After all, according to the accountant, the hardest part of their objective--getting the package to Juarez--had already been achieved, and they had very deep pockets. No, something else was afoot and if Tuco couldn't figure it out soon, the opportunity might evaporate.

Driving aimlessly achieved nothing, so he decided it was time to get Guero and break free of Cuchillo. He regretted not killing him in Juarez; the safe house hadn't really been necessary. After taking a circuitous route and doubling back on himself to ensure he wasn't followed, Tuco arrived at the gang's hideout and parked the big SUV around the corner.

Guero was sitting in the cramped living room watching his buddy Sponge Bob in hi-definition.

"*Hola, 'mano.*"

"Tuco! Did you get me a puppy? Squidward is mad at Sponge Bob!"

Fucking cartoons, thought Tuco. "No puppy yet, do you want to go find one now?"

"OKAY!"

"Where's Cuchillo?"

He saw Guero's head turn with widened eyes as he felt the sting of the hypodermic needle and the hot electric flow of the drug as it spread through his neck and shoulder. Then nothing.

Chapter 14

Ronald Mitchell could not stop sweating.

He had hoped to get the Martin kid's signature that morning, but the son of a bitch wanted to "think about it."

What was there to think about? Sign the damn agreement and walk away with $600K for a bunch of car washes that weren't worth half that on the open market. What an asshole, he thought.

Then, to add to his trouble, a rather intimidating Mexican showed up wanting to rush the timetable. The visit was suspect, but he had the code and it was foolproof. Besides, the man looked very familiar. Maybe he'd been around some of the other transactions.

So here it was--Daniel Martin had an attack of conscience and stolen ten million dollars, the chickens were coming to roost, and young Martin was dragging his feet. Hopefully Katy could get some information out of him. A pang of jealousy shot through him at the thought.

It was no coincidence that Katy was one of the highest paid and underworked legal secretaries in El Paso, and probably all of Texas. Her exceptional--make that incredible--oral talents, administered weekly, ensured her tenure at Sampson, Mitchell & Mitchell would be long and lucrative. Mitchell's jealousy stemmed from the fact she would probably screw the good-looking Martin kid, a pleasure Mitchell would never know. She made it clear that the blowjobs were as far as it would ever go between them, and the risk of losing them prevented him from pushing the issue.

Katy was very handy for extracting information that Mitchell would never be able to get on his own. That a smart, pretty girl like Katy would whore herself out for some extra cash and an easy work schedule surprised the lawyer, but not nearly as much as the information her targets revealed while chasing, catching, or basking in the afterglow of a ride with Katy.

So while he waited in sweaty anticipation and hoped for the best, Ronald Mitchell sat at his massive, office-in-a-box desk chewing Tums. He fiddled aimlessly with a long-bladed letter opener, oblivious to the gouges he was carving in the expensive leather writing pad that his partners had presented to him after he won a long-forgotten case. The partners, Joshua Sampson and his own father John Mitchell, were dead and gone, and it had been a long time since Ronald's ass had polished a courtroom chair. The namesakes of the once-respected firm must be spinning in their graves over what Ronald Mitchell had become.

***

When the Guadalete Development Corps had first approached Mitchell, it was clear their representative was more than aware of the attorney's corruption. He came straight at the lawyer with a fifty-thousand-dollar gift, and didn't bother to warn him of the consequences of breaking the attorney-client privilege.

As the broker for the deal, it surprised Mitchell how little the Sinaloa leaders had demanded for the job--less than half of what he had been authorized to offer. The bargain he negotiated for Guadalete doubled his original commission, but now, with the money missing, he was screwed at both ends, and hoping a twenty-four-year-old with a golden pussy could pull him out of it. She wasn't the only card up his sleeve, but was certainly his best bet.

His mind wandered into the darkness as he considered the ramifications of failure. The Mexicans were a known quantity--

more than likely they would *only* cut off the penis he hadn't seen in years and jam it into his blubbering mouth, before putting a couple of slugs in the back of his head.

The Guadalete Development Corps was a different story.

He was terrified at the thought of one of those bastards drawing a dull blade across his throat and sawing his head off as he'd seen in a video released by a terrorist group in Iraq. The memory of the unfortunate victim's high-pitched scream--cut short by a liquid sound of rushing air when the knife cut through his larynx as masked terrorists praised Allah--still caused Mitchell's hair to stand on end and cold sweat to flow. He decided right then that if push came to shove, he'd rather eat his own cock and take a bullet to the brain.

The intercom buzzer startled him out of his macabre thoughts.

"Mr. Mitchell, will you be needing anything else today?"

"No Ka…er, no. Thank you. You can call it a day. I'll close up." He had forgotten the temp's name.

"Will you need me tomorrow?"

If Katy were earning her money, then he most definitely would. "Yes, please be here at 10 a.m."

"Thank you, Mr. Mitchell. I'll see you in the morning," she lied. Fifteen dollars an hour wasn't enough to put up with the likes of Mr. Mendoza.

He listened to the temp gather her things and shuffle out, and felt a sudden uneasiness once alone in the building.

"Easy, Ron," he whispered to himself. "Nobody knows yet."

He was wrong.

Chapter 15

It didn't take long to confirm my suspicion about the drugs. Chico's Tacos were doing a number on my duodenum and I wasn't sure I was going to make it the last couple of blocks to my new house. It wouldn't have been an issue if I hadn't stopped for a twelve-pack of *quality* beer, but a little prolonged intestinal discomfort was better than drinking more Schlitz. To complicate matters, just as I pulled into the driveway, two government employees were walking down the front porch steps toward a government-issue car parked at my curb.

Actually, as far as I knew, they could have been from the Church of Latter Day Saints, wondering if I'd heard The News, except they weren't walking towards a couple of ten-speeds. The car, the badges at their hips and the fact that one of them was a fairly attractive blonde with a ponytail and nicely tailored suit meant that they probably weren't Mormons. Mormon women on a mission rarely wear tailored suits. The man with her may still have been a Mormon.

"Douglas Martin?" the Mormon asked. Come to think of it, he did look like a young Mitt Romney.

"Yes, but call me Jake." *And I really have to take a crap*, I almost added.

I was distracted by the blonde when the Mormon introduced himself as Special Agent Bill or Bob or something Johnson--yeah, let's say Johnson.

"--and this is Special Agent Christa Adams from the Drug Enforcement Agency. Do you mind if we ask you a few questions?" They both held up their government "creds."

"I guess not, but you're going to have to wait a few minutes," I answered as I moved toward the door. I hoped that they weren't mistaking the beads of sweat on my forehead for a nervous reaction.

My biological need was interfering with my dexterity, and I fumbled to get the key in the lock. "I think I got ahold of a bad *taquito*, and have some urgent business to attend to." To punctuate the statement, my stomach growled like a pissed-off pit bull.

"Chico's?" the woman asked and smiled with a mouth that was a little too big for her face, but in kind of a sexy way.

I nodded as I got the door open and almost stepped in a pile of...

"Crap!" Blu was sitting just beyond his creation with a smug look of satisfaction.

"Sorry about this, watch your step and please have a seat. I'll be right back."

The alone time gave me the opportunity to gather my thoughts about how to play it with the DEA. Not wanting the day to get any shittier--pardon the pun--I decided to play it as straight as possible without giving them too much. I finished up and went to the kitchen to get some cleaning supplies.

"Sorry about all of this, I thought he was housebroken," I said as I filled a plastic bag with dirty paper towels and Blu's poop.

The Special Agents were sitting on the living room sofa. Blu had his head between Miss DEA's knees and she was petting him like she was afraid to catch leprosy. Not a dog lover. Strike one.

My eyes traveled up the shapely thigh in tight blue wool but the .40 on her waist snapped me back to reality.

"What can you tell us about your father?" It was Bill/Bob.

"He's dead." Pretty straight, right?

"Yes, sir, we know that," Christa replied this time. Did I mention her voice was deeper than I expected? Kinda' sultry. "What can you tell us about what he did before he died?"

Probably pissed his pants, I thought, but couldn't bring myself to be that sarcastic. "Well, from what I can tell, he was pretty good at washing cars."

They just looked at me, trying to create an uncomfortable silence that I would fill with useful information. Instead of falling for the bait, I imagined Miss DEA working undercover as an exotic dancer in short-shorts and clear plastic hooker pumps. Sexist, I know, but half the battle is admitting you have a problem, right?

Bill/Bob broke the impasse. "Yes, he was very good at it. His business was quite successful. Maybe a little *too* successful." So I wasn't the only one who knew my dad was a loser.

Blu moved on from the lame head rub and hoped for better from Bill/Bob but wasn't getting it.

"So what does that have to do with me?"

"Well, Mr. Martin…"

"Jake," I interjected, looking straight at her.

"…Well, Jake, your father was a very important part of a money laundering investigation, and even though he is… gone… we think that you can help us moving forward. If you cooperate, we are prepared to allow your father's estate to pass to you unchallenged."

So there it was. I was a thread holding their investigation together and they were hoping that I would play. They probably wouldn't have mentioned the laundering if they hadn't already checked me out and discovered that I wasn't involved, but they were using the money, house, et al. as a carrot to buy my complicity. Just in case. I think I knew the answer, but I asked anyway, "What do you mean, 'unchallenged'?"

"Your father made his money illegally," Bill/Bob answered this time, "and his assets are forfeit at the discretion of the U.S. government in accordance with provisions of the RICO Act."

I'd heard of RICO--the Racketeer-Influenced and Corrupt Organizations Act--they could seize your property based on *suspicion* of trafficking or illegal organized activity. No trial, no proof, *nada*--just take whatever they want without so much as a "thank you."

"Maybe so, but he's dead, his assets were passed to me, and you know I have no idea what he was up to." I pulled that little peach right out of my ass.

"You do now," pointed out Christa. Strike two. I was really starting to dislike this large mouth dog-hater.

They were holding all of the cards, and I realized that being a smart-ass wasn't going to help my cause.

She assumed a softer tone and continued. "I'm sorry, we realize that this is a lot to process, and we want to make it clear that you are not under investigation. You do, however, have insider access to information that could help us shut down the flow of millions of dollars across the border.

"We're not asking you to wear a wire or anything, just help us answer some questions about the nature of your father's business, and gather some information about Ronald Mitchell and the people who are offering to buy the car washes."

"It seems like you know quite a bit already."

Bill/Bob responded, "We've been following this for a long time. Let's just say that your father's death set us back considerably."

"Should I oil up my Glock?"

"There's no reason to believe that you are in any danger," Christa replied. I didn't really have a Glock, but was thinking real hard about getting one, and her answer sealed the deal.

"Can we count on your cooperation, Mr. Martin?" Bill/Bob again. Did they rehearse the back-and-forth?

"Well, I assume you did your homework and know my background, so I'm pretty sure you know on which side of the border my loyalties lie."

"Yes, we do, and by the way, thank you for your service." Nice touch--appeal to my patriotism and let me know you did do your research. "When is your next meeting with Mr. Mitchell?"

"Friday... no... Wednesday." They shot each other a glance during my pause that said they already knew the answer to the question. I hoped they didn't catch on to my little fishing expedition, but screw 'em if they did. At least now I knew they had a lot more information than they were letting on. Bugs? Wire taps? It was the age of the Patriot Act.

They stood in perfect unison and Bill/Bob extended a business card. "Thank you for your time. We'll touch base Wednesday after your meeting with Mitchell. In the meantime, if you have any questions you can reach us at this number."

I took the card and read "Special Agent John Reynolds" under the embossed seal of the U.S. Drug Enforcement Agency. How the hell I got Bill or Bob Johnson out of the introduction, I don't know. Guess it had something to do with his partner. Pretty sure I had her name down pat, but she didn't give me a card with *her* number on it, so that was strike three.

Just before she walked out the door, Christa Adams turned and said, "Oh, one more thing, just out of curiosity--do you have any plans for your father's funeral?"

"Gonna send flowers?" A blank, expectant stare. "I really don't know yet. Right now his ashes are in a cardboard box, so I'm thinking something simple."

"Okay, well please let us know if you plan to leave town."

It wasn't the first time someone had grilled me about the disposition of Dad's remains.

***

So far it had been a pretty interesting day for a Monday, and I figured it was time for a beer. I let Blu out in the back yard where he made a big show of sniffing around, but not much else. He'd pretty much finished his business in the entryway.

"Well, come on then, Shithead."

I grabbed one of the IPAs on the way to the basement media room and settled into one of the soft recliners when it dawned on me that I forgot to open the beer, and it wasn't a twist-off. I muttered "fiddlesitcks," or something else that started with the letter "f" and got up to look for a bottle opener.

As I stood, the recliner rocked forward knocking the un-opened beer onto the carpeted floor. It rolled to the wall below the large projection screen. I said "fiddlesticks" again, this time loud enough to cause Blu to tuck his tail a little, and bent to retrieve the bottle when I noticed it.

It was subtle, and I never would have noticed it if I weren't on my knees fumbling around for the beer, but the nap of the carpet was different from the rest of the floor around it—like a hidden door had swung outward from the wall.

I realized now why the basement looked so much smaller than I remembered.

Even after retracting the roll-up screen, the door wasn't obvious, but knowing it was there helped. I pushed on the panels and one sprung outward enough to allow me to pull it open.

The door led to a small room about five feet deep that ran the width of the basement. It was empty except for some gray metal shelving along the wall and a photograph of a small kid in an oversized t-shirt holding a huge trout. Tacked to the wall over the photo was bumper sticker that read "Eat at Irma's."

It was another message from the man in a cardboard box on the front seat of my truck.

Chapter 16

The impossibly large ball wobbled on its axis and crashed with a loud thud against the resonant wall of a box just slightly larger than the ball itself. Each wobble and bounce thudded louder and resonated deeper than the last, and was accompanied by a flash of searing light. As he slowly eased into lucidity, Tuco realized that the ball was his brain, figuratively lurching from side to side within his skull, slamming the soft gray tissue against the unforgiving bone in time with his heartbeat.

A low moaning wail beckoned him as the drug wore off and he slowly regained consciousness. He felt like the ball would burst out of his skull at any moment.

The rhythmic wail grew louder and he started to hear his name tucked within the plaintive cry. He lay on his side with his back to the sound, but didn't have the strength to turn over. Simply opening his eyes sent a stab of pain through his forehead, followed by a wave of nausea that made him wretch the contents of his belly into a watery pile on the canvas cot. Just before he passed out again, his muddled brain registered Guero's plea.

***

The kittens.

Manny brought them—a present for the boys who he had begun to see as his own.

They were the first real gift that the boys had ever received, and Tuco was thrilled. He and Guero played with the cats for hours until Manny, finished with their mama, tucked them each into bed with the sleeping kittens curled on their pillows.

When they woke, Tuco noticed something different about Guero's cat. It wasn't moving like Tuco's, but as a five-year-old, he had no way of knowing his brother had rolled over in his sleep and smothered his kitten. It was the first in a long line of dead pets.

Their mother found the boys in the kitchen, Tuco playing with a squirmy kitten, and Guero pushing his dead cat around the floor like a stuffed animal.

"What the fuck, Guero?" She roughly grabbed the dead kitten and placed it in a plastic bag.

"God, what a pendejo!" she mumbled as she threw the bag in the trash. "You stay away from that, do you hear me? If you touch that trash, I will beat your ass!"

Sitting cross-legged on the floor, Guero sobbed and rocked back and forth. "Sorry Mama, sorry Mama…" devolving into incomprehensible moaning as the tears poured down his face. Tuco watched uncomprehendingly from across the kitchen, holding his own wriggling kitten.

She made coffee while Guero lay curled and crying on the floor. When Guero's rhythmic sobbing grew into a wail, she screamed, "Shut up, goddammit!"

Tuco was watching his brother, and didn't notice that his mother had turned her attention to him. She was nearly on him when he saw her coming at him with wild hair and dark circles under red-rimmed eyes, but what scared him most was the look on her face. He wouldn't have recognized it at his young age but she had the crazed look of triumph, like she just discovered how to turn lead into gold.

He scooted backwards across the linoleum, with wide eyes and a quivering lip, scared of his insane mother. Without a word, she grabbed his kitten, turned away, and bent over his crying brother.

"Here you go, Guero, your kitty is all better."

Just like that his kitten was gone.

Guero quit crying and played with his new kitten, oblivious to what had just transpired. Tuco left the kitchen and sat alone in the living room, staring at the darkened TV set with tears streaming down his face. Emotions swirled around his little heart like the clouds of creamer swirling in his mother's coffee cup.

It was the first time that he resented his brother.

Later that evening, the boys went unsupervised while their mother entertained in her bedroom. Tuco sat on the sofa, watching television while Guero, on the floor, teased his cat with a piece of string.

The kitten, his little paws splayed, lunged for the string and raked his claws across the back of Guero's hand, drawing a dew-drop line of blood. In reaction to the sudden pain, Guero backhanded the tiny cat, flinging it forcefully towards a small coffee table. The kitten hit the table at just the right angle and the impact with the hard wooden leg broke the creature's back but didn't kill it outright.

Guero left the room hurt and crying, and curled himself on the floor in front of his mother's door, ignored.

Tuco sat on the couch and watched the mortally injured kitten with morbid curiosity. It mewled weakly and was trying to walk on its forelegs, dragging its limp and useless lower half, looking for comfort but not finding any. The kitten finally collapsed, fearful, alone and in pain. It took ten minutes for the small cat to die, and Tuco watched clinically, like a doctor in a surgical gallery.

His stoicism hid his hatred of Guero.

Tuco became Richie, who years later would pelt his brother with a water balloon and ridicule the one who loved Tuco most.

***

Their grandparents had been strict, but kind. The boys shared a room. The three-room shack in Francisco Villa made their mother's apartment in the projects seem like a mansion.

Life in Juarez was different and despite his doting brother, Tuco felt isolated and alone. Tuco enrolled in school, but no one warmed to him. Richie became Ricardo. He was an outsider, an Americano. No more football, movies, or riding in cars. Just day after day of school, meager meals and Mexican television on a snowy, black-and-white set.

He missed Manny.

The only bright spot for Tuco was that he no longer had to take care of his brother. Their grandmother assumed the duty with one exception; In Juarez there were no special classes for Guero, so Abuelita allowed him to walk to school with Tuco. He would find his way back to the house and then reverse the process at the end of the school day.

Guero loved the time with his younger brother.

Tuco would rather he stayed at home.

Sometimes Guero had a hard time getting out of bed to make the walk to school, but he never failed to meet Tuco after classes ended. Then one day he wasn't there.

Tuco thought little of it and started on his way. Halfway home he found him. On a tumbleweed and trash-covered lot, four boys were gathered around Guero, who lay in the sand, curled like a fetus. They taunted him, and occasionally one rushed in to deliver a vicious kick. The sight of tears, snot and blood on his brother's bewildered face cut something loose in Tuco.

Without thinking he rushed them. Caught by surprise, the bullies turned to face him, but before they could react he tackled the closest one and came up swinging. He landed a few blows and bloodied a nose, but had no hope of winning the fight. Two of them managed to flank him and grab his flailing arms while a third got his arm around Tuco's neck from behind. Their leader, nose bloodied, reached into a dirty khaki trouser pocket and pulled out a short knife with a rusty blade.

He wiped the blood from under his nose with the back of his free hand and hissed, "Now I fuck you up, maricon."

As the khaki pants moved threateningly toward Tuco, Guero, forgotten in the commotion, moved in behind him and swung a heavy piece of lumber downward with all his might. Tuco heard his collarbone snap when the blow connected just above the arm holding the outstretched blade.

The bully screamed and dropped to his knees, the knife stuck at an odd angle in the sand. At the sight of their leader bent and cradling his shattered clavicle, his three accomplices fled the scene like roaches scattering in the light. Tuco walked up to him and kicked him square in the face. He tumbled over backwards, unconscious with blood pouring out of his nose and mouth.

"Now you are fucked... maricon."

He gathered Guero and they started for home.   A kid who stopped to watch the commotion fell in beside them, "No one has beaten him like that before. He deserved it. I'm Raul, what is your name?"

"My name is Tuco, and this is Guero."

His brother smiled.

***

"…Tuco! Wake up, Tuco!"

Chapter 17

Cuchillo had heard more than he let on. He knew that his shaggy appearance and crude mannerisms led most to believe he was an imbecile, but more than a few *pendejos* had died for making that mistake. Tuco would join them soon enough.

The Knife had eaten enough shit from that prick to last a lifetime; his death would be slow. He would die with his own guts wrapped around his throat like a necktie, begging for mercy like they all did, but not before he saw the retard carved up before his eyes.

When Cuchillo hit him with the etorphine injection, it seemed for a moment like he had overdone it and Tuco would die on the spot. The drug, also known as M99, was a large-animal tranquilizer that killed more than half of Cuchillo's "patients," but for instant immobilization, it couldn't be topped. The retard just giggled and clapped at the "joke," completely unaware that his brother's life hung on a chemical thread.

He tied the compliant big man to a chair before attending to the incapacitated Tuco. By the time he was stretched out on a folding cot with his wrists and ankles zip-tied, the *Patron's* pulse and breathing had dropped precariously. Cuchillo injected him with a small amount of Revivon to counteract the killing effect of the M99, but not enough to restore him to consciousness. Satisfied that the asshole wouldn't die before he could have his fun, Cuchillo left his boss and the imbecile brother and started on the next phase of his plan.

As he closed and locked the door behind him, Cuchillo heard the dummy's pitiful pleading, begging his brother to wake up.

Guero could plead and cry all he wanted but his brother would be out cold for at least eighteen hours.

***

Cuchillo plugged the name he heard during the old man's interrogation into the SUV's navigation system and drove to the lawyer's office. He parked at the far end of the lot and retrieved a small black bag from the cargo compartment before searching for his quarry.

It didn't take long. That it was the only car parked under a five-stall metal awning was evidence enough, but the sign that read "Reserved for Ronald Mitchell" in front of the Jaguar sedan sealed it. He pulled a slim-jim from the bag, but before sliding it into the guts of the door, he took a chance and tried the sleek chrome door handle. It popped open.

"Thanks, *puto*," he whispered with a smile and took a quick look around the lot before sliding into the passenger seat. He rummaged around the glove compartment and center console, finding the owner's manual, some old gum and an insurance card with the attorney's home address. In the black bag he carried a small device about the size of a pack of cigarettes. It was a code-grabber, and he used it to learn the unique signals from the Jag's overhead console remotes in a matter of seconds. He took the insurance card, went back to the SUV and drove away. The entire operation took less than sixty seconds.

After parking the SUV a few houses down the street from the lawyer's sprawling Spanish-style villa in the foothills overlooking the high-rises of downtown El Paso, Cuchillo used the code grabber to open the main gate and garage door. Once inside, he started to go through the attorney's personal things looking for clues to the whereabouts of the money. Eventually the *sicario* realized that he was wasting effort, and decided to just wait and use his own "code grabbing" techniques to extract the information from the source itself. So he sat on the lawyer's comfy leather couch in his enormous living room, munched on chilé-and-lime covered *pepitas,* watched a *novella on* Mitchell's fifty-two-inch LCD, and fantasized about the doe-eyed *señorita* pining for her lover in High Definition.

Chapter 18

Traffic was lighter than usual on the streets heading north out of the downtown area, but not light enough to keep Ronald Mitchell's blood pressure under control or prevent the free-flow of profanity directed at his fellow commuters as he drove home.

"Fucking ASSHOLE!" he shouted as he shot the bird at a driver who had the temerity to pull into his lane in preparation for a turn.

When he arrived at his house still brooding over the traffic and his predicament, the big man's blood pressure and fat-clogged arteries were dangerously close to teaming up for a devastating stroke. It would have been a merciful end to the day.

In his agitated state, he didn't notice that the mechanized driveway gate was already open before he pressed the button on the Jag's overhead console.

He pulled into the garage and sat listening to the last few lines of a Dave Matthews tune before killing the ignition. He never did understand why that guy was so popular, but he did like the melody of *Crash,* and the line about "hiking up your skirt" always got him to thinking lewd thoughts about Katy.

The pressure in his forehead subsided and was quickly replaced by a pressure spike between his thick legs. He considered rubbing one out to the sultry styling of Sadé's *Smooth Operator* right where he sat, but opted instead to go inside to watch the hidden camera videos of Katy in the women's bathroom at the office. His hard-drive also had several hours of videotaped "oral dictation" from Katy. He was confident she knew about the blow-job vids, because at times she seemed to ham it up for the hidden camera, but the women's toilet scenes were way past the line, which made them that much more stimulating.

With his short staff at full attention, he grabbed his briefcase and opened the door leading from the garage to a kitchen that had never seen a home-cooked meal. As he rounded the corner leading to his home office and the hard drive loaded with Katy in various stages of dress and fellatio, his erection went limp and he let out a girlish squeal at the sight of a stringy-haired Mexican standing behind a large pistol. He dropped his briefcase, raised both hands and took a rubbery step backwards.

"T-t-take anything you want," he stammered.

"Oh, don' worry, *compadre*. I will, I will," replied the Mexican with a smile that revealed a mouth full of yellow teeth set in a crusty black gum line.

Chapter 19

"How big?" I asked before shoveling in another fork full of enchilada.

"At least two hundred, or she didn't weigh an ounce. She 'friended' me on Facebook and her pictures were pretty hot. The Photoshop work would have made Hugh Hefner proud."

"No, say it isn't so! Those girls are airbrushed?"

Paul Castañeda just shook his head smiling and continued. "Either that or the pics were ten years old. Time had done a number on her."

"Well that officially sucks. Missy was the gold standard."

"Not anymore, my friend," he said while spreading his hands apart melodramatically.

He took another bite, finished chewing and asked, "Have you heard from Alex?"

I shook my head and he wisely dropped the subject.

An hour or so before, Paul called and said a meeting had been cancelled, and asked if I'd like to join him at The Riviera for some beer and enchiladas. Now El Paso has a lot of faults, but food is not one of them, and The Riviera makes some of the best enchiladas on the planet. I know that the meat, cheese, tortillas and red *chilé* are just a variation of the meal I ate for lunch, but if an airline pilot turns down free food and beer, the universe might just implode. I didn't want that on my conscience, so I accepted his invitation.

Paul was my best friend in high school, is the smartest man I've ever met, and is about the only one in El Paso who I've stayed in regular contact with. We had been pretty much inseparable back in the day--playing ball, getting snotty drunk in Juarez bars, hunting jackrabbits in the desert, and chasing the finest daughters of El Paso society. Paul and I were pretty good at football, under-age drinking and hunting rabbits.

When we graduated, I headed off to Austin, the University of Texas and a life in the Navy. Paul, the son of first generation Mexican immigrants, couldn't afford to get out of El Paso, so he worked his way through college at UTEP and started a telecommunications business. He invented some kind of explosive space modulator that allows him to transport small children via telephone lines. Or maybe it was just a gadget that makes phone calls cheaper. Whatever it does it earned him a shitload of money, enough to buy a third world country. I didn't feel guilty about letting him buy the beer and enchiladas.

He was a loyal friend who had always been there for me. When I was furloughed from the airlines, he offered me a job as a consultant even though I didn't know diddly about telephones: it was an example of how he would come through for a friend in a pinch. But before I could accept, the Navy came through with my Magical Mystery Tour.

Paul had it pretty good, but he made some exceedingly poor choices when it came to women. He married a perfectly charming young woman named Maria who suffered from a little known affliction--she just couldn't keep her legs closed in the vicinity of a penis.

Once Paul hit pay dirt, she decided that she would be better off managing her half of the fortune free from the bonds of holy matrimony. To announce the split, she had Paul served with papers and a videotape of her being double teamed by a pair of Nubian swordsmen, with the words "Fuck You" scrawled in lipstick across her back. It was a class act. However, Texas is a no-fault state, so despite the incontrovertible evidence of adultery, Maria rode into the sunset after six years of infidelity with a check for $100 million. Ain't the legal system just grand?

I would have hunted her down and killed her, but Paul took it all with the patience of a Tibetan Monk. The money just wasn't that important to him; he drove an older model Land Rover, lived in a nice but modest house, and dressed in the latest styles from JC Penney. What Ms. Katy the receptionist didn't realize is that yes, I *did* know the richest guy in El Paso, but why he was still here I'll never understand.

With tongues still burning from the New Mexico Red and noses growing numb from the beer, Paul paid the tab and we headed across the parking lot to a hole in the wall from our past. Aceitunas was the perfect place to continue the drinking and deep conversation. On a Friday night it would be full of thirty and forty-somethings in gaudy Ed Hardy and Tapout t-shirts trying to recapture the glory of their pathetic adolescence. Monday nights, on the other hand, were pretty quiet.

He filled me in on the goings on amongst our former class-mates. It was amazing how people tend to stay in touch when they know you have a wildly successful business and a personal worth in excess of $500 million, but that is selling Paul short. He was very popular before hitting it big.

I urged him to act like most gazillionaires and hire a top notch security team--you never know what kind of crazy rich-boy groupies are lurking about, but he politely blew me off, preferring to keep his down-to-earth profile.

As the beer flowed we moved on to headier stuff. He sat enthralled by my stories about Afghanistan, and I tried my best to return the favor and ignore the vibrating phone in my pocket as he rambled on about some gizmo they were working on that would save the world, or at least reduce your long distance bill. Then he waxed poetic about his ex-wife ripping out his heart and using it as a purse. Eventually we moved on to current events.

I filled him in on my visits with Ronald Mitchell and my friends from the DEA.

"It seems like my dad had aligned himself with some pretty bad people. I guess it doesn't surprise me, but I am a little surprised that he screwed it up so badly."

"Yeah, that is a surprise," Paul replied. "It just doesn't make sense that he'd cross the cartel. Sounds like he had a pretty good gig."

"Didn't seem that great to me. Four of the car washes are in neighborhoods where they can't afford to gas up their cars, much less pay to wash them."

"Hey, *esé*, never underestimate the power of a clean low-rider," Paul said in an exaggerated accent.

He continued, more seriously. "Carwashes are an all-cash business that are great for cleaning a little dirty money. Get enough suckers like your dad to run those kinds of outfits, pay them well, have a lawyer or accountant oversee the details and bingo, the laundered cash rolls in. A bunch of little businesses are a bit harder to keep track of, but they reduce large-scale exposure for the operation. Spreading the wealth over a lot of small businesses also prevents temptation."

"How much money are we talking about?"

"All in all about a hundred billion a year."

"No friggin' way!"

"Not your dad--his set up is just a small part of that—maybe three to five million a year in laundered funds. But the Mexicans have hit the big time. Remember a drug lord from Colombia named Pablo Escobar?"

Not really. "Yes."

"When they killed him off, everybody seemed to think it put the Colombians out of business, but all that really happened was they shifted the cocaine traffic to Mexico. A guy named Felix Gallardo built himself a nice little empire, but he also learned from Escobar's mistakes, and decentralized power. If a leader was taken out, the machine would still function. The cartels were born.

"Unfortunately 'The Godfather' Gallardo didn't leave a succession plan and when he was sent away in '89, each of the egomaniacs leading the individual cartels thought they were in charge.

"At first, it didn't hurt the business much. They branched out from pot and coke into heroin and meth. Their customer base north of the border expanded and a boatload of cash flowed south. 'El Chapo' Guzman, head of the Sinaloa Cartel, is on the Fortune 100 list."

Looks like I picked the wrong line of work. "So if there's so much money, why the hell are they fighting? And why the hell did their President go after them--don't they usually just pay off government leaders to keep the peace?"

"Usually, but Calderon was different, at least at first glance. He really seemed to want to clean it up, and he went hard after the cartels on the border, upsetting the delicate balance between the cartels. It made them weaker, and sensing blood in the water, Sinaloa used the opportunity to boost its export capacity. Whether by design or pure accident, Calderon's effort to clean up has sparked a war between Sinaloa and Juarez that claims ten lives a day. Now that Calderon is gone, we'll have to see what happens with the new President, but I'm betting the monster will be hard to subdue."

"You sure seem to know a lot about this stuff, Professor," I quipped.

"I have some important customers... friends... across the border, and they are living through all of this every day. Well, most of them are living. Hard not to take an interest."

His statement wasn't harsh or defensive, but I felt shamed by it nonetheless.

My thoughts turned back to my father and his role in the whole thing. It sure looked like he just got greedy and crossed the wrong guys, but something about it didn't add up.

"You know, now that I think about it, Mitchell was pretty eager to get me to sign over the business, and he stumbled all over himself when I said I might consider running the business myself. Oh, and the DEA was very interested in his activities."

"I would be, too. Mitchell probably knows quite a bit about how the money flows south, but they can't question him directly--attorney-client privilege and all. They have to catch him with his hand in the cookie jar. They had probably set up on your dad to get to Mitchell."

"Do you think there's anything to all the RICO threats they are throwing around?"

"Probably a stretch, but I'll have my legal team do some research. If I were you, I'd take the money and run. Throw the DEA a bone on what's-his-nuts, and if you're feeling guilty about the source of the money, make a big donation to Greenpeace, the Special Olympics or Gay Whales for Jesus."

"Yeah, you're right, but I think there's more here than meets the eye. I told you about the Florida thing, right?" He nodded and I continued. "Well, both Mitchell and the DEA are very interested in when--and *where*--I'm going to scatter my dad. They think that it's Florida, as in the land where old New Yorkers go to die, but that's just because they never went camping with my dad. I feel like he's leading me to something, and apparently, so do they. So whaddaya say, want to head out to the mountains tomorrow? I'll buy you lunch at Irma's."

"Sure, but I can't leave 'til afternoon."

We worked out a couple of the details and turned back to our beer. Except for a couple making out in a corner booth, we were the only ones in the place. The bartender was leaning against the other end of the bar and watching the late news. Paul nodded up at the screen as my phone vibrated again.

"They hardly even cover that nonsense anymore," he said about the TV, "but this one caught some attention."

The perfectly groomed local newscaster cut away to a grainy image of a dark haired man dressed "business casual" pointing a pistol at what looked like a cop in tactical gear sprawled on a dirty sidewalk.

Paul narrated. "A week ago these guys whacked a whole convoy of Mexico's finest in broad daylight just a couple of blocks from Fred's Rainbow Bar."

Fred's was a favorite hangout when we were kids. I bought my first beer there when I was sixteen, and Fred himself made these awesome little sandwiches on Mexican bread with fresh avocado and jalapeños spread on mystery meat. Many a high school kid puked up those sandwiches on the long walk home over the bridge to El Paso.

"Then a couple of days ago," Paul continued, "one of the TV stations aired a low-res security video of this guy blowing the cop's brains all over the sidewalk. It was a classy move, with people eatin' their dinner, watching the news, then BLAMMO, another win for the sensationalist media. I think someone's gonna get fired for it. Anyway, now all they show is the still shot of the moment before he pulled the trigger. Turns out the guy grew up in EP--the bad guy, not the cop. He went to school at Morehead."

"No kidding? My mom taught there way back when."

"Yep, small world. Anyway, the *narcos* took out eight cops and only lost three of their own. One was a clown who stood too close to his own grenade. Whole thing was a big mess, but just another day in the Drug War."

"Grenades? Holy crap."

"Yep, and you have some of *their* money, Chato."

That was a pleasant thought, and for the first time I thought I might be into something over my head.

"Ten per day are dying on that side of the river, and that's just Juarez," he said.

"That's pretty screwed up. All so some stupid asshole can smoke a joint or fry his brain with the smoke from a burning shard of methamphetamine." I took another swig of my beer, suddenly aware of the irony in my outrage. After all, my drug was legal. "It's Prohibition all over again--when are they gonna learn? Billions of dollars are spent on interdiction that only keeps prices up and puts more money in the pockets of the drug lords!"

Paul nodded in agreement, or maybe just to shut me up, and finished his own beer while ordering us another round. He was used to my alcohol-fueled rants. "But unfortunately, *amigo*,

Prohibition is here to stay. Hell, even the whackos out in California voted to keep pot illegal."

"Well, if it ever gets legal, I'm sure someone will be ready to capitalize on it, but in the meantime the poor Mexicans will just keep having to take it in the ass."

"Well here's to capitalism and taking it in the ass!" We clinked bottles a little too loudly and the bartender shot us a stony look of disapproval. We just laughed and my phone vibrated, again.

Over yet another beer we confirmed our plans to scatter Pop's ashes in the Florida Mountains. Paul said he'd bring his guns, and then added, "It'll be like old times--we can pop some jackrabbits and rattlesnakes."

"Well, Buddy, my rabbit killin' days are over, but I wouldn't mind getting me a snake or two." I didn't explain that the last time I shot a rabbit, the scream of fear and pain that came out of that little body touched something in my core. I vowed to never shoot another living creature, but would be more than happy to make an exception for snakes or terrorists--whenever I got the chance.

Chapter 20

When Tuco cautiously opened his eyes, the pain had ebbed to a dull, pulsing throb. The cobwebs cleared and his thoughts, just random bits and pieces at first, consolidated into a lucid stream. He lay on his side, tied at the wrists and ankles, and the bitter, caustic smell of bile assaulted his nose.

Tuco rolled away from the fetid mess and saw Guero sitting upright, asleep with his mouth open and chin on his chest. In the fading light, he barely made out the duct tape that bound his brother securely to the stout chair. He held his breath and listened for signs of someone else in the house, but aside from Guero's soft snores and the ticking clock in another room, all was quiet.

Convinced they were alone, he called out to his sleeping brother, "*Mano*, wake up!"

He stirred, but continued to snore.

"Guero! WAKE UP!" The effort hurt his head but had the desired effect.

The large man opened his eyes, and Tuco sensed more than saw the confusion in them. As he came awake, Guero struggled against his bonds and fear supplanted confusion.

"Guero, it's okay, you are okay."

"Tuco? My arms hurt. Cuchillo hurted you, Tuco. I'm scared of him."

"Don't be scared, Guero--" his head screamed, "--I won't let him hurt you. Can you move your arms?"

He watched his brother struggle, the effort clear in his reddened face.

"They hurt, Tuco."

"It will be okay, Guero. Stop trying to move your arms, just wriggle your fingers, okay?" He hoped that would help restore some blood flow and ease his brother's discomfort.

Guero started to sob.

"Stay strong, *hermano,* I'll get us out of this," he said softly.

Tuco considered his own restraints. The thick zip-ties were very effective, and struggling against the heavy nylon bands usually just made them tighter. But Tuco had once heard a special ops policeman say that you should never turn your back on a suspect in plastic cuffs.

"Most will just sit there, docile as a rabbit once you've caught them, but don't be fooled, a smart one will be out of them in less than a second," the veteran cop said. "I always use the metal."

He didn't really pay much attention to the old cop--most of what he said was a load of crap anyway--but despite the lingering fogginess from the drug, Tuco remembered his old colleague's pantomimed demonstration and put it to the test.

He rolled onto his back, tucked his knees as close as he could get them to his chest, and worked his bound arms over his buttocks. It took some effort, but Tuco managed to get his legs through the loop of his arms. He sat up on the edge of the cot and paused while his head filled with pain. It was the mother of all hangovers.

Tuco raised his arms as high as he could, paused to take a deep breath and steel himself to the impending agony and brought his wrists down across his knees with all the force he could muster. The nylon tie bit into his wrists and the impact jarred him to his shoulders, but it held fast. He cried out in pain.

"Stop it, Tuco," his brother pleaded, but after a full five minutes of recovery, he stood to try it again, hoping the extra swing distance would make a difference.

With a short, powerful scream, he raised his arms and swung them downward once again. For an instant the band felt white hot on his wrists, but it parted with a satisfying pop and Tuco's hands were free.

To his relief, the boastful cop had been right.

He took a moment to recover.

"Listen for the car, Guero, or any noise."

He used the broken zip tie as a friction saw, and worked quickly through the strap around his ankles. He unwrapped the tape securing Guero's arms to the chair and massaged them to get the blood flowing.

"Does that feel better?"

Guero stopped crying, but was still very scared. "Yes, but I want to go home."

The room had no windows. He tried the door, but as he expected, it was solid and bolted from the outside. It had been built to cartel specifications and he knew there was no chance of getting out without assistance from the outside. He fought past the lingering pain and devised a plan to escape his traitorous *sicario*.

"We can go home very soon, but first we have to play a game with Cuchillo."

While he continued to rub the blood back into Guero's numb hands and fingers, he explained the rules.

Chapter 21

Ronald Mitchell was not ready for this, not yet anyway. He hadn't expected the appearance of this evil, skinny Mexican with stringy hair and rotten teeth for at least another week, but here he was.

Despite the unexpected intrusion, the initial shock faded and he wasn't overly concerned, this was just another scare tactic to show they meant business. His concern increased a bit when the Mexican forced him to strip down to his socks and boxers, a bit more when he duct-taped him to one of the sturdy, mission style dining room chairs, and a bit more when he pulled out a gleaming straight-blade razor.

Though concerned, Ronald Mitchell didn't panic until the Mexican leaned in close with a vulture's breath and whispered, "Where's the ten million dollars, *maricon*?"

It was then that he realized something was terribly amiss. Someone else knew about the deal. In a moment of crystal clarity, he remembered where he had seen Mr. Martinez, a grainy video of an ambush in Juarez. He was NOT a member of the Sinaloa Cartel.

"Start talking, motherfucker, or things will become very unpleasant for you." Cuchillo had trouble pronouncing the word "unpleasant," but Mitchell got the point.

The attorney's eyes darted around the room like he was looking for the cash. Panic seized him when he realized that no matter what this man did to him, he didn't have the knowledge to make him stop. Mitchell simply didn't have the answer the interrogator wanted to hear.

"I-I d-don't know," he stammered through a building lump in his throat.

When the blade sliced into his flabby breast and bisected his pink nipple, Ronald Mitchell's bowels released in a watery mess that spilled over the edge of the oak chair onto the hardwood floor.

Over his own sobs he heard the Mexican's high-pitched voice. "Fucking gross, you sick piece of shit!"

Chapter 22

"Another round?"

"Seriously? I can't feel my nose." I was well past half-schnockered.

"So much for the hair-on-fire, bad-ass pilot. Would you like a Geritol with the last of your beer?"

"Better make it two. I'll be back, need to pee."

I made my way to the one-holer at the back of the bar and fished my phone out of my pocket. There were two text messages and a missed call from the same unfamiliar number.

"Does the richest man in El Paso like margaritas?" and "Call me. I stay up late," could only have been from Katy, Ron Mitchell's receptionist. Unless I'd used that line on the girl working the counter at Chico's Tacos--nope, it was Katy.

I thought over some smooth opening lines and dialed the number.

"Hello, Jake."

Damn, she stole my opening line.

"Hi, this is Jake--" *arrgh*, "--I mean, I hope I didn't wake you."

"Not at all, I rarely get to bed before two."

"Is that offer for margaritas still open?" I knew from the gist of the texts that margaritas were incidental.

"Well, eleven is a little late on a weeknight to find a good one… but we can try." *That's the spirit!* "Where would you like to meet?"

"Well, as it turns out, I'm already at Aceitunas, on Doniphan, do you know it? The bartender assures me he makes the best margarita on the block."

"Yeah, I know it, isn't that kind of a dive bar for the Ed Hardy crowd?"

"Ummm, yeah." I was glad at the moment that I didn't own one of those shirts. "But I'm not in much of a condition to drive anywhere else."

"Okay, I'll be over in about twenty minutes, but I'm not dressing up or anything."

Don't dress at all, I thought. "Cool, see you soon."

"Have one ready for me."

I managed to pee without getting my shoes wet or dropping my iPhone in the toilet and strolled--no strutted is a better word--back to the bar.

"You know, I think I will have one more."

"You were in there for a while, did you make room for another?"

"No, but a friend will be joining us in about twenty minutes."

Paul shook his head. "Jesus, you couldn't walk through a convent without being hit by a piece of ass."

"I wish, but this is a live one. On second thought maybe I should have a glass of water. *Garçon!* Tall water and your best margarita, *s'il vous plaît.*"

The bartender smirked and went to work on the order, unimpressed by my flawless French.

Two more trips to the urinal and about forty-five minutes later, Katy walked in the front door. She was wearing sweatpants and a tight fitting t-shirt printed with something I couldn't read.

As she walked across the bar, Paul leaned over and whispered something along the lines of "Good luck."

Maybe it was "You suck."

"Sorry I'm late," she offered as we stood to greet her.

"Not at all, he just finished making your margarita." I handed her a fresh drink. I had finished the first and second attempts before she arrived.

"Katy, this is my friend Paul." His irises bounced like a rubber ball between her face and boobs.

"Nice to meet you. Jake didn't tell me how pretty you are."

She blushed a little and rolled her shoulders back a bit. "Thanks, nice to meet you, too."

We moved to a high top table in anticipation of her arrival, and I pulled out a stool. She and I sat but Paul remained standing.

"Well, I have an early day tomorrow so I'll let you two get on with your evening. Call me in the morning, Jake."

"You got it. Thanks for the enchiladas and beer." After a few more pleasantries, he made his way out of the bar.

"How do you know Paul Castañeda?" Katy asked.

"Childhood friend. How do you know him?"

Her big blue eyes looked around the room for an answer. "I follow local business." She changed the subject quickly, "This margarita is kinda' weak, what do you have at your place?"

I missed something important as my libido took charge. "Just beer."

"Works for me. Should I drive?"

"Only if you want me to be there, too."

I followed her perfectly proportioned cotton spandex-covered ass to a Mercedes sport coupe parked next to my truck. Either Mitchell paid her very well, or she had a hell of a side job. Maybe one that required a shiny brass pole?

We made small talk on the twenty minute drive to my dad's place, but what I remember most is how her full lips glistened in the dim light of the car's instrument panel, and how she playfully touched my thigh at all of the right moments during the conversation. By the time we pulled into my driveway, I was pretty sure that if I managed not to pass out or throw up on her feet, I might get lucky enough to kiss this girl.

Chapter 23

"*Pinche* lawyer."

There was no tequila and the only beer in the refrigerator was some dark stuff from a country Cuchillo had never heard of. He slammed the door in disgust and started out of the kitchen, but only took a couple of steps before he stopped to reconsider.

He muttered, "*Pinche* fucking lawyer," oblivious to the redundancy as he yanked open the refrigerator door and grabbed one of the Belgian ales. His supply of cocaine had run out halfway through his interrogation and he needed something to keep the buzz alive.

The *sicario* sat at the attorney's desk and tried to twist the top off of the bottle. The sharp pleats of the cap cut into his palm instead of twisting off as expected. He yelped at the pain and hurled the bottle across the Mitchell's study. It exploded in a spray of foam and glass against a bookcase full of leather-bound legal tomes.

"FUCKING LAWYER!"

Always a fast learner, Cuchillo settled back into the chair with a fresh beer that he opened in the kitchen, and fished around in the bag for the last of his pumpkin seeds. The room smelled of hops and soggy paper.

Cuchillo didn't care much for beer and this one was particularly bad. A little more coke or a few shots of tequila would do the trick, but he was forced instead to sip the beer with a grimace while he waited for the computers, a laptop and desktop, to boot up. The lawyer gave him the login passwords and they worked. He knew they would.

Cuchillo's unfamiliarity with Apple products cost him a little time, but he eventually found what he needed on the computer. He also found a bonus in the form of a file folder titled "Katy."

Mitchell's tormentor worked his way through three of the strong beers while he watched the highlights of four years' worth of hidden camera work. Folder after folder of voyeuristic bathroom scenes transfixed Cuchillo and left him aroused. When he opened the clips shot in the attorney's office, he was even more titillated by the sight of the young secretary removing her top for the camera, but his arousal waned when the corpulent lawyer came into view and violated her pretty mouth. It reminded him that he had unfinished business.

"You are a twisted *cabron*," he said to the empty study. "But at least you have told me the truth."

He rose unsteadily from the desk, the European beer much stronger than anything he was used to, and made his way back to the dining room. Ronald Mitchell, much worse for wear, was strapped face-up and naked on top of his weathered-wood dining table. Blood, piss and watery feces mingled in a pool around the base of the chair where his ordeal started.

He tensed as Cuchillo circled the table, his eyes rolling frantically in their sockets as he tried to keep his tormentor in sight.

"You know, *maricon*, when I was little, me and my sister were sent to live at a…what you call it…a *orphange*? The *padre* that run it was a fat piece of shit like you. Sometimes he come and make my sister to suck on his dick, I try to stop him, but he just beat me like a dog, the fat bastard.

"My sister was pretty, like the one you like to watch make piss. Too pretty for you, *Maricon,* and too pretty for that fat fucking priest. When I got older, you know what I did to him?"

He grabbed Mitchell's face and hissed, "I cut his fucking throat."

Mitchell started to hyperventilate and his nostrils flared frantically, whistling with each panicked breath. He let out a muffled cry when Cuchillo grabbed his flaccid member and stretched it to its limit.

"Maybe I let you see how it is to be the girl," he whispered into the lawyer's bloody ear.

***

Cuchillo transferred the important files from Mitchell's desktop to the laptop, including some of the "Katy" files to watch later. He stuffed the computer into a duffle bag along with twenty thousand in cash and some Krugerrands that he had looted from the attorney's safe.

Still a little drunk and freshly washed, he loaded up the SUV and left Ronald Mitchell's hillside villa. It was a short drive around the southern tip of the Franklin Mountains to his next destination, and the roads virtually deserted.

Satisfied he had the correct address, he parked on the street a couple of doors down and waited. When boredom set in he remembered the prurient video clips and fished out the laptop. He was opening one of the bathroom scenes when a small, sporty car pulled into the driveway of the house he was watching.

The driver's door opened and there she was. Even in the poor light he recognized the hair and curves of her build. A man joined her from the passenger side. Cuchillo knew that this man was the key to his success but he would have to play him differently than he had the attorney: strike too early, and the victim wouldn't know anything useful.

That Mitchell didn't have the money, or even know where it was hidden, had taken Cuchillo by surprise and he was now out of his element. His strength was extracting information, not waiting for it, but for ten million dollars, he would learn quickly.

He watched the girl help his staggering quarry up the steps and into the house, and the thought of what she would do with him there intensified his arousal.

Confident they had settled in for the night, Cuchillo turned his attention back to the laptop. Thinking of Katy, his sister, his first, last and next kill, he pleasured himself before starting the SUV and driving to the safe house to bring the latter to fruition.

Chapter 24

Blu greeted us when I opened the door, and thankfully hadn't left any new piles on the floor.

I let him work his canine magic on Katy while I rustled up a couple of lagers and put on some Ottmar Leibert. Smooth Spanish guitar always helps to break the ice, not that there was any ice.

Katy sat sideways on the sofa, with one leg tucked under the other, her head propped up by and elbow on the back of the couch. Her hair had been in a ponytail, but was now free and spilling down her forearm like a silky brown river.

The tight cotton of her t-shirt was stretched near its limit over her clearly braless breasts. Whether God-given or surgically enhanced, they were quite exquisite.

"I really like your place."

"Thanks, it was my father's."

She flashed a sad, puppy-dog look. "Oh, I'm so sorry, I forgot. I met him a couple of times, he always seemed very nice."

"No worries, we weren't close. He left when…" My feel-sorry-for-me story was cut short by her soft lips and gently probing tongue. She smelled of Chanel and tasted like strawberries dipped in beer.

This was way too easy.

Chapter 25

Special Agents Christa Adams and John Reynolds pulled up to the Spanish villa on Crazy Cat Mountain Road dreading what they would find. Nearly a year's worth of work was swiftly circling the drain.

Adams ended her cellular call and looked at her partner. "We could be royally screwed."

"What happened?" Reynolds asked as he pulled the car into a driveway crowded with El Paso police cars and DEA vehicles.

"The van was delayed on a higher priority op. When they finally got here and did an IR scan, the house was clear so they entered and found him. A nosy neighbor called EPPD and our guys couldn't justify keeping them out, so it's a fucking three-ringed circus now."

They had watched Mitchell for months, but couldn't get the brass to sign off on around-the-clock surveillance. The El Paso Office was stretched thin as it was, and there were some very promising leads on some Juarez Cartel shipments. Seizures make better press than shutting down cash flow, so the attorney was pretty low priority. Appearing to win the War on Drugs was much more important than actually winning it.

Despite the prevailing attitude about glory busts, Adams had held onto Mitchell and the money flow angle like a tenacious pit bull, and her persistence had been starting to pay off. The Martin murder and his connection to the car wash laundering gave them some much needed leverage on Mitchell, it also opened the door for Adams and Reynolds to get warrants authorizing them to wiretap his home and office. Weeks of handstands and jumping through hoops had culminated in the scheduled installation of electronic monitoring devices earlier that afternoon--scheduled but not yet done.

They worked within the constraints of their system and built a surveillance plan that relied heavily on probability and luck.

But luck is a cruel bitch. Luck ensured they were interviewing Martin's son while Tuco, and later Cuchillo, visited the lawyer's office. And luck ensured that Cuchillo was "interviewing" their best lead in years, while they were busy on a bust that promised fifty kilos but netted a scrawny kid smuggling two dehydrated hyacinth macaws and a dozen emaciated boa constrictors.

"Is it bad?" Reynolds asked as they made their way up the driveway.

"I think so. Ned said it was pretty ugly, and he's seen his fair share of Colombian neckties. There he is now."

Ned Suarez didn't look like much, but the slight, gawky agent sporting faded jeans and a sparse goatee was a living legend in the DEA. His deep undercover work had led to the arrest of Felix Gallardo, godfather of the Mexican cartel system and the man who ordered the torture and murder of Ned's close friend, Agent Enrique Camarena.

Ned had also spent time in the poppy fields of Afghanistan.

Highly intelligent, with a degree in computer science from Cal Tech, he had paid his undercover dues and currently headed up the El Paso Field Division's Technical Service Department.

"Hi Christa, looking good. Still hitting the road?" Ned held out his hand.

"Not so much. No way I could keep up with you," she replied, returning the handshake. In fact, she could run a marathon in just under two hours and forty minutes, ten minutes faster than Ned's lifetime best.

"I doubt that. Who's the stiff," he said with a wink and smile.

"This is my new partner, John Reynolds, fresh out of Quantico."

"I'll give you the rundown here before we go in," Ned said. "Lots of extra ears in there. We were supposed to rig the house early this afternoon, but got called off on a higher priority. I was feeling kind of bad about it, so decided to swing by tonight on the off chance he was out. The inside work would have only taken a couple of minutes and we had a good view of the approaches if he happened back to the house.

"Anyway, the IR scan was clear, so we decided to go for it. Once we got inside, we found him.

"I had John pull the van in the driveway, and that's when the nosy next-door neighbor called in the local boys." He waved and flashed a Wink Martindale smile at a short, older woman in slippers and a nightdress covered by a shabby red, faux fur-lined wool coat. She smiled and waved back like Ned was her best friend.

"P.D. said she called in about a bunch of suspicious vehicles and loud noises at the Mitchell residence. Guess she missed the large yellow 'DEA' plastered all over our backs. Anyway, once they got here I couldn't justifiably keep them out, so it's been pretty busy. The good news is I threw around a bunch of B.S. about Homeland Security and the Patriot Act so they've pretty much been on the perimeter, but unless we get some high-level support real pronto-like, we're going to have to turn this over to them as a murder investigation."

"How bad is it?" she asked.

"Pretty messy, but that's the name of the game these days. Whoever did this is one sick puppy. He got what he wanted and then enjoyed a beer or two. Found a bottle with some blood on the label, and it wasn't the same type as the victim's. We took it to be processed for blood and saliva." He put his finger to his lips and turned towards the police cars.

"They'd raise hell if they knew, but screw them. I have a friend or two at the local FBI lab that can run the DNA against the criminal database. It's a long shot, but worth a try. Aside from a broken bottle in the study and the mess in the dining room, the place was pretty pristine. Ready to take a look?"

Ned took them through the garage and into the kitchen. The polished granite and stainless steel shone in contrast to the carnage visible in the dining room.

"Holy crap." Reynolds enunciated the words very slowly.

"Yup, great view, isn't it?"

Floor-to-ceiling picture windows were filled with the night-time vista of the gleaming cities of El Paso and Juarez, obscured by large patches of human skin pasted to the glass like self-clinging decals. The odd angles and random placement looked like a macabre Picasso mosaic.

Splayed on the table was the late Ronald Mitchell, Esq. Most of the skin on his arms, legs and torso had been removed and was presumably blocking the view of Downtown El Paso.

"Judging from the arterial spray and bleeding from the other wounds, he was skinned before the bastard cut his head off. By the way, can you confirm that this is Mitchell?" Ned gestured to the bald lawyer's head, sitting on the table, wedged into his own crotch between oozing, skinless thighs.

"Yes, that's him. Or was," Adams replied. "Whoever did this really has some issues."

"Yep, we checked, and it's in his mouth." Ned moved towards the severed neck. "It was a clean cut, probably a single blow with a very sharp and heavy blade, machete maybe. You can see a cut in the table consistent with the wound. I wonder if what they say is true about staying conscious for a while after losing your head? I'd hate for the taste of my own prick to be my last memory. You okay, sport?"

A greenish-looking Reynolds was standing a couple of feet back from the two senior agents. "I'm good," he replied, but when a platter-sized flap of skin peeled off of the window and plopped to the floor like a wet pizza dough, he puked down the back of Christa Adams' pant legs.

Chapter 26

All in all it had been a very satisfying day and was only going to get better. The attorney had provided hours' worth of fun and now it was Tuco's turn.

Cuchillo would never be able to articulate what motivated him to be so cruel, but was well aware of the power that it gave him. More than just an equalizer, his cruelty elevated him. When he had killed the abusive priest, he felt a power akin to God.

For the brief time that the *padre* lived after Cuchillo's brutal, slashing stroke, and he sat against the orphanage wall trying in vain to keep his guts from spilling to the floor, the young killer reveled in the glory of what he had done. When the last breath left the priest, the moment--the feeling of divine power--was lost.

Very few of his victims received the mercy of a quick death, and those who did, only out of necessity. Mercy robbed him of the power; it stole from him the sweet arousal of feeling his victim writhe as his blade sliced.

If he moved towards his prey, they flinched: when he touched them, he could feel their muscles clench: when he cut, they screamed, fainted or lost control of their bodily function. THAT was power.

Most of them had held him in contempt and looked down their noses at his unkempt appearance and uncultured manner-isms. But, once they were on the table, their disgust turned to primal fear. Much as it would with Tuco. The thought excited him more than the up-skirt shots of the pretty secretary.

The safe house was exactly as he left it, except for the smell of bile mixed with body odor and stale cigarettes.

The drug, he thought, *I hope he didn't drown himself.*

He turned on the light in the small bedroom and found Tuco and his brother right as he had left them. The sudden brightness woke Guero, but Tuco did not stir.

Dead?

"Shit, is he breathing?" he asked the retard, who blinked at him silently.

Cuchillo moved over to the big man taped in the chair and Guero cringed. "IS HE DEAD?" he shouted. Again, no answer.

"*Idiota!*"

He moved to the bed and bent to place his fingers on Tuco's neck. His boss' hair was matted and sticky with vomit.

"Not so pretty now, eh *patron?*"

As he registered the strong pulse, he caught movement from the chair.

"BOO!" Guero yelled as he raised his arms and stood out of the chair.

Cuchillo turned towards him and reached to his left front pocket but realized the mistake a second too late. Tuco had taken the karambit.

Cuchillo heard the metallic click and felt a tugging at his abdomen that turned into a searing pain. When he tried to scream, the breath wouldn't come.

Chapter 27

Alex lay half-covered by the white sheet, propped up on one elbow and looked down at me. The sun streaming in the window behind her kept me from making out the details of her face or the expression in her fiery green eyes. Her firm breasts looked as if they weren't affected by gravity or the twist of her body. It was the last time I would see her naked.

We had alternately argued and made love for most of the night, stopping only when exhaustion, or exasperation, forced us to sleep.

She lightly traced her fingers over my chest. "You know this is something I have to do, and it has nothing to do with us. You knew it was coming."

The tickle of her fingers on my skin would turn me on under normal circumstances, but I sat up abruptly to stop her caress.

"It has everything to do with us!" I was acting like a petulant child.

It had been over a year and a half since we first met at the park. In the days that followed that first encounter, I found myself hanging out there much more than usual, hoping to run into her again. She ran at the same time most days, so my challenge was to not look too eager.

It took a few conversations in the park, and I never could have done it without Blu, but she finally agreed to join me for dinner and drinks. As pretty as she was in her jogging attire, she was absolutely stunning in a cocktail dress and make-up.

It turned out that in addition to her looks, she was armed with an equally impressive intellect.

As the only daughter of the epitome of old Mexican money and power, Alex was determined to stray from the norm and make it on her own. Unfortunately for me, "making it" meant changing the system that had kept her family rich for generations.

There is a great disparity in the standard of living between the relative few who control the wealth of Mexico and the working classes. With few notable exceptions like drug lords and successful politicians, it is very difficult for the average Mexican citizen to break out of the cycle of poverty. Those who do are unlikely to be accepted by the paragons of the Mexican Aristocracy.

An inefficient education system, cronyism and outright corruption conspire to keep the poor toiling to fill the pockets of the rich. Like most Americans, I normally wouldn't give a rat's ass, but after a year and a half with Alex, I couldn't help but be a fountain of statistics regarding the plight of Mexico.

She thought she could help change it all, and unlike most of the Hollywood bleeding hearts who spout meaningless sound-bites, she put her money where her mouth was. Alex felt that change must come from within, so she shed the trappings of wealth and fled to the U.S., where she managed to wean herself from the teat of privilege and earned scholarships to pay her own way.

When I met her, she was starting her last year of law school at the University of Texas, which would have set her up nicely to land a high-paying job anywhere in the States, but that wasn't her goal.

Mexico was on her mind, and it was there she was going to make her splash.

She told me over and over again what she had planned, but I ignored the warning signs and fell hopelessly in love.

In all fairness, so did she, but it wasn't enough to pull her eyes off of the prize: a personal crusade to draw her country into the twenty-first century.

Her plan was simple. Alex was going to earn credibility by fighting corruption on the front lines, and use that to enter the turbulent world of Mexican politics as a reformer.

I thought it was a bit idealistic and would have been much happier with a plan that involved her working as a high-power attorney. I assured her that I'd quit my airline job and be her sexual slave, but my ploy didn't work.

Alex was different than any woman I had ever known. She challenged me intellectually, was there for me emotionally and had become my best friend. I could not imagine my life without her but was faced with the prospect of losing her to a quest worthy of Cervantes.

As the end neared and she graduated *magna cum laude*, I fought harder to keep her with me, but it was like catching water in a net, so there we were on our last morning together.

I couldn't see her face for the halo of light behind her, but I knew she was pursing her lips in the pout that she knew I couldn't resist. I capitulated easily. "I know this is something you have to do, and I'll be here to support you."

She flashed me a sad, executioner's smile and kissed my cheek. The weight of her bare breast brushing across my chest stirred something a little carnal, her tongue teasing my earlobe really got the blood flowing, and her soft fingertips teasing me under the sheets got my full attention.

By the time she poured herself on to me like warm syrup, I'd completely forgotten that she was leaving for Mexico later that day to join the *Policia Federal*.

I woke from the dream with a start and it took a few minutes to figure out where I was.

Chapter 28

Tuco sat at a wood grain Formica table and stroked the keys on Ronald Mitchell's laptop. Guero slept under a cheap duvet on one of the two double beds in their hotel room.

The expected fight with Cuchillo had never materialized. Hoping to surprise him with the first strike and throw him off balance, Tuco was the one surprised by the karambit's lethality. His upward thrust with the claw-like weapon opened Cuchillo's skinny midsection like it was made of butter, transected the abdominal wall and severed his diaphragm. The *sicario* spent his last moments sitting against the wall, holding his own purplish, glistening guts cradled in both hands and gaped for air like a landed fish. The look he gave Tuco as he died was filled with a mixture of surprise, hatred and resigned comprehension.

Without the muscle he needed to draw the air into his lungs, Cuchillo asphyxiated within minutes.

A quick inventory of Cuchillo's bag revealed the tools of his trade, including a bloody machete, and a laptop computer. It was clear to Tuco that a visit to Ronald Mitchell would be a waste of time. He knew that the information he needed was probably in the bag; Cuchillo was nothing if not thorough.

Back at the safe house, Tuco carefully removed any traces of their presence, including the vomit-covered sheets. After taking a shower and donning fresh clothes, he removed the GPS tracker that he himself had ordered installed in all cartel vehicles, loaded Guero into the SUV and left Cuchillo to rot in the safe house.

They checked into a nondescript chain hotel near downtown, and still a bit groggy from the anesthetic, lay down to catch a few hours of much-needed sleep. He drifted off to the lullaby of Guero's ascending snores. It was four in the morning.

Chapter 29

As I gained my bearings in the muted, muddy light of pre-dawn, the only thing left of Alex was a hollow emptiness and some morning wood. It took a few seconds for my sleep-addled brain to figure out where in the hell I was and who was purring like a kitten wrapped in the sheets beside me. The vague, musky smell of sex tickled my nose with every other breath. When I realized that it was Katy snoring softly beside me, the emptiness from the faded dream became more acute and I felt a little guilty, as if I were betraying Alex. But not guilty enough to make me lose the hard-on.

The night's activities were coming back to me and the replay had me ready for more. She did things with her mouth that defied all laws of science and logic. I was so lost in the mental re-run that I hadn't noticed Katy had stopped snoring and I nearly jumped out of my skin when she ran her fingers up the inside of my thigh.

"Good morning," she purred.

Why did I suddenly feel like a male Black Widow spider?

"Mmmmm," was all I could manage.

"Really good morning," she giggled when her wandering hand found the boner peeking out of my boxers.

Without another word, she slipped her fingers under the elastic band, ducked her head under the sheets and went to work.

After she'd finished, which didn't take long—have I mentioned she was *really* good with her mouth?—she popped up like she'd done nothing more than blow some lint out of my belly button.

"I just love that first thing in the morning."

I agreed, the best part of waking up has nothing to do with Folger's, but all I could manage was another, "Hmmmm."

"Thanks for last night. None of the others ever pushed my buttons like you do."

Something about that statement got my attention. Others, not "other men," "other boyfriends" or "other guys I've screwed," just "others." It had a clinical ring to it, the kind of matter-of-fact statement you might hear from a professional.

"I aim to please, ma'am."

"Well you definitely hit your target," as she said it she lifted her knee slightly and rolled towards me, brushing her clean-shaven womanhood across my thigh. She oozed sexuality like Niagara oozes water.

I thought for a split-second that she was going to resurrect Lazarus for yet another ride, but she leaned back over and started an interrogation worthy of Mata Hari.

"I'm sorry, I keep forgetting why you are here. You must be devastated."

Devastated? Not so much, but only a fool wouldn't play it up a little. "I'm okay, it's just all come as a big surprise."

She leaned in and kissed me. Considering the early hour and where her mouth had just been, I was surprised at the sweetness of her breath. I wondered where she hid the mints.

"When you left the other day, you had a box. Was that… him?"

"Yeah, your boss had him cremated in accordance with his will. Guess he was too cheap to spring for an urn…I mean my father, not your boss."

"Ronnie's pretty cheap, too. He told me you're supposed to take him to Florida to scatter his ashes. My family used to vacation there when I was a kid. Did you go there a lot?"

Yeah, but not the Florida she thought. "Eh."

"Are you going to take him there?"

"I guess, wouldn't want to ignore his last wishes."

"I can go with you if you want…you know, to keep you…company." She reached down and lightly stroked my dead soldier, and much to my surprise the fight wasn't totally out of him. I don't think this girl had much to do with Jesus, but she *could* raise the dead.

The idea of her sprawled naked on a secluded Florida beach nearly obliterated the feeling that I was being interrogated, but then I guessed that was part of her tactic. It was the word "others" and the off-handed way she referred to her boss as "Ronnie" that brought me back. Why the hell was "Ronnie" telling her anything about Florida?

"Maybe. Yeah, that would be nice."

"Where in Florida? I mean it would be kind of creepy if he wanted you to sprinkle him on Disneyland or something."

"World."

"Oh, is that near Miami or something?"

"No, I mean it's Disney*world*. Disneyland is in California." Or something.

"Right. But seriously, like where in Florida? I need to know what kind of clothes to bring."

Like you need to choose between sweaters or shorts? It's freaking Florida for Christ's sake! This conversation was well past inane. But the recognition that I was being interrogated, or at least pressed for information, made me follow a hunch.

"You won't need anything but a beach towel and a toothbrush, but make it a black towel, in light of the occasion."

I sighed as if reminiscing and continued. "It was near Panama City, on the Redneck Riviera," I lied. "A little beach near where the Chattahoochee River spills into the Gulf." Or something. I had no clue where the Chattahoochee River was, or whether it spilled into the Gulf, but figured she'd never know the difference.

"Oh wow! That's where we used to go!"

What an amazing *coincidence.*

"Really? We used to rent a cabin for a couple of weeks every summer, right on the beach," I continued the embellishment.

"Wow, us too!"

No shit?

"Which rental company did you use, I mean wouldn't it be just crazy if we were at the same place and didn't even know it?"

Yep, crazy beyond words.

"I'm not sure, I think it was called Big Al's." I never said I was a good liar. "I'd recognize it if I saw it…it was right on the main road out of Panama City."

"So Big Al's on the main road out of Panama City?" If she were a reporter she'd be scribbling furiously in her notebook. "When should I pack my towel and toothbrush?"

"Just have them ready and I'll let you know. Probably sometime in the next couple of days. Will you have any trouble getting away from work?" I already knew the answer to that question.

"No, Ronnie will let me go. Your dad and you are…" she paused awkwardly, "were… important clients. Besides, he owes me."

I bet he does. I wondered for a second whether or not good ol' Ronnie knew just how skilled his receptionist was at the oral arts. Silly me, of course he did.

"I have to get going." At that she got up, all business, and got dressed.

Chapter 30

Tuco rose at eight feeling surprisingly refreshed, and he let the hotel room instant coffee cool while he perused the late attorney's files. Guero would soon be asking about breakfast, so he wanted to learn as much as possible before the quiet was shattered and he was forced to run across the street for a bag full of "egga-muffins."

He had been right about Cuchillo's attention to detail. The laptop alone was a treasure trove, complete with a sticky note full of URL's, user names and passwords scrawled in Cuchillo's primitive handwriting tacked to the palm rest. A brown smudge of what Tuco assumed to be the lawyer's blood obscured the return key and matched a similar stain on the small yellow paper.

The *sicario* had left several video panes open on the computer desktop, all of them framing a pretty brunette in various stages of dress and sexual activity. Clearly she was Mitchell's secretary, and not the frumpy old hag who had spilled her Starbucks during his office visit. Something about the girl might bear closer scrutiny.

He found an encrypted file that detailed the Guadalete Development Corps transaction and corroborated the information provided by the Sinaloa accountant. It contained several references to an individual identified as "DM," which Tuco cross-referenced to a file labeled 'd-Martin.'

The files painted a comprehensive picture of the "who, what, when and why" of the ten million dollars, but left out the most important part—where.

It neared ten o'clock when Tuco finished with the computer and moved to the attorney's hand-written notes. Still plenty of time left to get Guero's favorite breakfast sandwiches.

At eleven, Guero's whining could no longer be ignored and Tuco went across the street to get Quarter Pounders for breakfast.

Things were starting to clear up for Tuco. Martin was the money man who had stolen the cash and was killed for it; Mitchell had arranged the murder but made the rookie mistake of pulling the trigger before asking the questions; the Guadalete Development Corps were bad people even by Tuco's sense of values; and the launderer's son seemed to hold the key to a ten-million-dollar treasure chest somewhere in Florida.

According to the cartel GPS track, Cuchillo had visited the late Mr. Martin's residence just before returning to the safe house to meet his demise. In the only commonality that Tuco would concede, Mitchell also had a penchant for GPS tracking. One of the URLs from the sticky note was a GPS tracker that had real time and historical tracks for three separate devices. The device labeled "RM" had been parked at his residence since the evening before, and Tuco assumed that it wouldn't be moving anytime soon. Another labeled "DM" had been parked at a Westside restaurant for over twelve hours, but by far the most active was "KO." It had gone to DM's address, stopped at a high rent apartment building, joined up with the DM tracker at the restaurant, spent the night at the DM residence and after a short stop at the aforementioned apartment, was back at the law offices of Sampson, Mitchell and Mitchell. She would warrant a visit.

Chapter 31

Her mission was *fait accompli*, and she wanted to gloat over it. For a moment or two she had debated going straight to the lawyer's house to share her success, but decided against it.

If she had gone to his place, he would have surely demanded a wake-up call or maybe some help cleaning himself in the shower, and after a good night with Jake, the thought of her boss brought with it a bit of nausea. Besides, she was pretty sure she smelled like a porn star after a two-day shoot, and that would only enrage Mitchell. So she decided to save the good news for the office.

Katy dropped the thick Turkish towel and admired her own nude body in the full-length mirror. Normally at this juncture, she would lie back on her elegantly appointed bed and bring herself to climax with two flawlessly manicured fingers, but not this time. Jake had actually known his way around a woman, and the indulgence was wholly unnecessary. So she simply stood and watched the water drip off of her hair and flow lazily over the ridges and valleys of her shoulders, breasts and impossibly flat belly. She was enrapt in a moment of self-admiration that made Narcissus look like a rank amateur.

As she dressed, she came to the conclusion that this payoff should be much higher than the others. This wasn't the typical run-of-the-mill blow-for-info or blackmail photo session. Ronnie was really sweating this one, and there was big money involved. Big Money. Yep, if she planned this right, the time on her knees in front of that bastard might be drawing to a close.

Katy applied bright red lipstick she found whorish and liberally splashed on Obsession she found adolescent, but knew they were his favorites and today she was pulling out all the stops. After a final look in the mirror she headed off to the firm.

When she arrived, it was a few minutes past her regular show time and there was a woman sitting outside the office door. The lady's shoulders sagged at Katy's appearance.

"Mr. Mitchell isn't here yet?"

"No. Are you Katy? I'm Martha, LegalTemp sent me."

"Hi. Sorry, but we won't need you today."

Katy unlocked the door and walked in, leaving the deflated temp in the hall. Martha sighed, gathered her things and walked dejectedly away.

Katy sat at her desk and looked up flights between El Paso and Panama City. *Might as well nail Jake down*, she thought, *and it will be easier if I'm armed with flight numbers and times.* Once she had a few options, she turned her attention to the latest Hollywood scandals on TMZ.com.

She was so fully engrossed in a story about a starlet's Chihuahua who was squashed inadvertently by a bad-boy movie star on a rented Harley, that she was startled when the office door opened. Katy jumped up expecting to see Ronald Mitchell but was instead greeted by a pair of federal officers.

"Hi, Christa. Who's your friend?" she replied looking at John Reynolds warily. Adams, standing a step behind her partner gave Katy a conspiratorial shake of her head.

Reynolds thought that 'Linda Lovelace' was hotter in person than in the videos the forensics team had found on Mitchell's iMac, and much hotter than the porn star whose moniker had been assigned her by one of the techs. Based on the video evidence she was also much more talented than the *Deep Throat* actress. His fascination with her full red lips caused him to miss the fact that she and Christa Adams were not strangers.

"We have some bad news for you, Miss Olsen." Reynolds tried to be as sensitive and smooth as possible. "Ronald Mitchell was found dead at his residence."

Katy sank slowly back into the chair, and Reynolds mistook the look of shock on her pretty face as one of concern for her late boss.

"No. I can't believe it. W-what happened?" she stammered as her mind raced through the ramifications of his demise. *No more blowjobs for Ronnie: good. No more fat paychecks and bonuses: bad. Might have to find a real job: bad. Plenty of horny attorneys out there who would pay dearly for her services: not so bad.*

She used the thought of the poor Chihuahua, broken and bleeding in a Hollywood gutter to get the tears flowing.

Reynolds handed her a handkerchief from his coat pocket and prayed it was clean. "What can you tell us about Mr. Mitchell's activities yesterday?"

"Not m-much really," she replied through an over acted sob. "He met with a client early, a probate case, I think, and then I wasn't feeling well, so I took the rest of the day off. I left before lunch." She sniffed loudly.

"Who was the client?" asked Adams.

"I'm not sure," she lied.

"Don't you log appointments?" Reynolds called her on it.

"Uh, yeah. Sorry, I didn't think about that." She made a show of shuffling through the desk planner.

"Here, here it is, Doug Martin," she offered, and then realized that she just violated the client's right to privacy. She cursed herself for not thinking of that as her first response.

"Thank you. Did you talk to Mr. Mitchell at all after you left?"

"No, sorry. You might want to talk to the temp who filled in for me." She shuffled some more papers. "I can give you the company's number." She continued, "What happened to Ron… Mr. Mitchell?"

"It appears he was murdered." *Unless he skinned himself and his head popped off during auto-fellatio,* Reynolds didn't add.

Adams held out a small card with two pictures. "Have you seen either of these men over the past couple of days?"

Katy looked them over and slowly shook her head. She would have remembered either one of them, one for his good looks and the other for precisely the opposite. For a moment she thought she could actually smell the ugly one.

Had they interviewed the temp, they would have discovered that Ricardo "Tuco" Medrano, the handsome one, had indeed stood in that very spot less than twenty-four hours before.

"Who are they?" Katy asked.

"Just someone we want to talk to. We have reason to believe they may have tried to contact Mr. Mitchell. They may still. If they show up here, will you please notify us?" Reynolds replied.

"Yes." Katy wouldn't be around the office any longer than it took the feds to drive out of sight. "Did they kill Ron…Mr. Mitchell?"

"We'd just like to talk with them, Miss Olsen."

"They aren't dangerous, are they?"

"We don't believe you have anything to fear. If they *were* the ones who killed him, they probably wouldn't show up here," Adams' response was less than convincing. "Please, just let us know if they do."

Reynolds handed her his card.

"Thanks," she paused, "Don't forget this."

"Huh?"

"The temp." She held out a sticky note on which she had written a name and number. "Here's the number for Legal-Temp."

"Thank you." Adams took the note and continued, "I know this is terrible news, and we are very sorry about Mr. Mitchell. Are you going to be all right here by yourself?" She doubted the girl would miss the closed-door sessions with her late employer.

"Y-yes. I'll try to stay busy and clear all of his appointments." *And clear out the safe in his office.* "This is just all so horrible," she added with another theatrical sob.

Reynolds preceded Adams out the front door, and as the latter stepped out of the office, she turned back to Katy and pantomimed the universal sign for "call me." The receptionist nodded her assent.

After the Feds left, she made a beeline for the floor safe hidden under Mitchell's office chair. Katy had known the combination since her second week on the job. Mitchell clumsily fumbled through it while retrieving the wad of cash that was her first bonus for "services rendered." Katy watched him surreptitiously through her compact mirror and he had never been the wiser for it. He also had never bothered to have it changed.

She found over fifty thousand dollars in cash and a .38 revolver stuffed in the safe, along with a DVD labeled "Katy's Greatest Hits."

"Rot in hell, you fucking pig," she muttered as she bent the disc until it shattered in a spray of sharp plastic shards.

Fifty grand was nice, but she was sure that whatever Ronnie was after was much bigger. Now that he was out of the picture, she would just have to play it out solo. Like any great fool who thinks themselves bigger than the world around them, Katy was more than confident that she could pull it off.

With her oversized purse stuffed full of cash and a snub-nose .38, she blew off his future appointments and decided that her tenure at Sampson, Mitchell and Mitchell, Attorneys at Law, had officially ended.

She didn't bother to lock the doors.

Chapter 32

Adams and Reynolds left the dead lawyer's office feeling like they were chasing their own tails.

The morning had seen lead after lead pour in, and the whos, whens, wheres and hows were falling into place for them, but not the whats or whys.

Cooperation from their counterparts in Mexico was largely a function of how much the flow of information served the source, and based on the relative deluge, there was something afoot that elements of the *Policia Federal* wanted to get their mitts into.

Taken alone, each report was an interesting look at the goings on in the world of drug production and export, but when lumped together, the tidbits coalesced into a story that was filling in a lot of the blanks for Reynolds and Adams.

According to their sources, the flannel-clad daughter of a senior Sinaloa moneyman had been found aimlessly wandering the dirt streets of a Juarez *colonia*. Though disheveled, barefoot and carrying a small squirming puppy she was able to lead police to a fortified home she described as a "death house." She claimed it was the site where she and her father were kept prisoner and compelled to watch the torture and dismemberment of her father's personal bodyguard.

Her description of the perpetrators amounted to *"un guapo, un feo, and un retardo grande,"* or a handsome one, an ugly one and a big retarded one.

Police broke into the house and discovered two fifty-gallon drums containing the dismembered remains of Arturo "El Clavero" Guzman and his unidentified bodyguard. El Clavero, or the Key Master, was a senior accountant for the Sinaloa Cartel, and in addition to being the girl's father, he was also a distant cousin of cartel leader Joaquin "El Chapo" Guzman. They also found several decomposed bodies buried in the back yard.

The torture and murder of a high-level cartel member wasn't all that unusual, but it did raise a flag considering the fact he was a key player in Adams and Reynolds' laundering investigation. What was unusual was that the subject of another tip might have been fingered for the murder.

The prime suspect, Ricardo "Tuco" Medrano had stepped on his own crank in a big way. In an otherwise unremarkable ambush of a Federal Police convoy, Medrano was photographed and identified as one of the assailants. To complicate matters, the man he had killed on camera was a highly-placed *Policia Federal* officer in the employ of the Sinaloa Cartel. The unsanctioned assault had both cartels buzzing.

When Medrano's image had gone public in the Monday morning paper, it didn't take long for the cartel's leadership to mark him for death. All of this came to the DEA via a confidential source deep within the cartel inner circle.

After killing the Sinaloa accountant and releasing his daughter, Tuco Medrano, his brother Juan and a cartel assassin known only as "El Cuchillo" seemed to have fallen off the face of the Earth. That was unless the trio had visited one Ronald Mitchell and pasted his bloody skin to the windows of his expansive dining room.

Reynolds and Adams felt confident that was precisely the case, but with Mitchell dead and no real clue how all of the pieces fit together, the late Mr. Martin's son was the best lead left to follow.

"Did you get the impression she was hiding something?" Reynolds asked his partner as they drove away from Mitchell's office.

"Definitely." *She's my Confidential Informant*, she didn't add. "As intimate as she was with her boss, I'd guess he sent her after clients, both for information and leverage. He probably put her onto Martin."

"The old man?"

"No, Jake. She tried to cover the fact that he had been there at the office. Wouldn't surprise me if that's why she left the office early yesterday, Mitchell gave her the day off to go fishing. I'm guessing she's just antsy that we'll discover what she does to help pay for that fancy little car, but probably doesn't know a whole lot. Now that Mitchell is gone, she won't hang out at the office for very long." She also didn't add that Miss Olsen's weekly check-in phone call was less than an hour away.

"How about putting a tail on her?"

"We can try."

"Should we follow up with the temp?"

"Nah, the temp will probably tell us what we already know, Medrano was there. He's a ghost. We need to stay on Martin. If he's the key, our boy Tuco will show up and maybe we can figure out what this is all about."

"What now?"

"Let's go back to the office and see what they pulled from Mitchell's computer, and we can get the ball rolling on a tail for our pretty little blowjob artist. Later we can track down Martin."

By the time their request for additional support had been denied, it would have been too late anyway.

Chapter 33

Jose Luis Fratello slammed his iPad on the desktop, turning the technological marvel into a useless piece of aluminum with a shattered glass screen. As head of *La Linea,* the enforcement arm of the Juarez Cartel, he was directly responsible for Tuco Medrano's transgressions, and the report from the soldier standing at his desk did little to help his cause.

When the news had broken that Tuco had autonomously choreographed the *Avenida Norgazaray* ambush, then disappeared across the border after torturing and killing El Clavero, *Don* Vicente Carrillo, Fratello's boss, had called in the trusted lieutenant to express his disappointment. The *Don's* voice was even and calm, but the message was crystal clear.

Failure would not be tolerated.

Fratello's only chance for survival was to rein in Tuco before the Don lost patience, and the clock was ticking.

The avalanche picked up speed and consumed everyone in its path. A hapless warehouse guard whose only transgression had been being on duty when Tuco left Juarez through the tunnel had already been beaten to death and the soldier who gave Fratello the bad news expected no better for himself.

He just returned from the *Azteca* safe house in El Paso where the GPS tracker was parked, and the news that Tuco wasn't there led to the iPad tantrum. It was not the end of the bad news.

The soldier swallowed hard and continued, "Cuchillo is dead Boss, and we found this." He showed him the small black GPS transmitter Tuco had pulled from the SUV.

Fratello took the small device, and stared at it while he hefted it in his palm, a vein pulsing at his temple like an angry earthworm.

He looked up abruptly and bellowed, "*Mierda!*"

The tracker sailed across the room and shattered against a wall.

"Get back there and find that *cabron!* I don't care how you do it, just find him, God damn it! Look under every rock, pay who ever you have to, but find them! Kill the fucking imbecile, but bring Tuco to me!"

Chapter 34

Katy shifted the bag on her shoulder and unlocked the door to the impressive apartment that, like her car, was well beyond the means of a legal secretary. The bag was heavy, but she hardly noticed and nearly skipped like a schoolgirl from the foyer to her living room. Her levity vanished at the sight of the man sitting casually on her off-white, Italian leather sofa.

"Miss Olsen, I presume?" It was the handsome man from the government photo. His delivery was smooth and measured, like the guy from the *Dos Equis* commercial.

"Yes," she replied cautiously while instinctively clutching the bag closer to her body. Doing her best to sound indignant and unafraid, she puffed up and asked, "Who are you and what the hell are you doing in my apartment?" She thought she saw his eyes narrow a bit at her tone. It was fleeting, but enough to shake her resolve.

"Please pardon the intrusion, but as I'm sure you are aware, your employer has come to... an untimely end. Mr. Mitchell was helping me with an important matter, and I think now that he is gone, you will be able to help in his place."

"Did you kill Ronald?" she blurted.

"No, and I regret that he is dead. I have already dealt with the animal who murdered him." He made the statement as if talking about a daily chore.

"The greasy one?"

He chuckled at the description. "Yes."

Katy sat slowly in an easy chair opposite the sofa. Perhaps it was her innocent face, or the way her blouse was unbuttoned at the top, but whatever the distraction, Tuco didn't notice her right hand fumbling in the bag behind her.

"What do you want from me?"

"Just some information, and the assistance you were giving your… former… employer."

"So what's in it for me?"

"I think you know the answer to that…" he started to reply.

Katy cut him off as she pulled the revolver from her purse and leveled it at Tuco. "I think I know too. Maybe some rough sex and a shallow grave in the desert."

Unfazed, he leaned forward slowly, "It's clear you misunderstand my intentions, Miss Olsen. I would like us to work together. There is plenty for both of us." He paused. "Do you even know what you are after?"

The confusion in her eyes gave him his answer, "Ten million dollars, Katy."

Her pupils dilated and she lowered the pistol a fraction, then just as suddenly she raised it again, "You *need* me, but I don't need you."

He smiled, "To find the money? No, you don't need me, but once you do, what then? Are you going to kill Martin? Then what about the cartel? You wouldn't last long enough to buy a new pair of shoes."

He could see her wheels spinning. She lowered the gun again and bit her lower lip. Tuco thought he had her.

The handsome *narco's* offer had some merit, but he had underestimated Katy's ego and greed. She wasn't the slightest bit worried about the cartel, but she needed to get rid of the man sitting in her living room. Her call with Christa Adams was just a few minutes away and she could kill two birds with one stone: drop the dime on the good-looking drug lord and keep Adams tied up long enough to execute her plan.

"I'm flying to Florida with Jake, Daniel Martin's son. We leave for Miami tonight or tomorrow, I'm not sure yet. I think that's where the old man hid the money. You can't stay here, the DEA came by the office looking for you, and they might be watching me. I'll call you when I know more." She hoped it was enough to get him out of her apartment.

Tuco didn't buy it, but he knew from Mitchell's files that there were some half-truths sprinkled throughout her story. He reached into his pocket for a pen and she raised her pistol.

"Easy, it's just a pen, for my phone..." his eyes widened, "...Guero, NO!"

She turned, but it was too late.

Chapter 35

After Katy left, I lay in bed and enjoyed the afterglow for as long as I could until a wet nose nudged my armpit and spoiled the moment. Don't ever get a dog.

I ran a hot shower and while I stood letting the water wash away the remnants of my night, I thought about the whole sordid situation. Sure, she was a mercenary, a greed-driven bitch, but man was she hot, and did I mention pretty good in the sack?

I shook my head in shame at the stupid rationalization. Katy would blow a billy goat if the money were right, and I was sure that Mitchell was paying her generously to get close to me. My best hope was for a little gratuitous sex and to gather some information of my own.

I finished my morning routine, fed my brain with some stale Starbucks I found in the kitchen, and checked my phone. In all the excitement I had forgotten my wall charger in Austin. The battery was down to about 20 percent, but I had a mobile charger in the truck. A message from Paul told me to stop whatever unnatural act I was committing and get down to his office. Pronto. He'd found some good dirt on drugs, money and the men who love them.

I fed Blu, tossed the Frisbee for him a few times, had another cup of coffee and headed out the front door to find...

"Crap!"

…that my car was still parked between The Riviera and Aceitunas. After thirty minutes and a cab-ride-of-shame to pick up my Chevy, I was on my way to Paul's office.

Chapter 36

Tuco loved the fall weather in El Paso, and this day was exceptionally spectacular. He sat in a chair on Katy's balcony overlooking the city and the sprawl of Juarez beyond. The sky was cloudless and clean, the temperature perfect and he could hear birds above the faint noise of traffic below. The buildings of downtown shone stark in the bright midday sun, and they stood out like actors in a spotlight on a darkened stage. Across the river, the gargantuan red, white and green flag of Mexico fluttered in slow motion. He had read somewhere that the flag was so large it could cover a football field; overcompensation for a nation with an inferiority complex?

Tuco thought so but he had to admit it was an impressive sight, waving regally against the crystal blue sky.

He couldn't blame Guero for killing the girl lying in the room behind him. In his simple mind, a bad person was pointing a gun at his brother, his Tuco, and Tuco had to be saved. Never mind that the gun wasn't loaded or that the girl didn't have what it takes to pull the trigger. Guero saw the need for action and he took it.

In the end, it was Tuco's shout that killed her. By calling out to Guero, Tuco had alerted her to his presence and she turned. Guero's meaty fist met the side of her face and her neck snapped with a dull, muffled crack. She went rigid for a moment and had the gun been loaded, the involuntary convulsion would have sent a bullet through Tuco's forehead. Instead, her legs twitched a couple of times, kicking the underside of the glass coffee table as she slumped back into the easy chair and lay still.

After countless puppies and kittens, Guero had taken a human life. He looked up at Tuco with teary eyes and a quivering lower lip.

Tuco comforted his brother, hopeful that his limited mental capacity and short memory would diminish the tragedy of the event. The large man cried like a child for several minutes, but eventually calmed and returned to the video game. Tuco left him in the second bedroom and stepped out onto the balcony to gather his thoughts.

If only life were as simple as losing yourself in an electronic trance.

Tuco turned his back on the symbiotic cities and walked into the girl's living room. She lay sprawled on the recliner where she had fallen thirty minutes before. Tuco closed her staring eyes and carried her limp form to the master bedroom, her head lolling unnaturally with each step.

He stretched her out on top of the large bed and she looked like she was taking an afternoon nap. Her skirt had ridden up when he moved her, revealing a pair of shapely, tanned thighs and nearly translucent lace panties.

"What a waste," he whispered with a sigh as he left the room.

Well, so much for getting out of the killing business, he thought sardonically. Nothing so far had gone to plan, and the trail of bodies was growing longer. Not that he really mourned any of them, but Guero's involvement gave him pause. Tuco knew his own soul was damned, but he hoped that God could forgive his brother.

He checked on Guero in Katy's spare bedroom. It was where he had been when she came home, playing a handheld video game that Tuco picked up for him earlier that morning. He'd only left the room at that unlucky moment to search out new batteries for the game; Katy had died shortly after Guero's first set of Duracells. He seemed fine, so Tuco went back into the living room.

He rummaged through her bag, but besides the cash, found nothing useful. In frustration he dumped the cash onto the easy chair. Five bundles of one hundred dollar bills tumbled out, followed by a folded sheet of yellow legal pad paper that he had missed in the initial search.

On the sheet was a list of flight numbers and times for a couple of different airlines. The last line simply said "Rental car to PC?"

She had said something about Miami before Guero broke her neck, but a quick check of airline websites on Mitchell's laptop showed that Katy had been planning to fly to Pensacola, Florida, and PC could only be Panama City. So Katy had it narrowed down to Panama City and had lied about it.

Was she in it with Martin? Would he miss her?

Too late to worry about it now.

Tuco turned back to the laptop and logged into Mitchell's GPS tracking account. RM and KO were right where he expected them, but DM was on the move.

Chapter 37

I stood in front of the steel and glass edifice and had to admit I was pretty impressed. Trident Communications' architecture was definitely atypical for Adobe and stone obsessed El Paso, but it blended with the desert foothill landscape like a piece of art. Whoever Paul had hired to design the place really knew their stuff.

The foyer was an eclectic combination of natural and polished stone, brushed stainless steel and glass dominated by a large reception counter staffed by several super-cool young techies who looked like they had been peeled off of a Benetton poster. One of the t-shirt-clad hipsters greeted me with a way too perky "Welcome to Trident, how can I help you?" just before I saw the espresso machine behind her.

"Hi, I'm Jake Martin here to see Mr. Castañeda."

She hammered on a keyboard. "It will be just a minute, can I get you anything while you wait?"

Sure, how about a skinny, hand-pressed cat-turd cappuccino with a lemon twist and an elderberry scone?

"No, thanks," I replied.

I heard that the pinnacle of the coffee experience is a bean that has been eaten and subsequently crapped out by a cat, or maybe it's a mongoose, that knows to eat only the finest beans at their peak of readiness. Peasants making pennies a day dig through the feces to find the undigested beans that sell for $300 a pound. That's a lot to pay for a shitty cup of coffee...

After a very short wait, they decided I was cool enough to penetrate the inner sanctum. One of the techno-nymphs with a lip ring and skinny jeans escorted me down a long, polished hallway and ushered me into Paul's office.

"Abercrombie and Fitch go out of business and you hire all their people?"

"That's some kind of funny." I could tell it irritated him a little. I'm pretty good at that.

"Sorry, guess I'm getting old and crotchety, it just looks like you've hired a bunch of twelve-year-olds."

"Yeah, they do seem to be getting younger, but it keeps us fresh. The one who escorted you in has a masters from M.I.T." Not bad for a receptionist. "It's all part of the game. Look hip and cool and you'll sell all kinds of crap. Steve Jobs pioneered it and it works for them, so I'd be foolish not to emulate success."

Paul's office was very unassuming, just a desk and a couple of comfortable chairs in front of an expansive window overlooking the river and Mt. Christo Rey. The decorations were sparse and understated, exactly what I expected from Paul. The only extravagance was a wall of big screens tuned to every news and business channel on the planet. One of them showed the President, looking worn but still imperious, wagging his finger and staring at his teleprompter.

"How are you feeling this morning?"

"Hot shower and some coffee and I'm good as new," I lied. "Hey, speaking of coffee, your kids out there got any of those mongoose-crap beans?"

"It's a civet cat, and no, we ran out last week." I knew Paul would know. He's a savant at useless trivia. "I'm surprised you're not still in bed with that innocent young girl. Did you check her license?"

"Twenty-two and three months."

"Bastard."

"Hey, don't be jealous! Now that you're on her radar, I wouldn't be surprised if she showed up here wearing nothing but a trench coat and a smile." And that was the truth.

"What, so I can play second batter after Jake's been to the plate? Not a chance, *amigo*."

"You'll be sorry…the girl's got real talent."

Paul picked up a folder and moved around the desk, gesturing to one of the chairs. He sat beside me and handed me the folder.

"You, my friend, have stepped into one huge pile of poo."

"Super." I opened the folder and saw a photo of a suave looking Latino. It's not my week for guys, but I have to admit that this was one good-looking man. Reminded me of the dude who always plays the bad Hispanic drug lord in most Hollywood movies. Imagine that.

"Meet Ricardo Medrano, aka Tuco. He is, or was, a head honcho in *La Línea*, a group of brutal SOBs that act as the enforcement arm for the Juarez Cartel. I know you'd had a few beers so you may not remember, but that's the guy from the news."

"I remember. He's really an American citizen, right? Went to Morehead Junior High?"

"Yep, that's him." Paul picked up a remote and America's answer to Hugo Chavez blinked off the screen and was replaced by an old image of a kid in a Morehead Jr. High football uniform. A bright white number twenty-one stood out against the plain red jersey.

"Medrano grew up in the Jackie Robinson Federal Housing project with his mother and mentally challenged brother, Juan."

"By mentally challenged do you mean 'retarded'?" Political correctness is not one of my strong suits. I'd order steak at a PETA luncheon.

"Yes. Mom was an anchor baby and had the brother when she was sixteen. It appears she had an affinity for the 'chemical lifestyle' and supplemented her federal stipend by turning tricks out of her taxpayer-supplied apartment. No father of record for either kid. The drugs explain the older brother's handicap, but Tuco somehow managed to dodge that bullet. By all accounts he is very intelligent."

"So how'd a smart kid from the projects end up in the cartel?" I actually managed to keep a straight face when I asked that.

"A jilted john took out the mother and a rival customer before eating one of his own bullets. Police report says that young Tuco witnessed most of it first-hand. He and Juan were sent to live with his mother's parents in Juarez. We don't hear from him again until he joined the army for a two-year stint at eighteen and then again here."

Paul flashed up a shot that I vaguely remembered from several years earlier. A newspaper photographer captured the image of a handsome and stoic young Juarez cop with his weapon raised, pointed at a suspect caught the instant before he fell to the ground. A pink mist lingered in the air where his head had been just a second before.

"The cop is Tuco Medrano, a rookie. He and his partner had stumbled into a bank robbery. The *bandidos* were armed with AK-47s and Medrano's partner was killed as they got out of the car. Tuco stood calmly amid the flying bullets, aimed his shotgun and put a slug through the eye of a bandit blazing away with a machine gun. Seeing their comrade's head disintegrate in a gory spray caused the others to drop their weapons and surrender on the spot.

"He was an instant celebrity and a public relations boon to the Juarez cops, who were still reeling from the inept handling of the serial murders of nearly three hundred young women. His good shooting, and the lucky presence of a photographer, earned Tuco a spot in the *Grupo Especial*—the SWAT team of the *Policia Federal*."

He flashed up a couple of shots of a young Medrano in a police uniform. It reminded me of the pictures of newly-minted U.S. soldiers, trying to look fierce but coming across as the awkward kids who they really are. The last shot was of Medrano and another officer dressed in fatigues, a trophy of some sort sat on a table between them. They smiled and had the relaxed look of seasoned pros.

"That's Medrano with his good friend, Ramon Cordona. You'll see him again at the end of this video."

The picture faded into a recording of a busy Juarez street that I recognized as a longer, unedited version of the attack on the police convoy that we watched on the news at Aceitunas. I was impressed with the coordination and precision of the whole affair, at least what the camera captured anyway.

The clip ended after our star lifted his mask and gave the wounded cop--Cordona--a frontal lobotomy. It was hard to watch and looked personal.

"Nine out of ten guys don't recover from something like that."

Paul agreed. "Yep... and that was one of his best friends. They turned into rivals at the *Policia Federal.*"

"Carries a grudge, does he?"

"You could say that."

"Why the fallout?"

"We're still working out the details of what went wrong between Medrano and Cordona," Paul explained, "but the result is pretty clear.

"After the death of his grandparents, the burden of his brother probably forced him to look for supplemental income. Moonlighting as security for rich Juarenses could bring in a few pesos, but nothing compared to the money from the *narcos*. The vast majority of *federales* were on at least one of the cartel's payrolls. It's crazy to us, but just part of the Mexican system that's been in place for centuries. They call it *La Plaza*. You scratch my back, I'll watch yours, and we're all good. As they say--everybody's doing it.

"Hell, for the most part—before the violence, anyway--the common man in Mexico saw the *narcos* as modern-day Robin Hoods. They made money off of rich, overly indulgent Americans, and drove an underground economy that ultimately helped the common Mexican. The system provided jobs and opportunities that fed families. There was no black and white, right or wrong, it was simply the way of things."

"Sounds like you'd have to be pretty stupid to get caught."

"Not if someone wanted you out of the way. Like I said, we're still working out the why, but it's clear that someone wanted Medrano gone, and all signs point to Cordona.

"Medrano was working for the Juarez Cartel, and his assault team was sent on an off-the-books raid of what they thought was a Sinaloa storage facility. It was a trap that had been set up by cops on the Sinaloa payroll operating under the guise of an anti-corruption operation. Medrano's team was caught dead to rights, but somehow he escaped. He avoided jail, but his connections weren't strong enough to save his career with the *Policia Federal*.

"I figure he somehow found out about Cordona's involvement and waited patiently for the opportunity to take revenge."

"Guess he got it." I thought about the cop's brains splashed across the sidewalk.

"Yeah, but it bit Medrano in the ass. Word on the street is he went rogue on the ambush, which doesn't sit well with his bosses. Then, so the story goes, he tortured and killed a Sinaloa Cartel money man and disappeared like a wisp of smoke along with his brother and a cartel thug."

"This is pretty good intel... where do you get all this stuff?" I was starting to wonder what my mild-mannered tech-weenie friend was really all about.

"Information pays, and I pay for information. Last night, someone paid a visit to your lawyer friend. They skinned him and stuffed his mouth full of his own penis. My money is on Medrano and company."

"They cut his crank off?"

"No, his 'crank' was still attached," replied Paul.

I worked through the mental gymnastics of that gem. "You mean?"

"Yep, they beheaded him."

"That's pretty twisted."

I paused. "So let me see if I have this straight. Dad was laundering money for a Mexican cartel and may have been killed for it. Now we have a rogue *narco* who's tortured and killed an accountant from a rival organization, then shagged-ass across the border to torture and kill my lawyer, who may have been the one that whacked my father?" The seriousness of the situation started to sink in, and again I wondered if I was in over my head.

"This guy's looking for something more, and I get the feeling that I'm between him and whatever the hell it is he's after. Maybe there's something more to Dad's final request than a resting place with a view?"

"You are smarter than you look, Mr. Martin."

"Maybe so, but what's the next step? Call the Feds?"

"Why would you do that? They've known about Mitchell for over twelve hours, and have they given you so much as a 'Heads up, Jake, a guy just skinned your lawyer and might like to have a word with you?'"

"Nope, not a peep." I peeked at my phone to make sure there were no missed calls. Nothing, but the battery was at ten percent. I had forgotten to plug it in on the way over.

"You, *amigo*, are a bloody bag of fish guts dangling on a line, and the feds are waiting in a cage for the shark to grab you so they can shoot him and take all of the credit."

"Those bastards." I was getting a little annoyed. Perhaps the bait analogy wasn't appropriate because frankly I didn't think they were smart enough to make all of the connections, but the fact they hadn't bothered to tell me that I might be in some danger really pissed me off. I wasn't going to trust Christa Adams and Bob, Bill, John or whoever-the-hell he was with something as precious as my silky-smooth skin.

"My people haven't been able to figure out what he's after. Clearly it is something your father felt was worth risking his life over and has Medrano playing his bloody game on this side of the border. We're working to find that piece of the puzzle."

"My father has left some clues for us, and I think we should follow the rabbit hole to see where it leads. Whaddaya' say we take a trip to the desert?"

"Yep," Paul replied. "I've put together some supplies for us, and the guns are oiled and ready."

Before I could tell him that I needed to run by the house and pick up my dog, a woman walked in.

"Jake, this is Sylvia. She's my Director of Investigative Services."

Director of what? Who the hell is this guy who I thought I knew.

"Nice to meet you," I said to perhaps the most unremarkable woman I've ever seen. She nodded, reached out and broke three bones in my hand with the most remarkable grip I've ever felt. Maybe I'm just a wimp.

Nothing except her crushing handshake really stood out about the woman. She wasn't tall, but wasn't short, wasn't skinny, but wasn't fat, wasn't ugly, but wasn't pretty, wasn't stacked--well, you get the picture. If I had to describe Sylvia to a sketch artist, we'd end up with a black-haired smiley face. I bet she was damn good at blending in.

"Sylvia and her team put together the little presentation you just watched."

Her team?

She handed Paul one of two black folders.

He looked up from the open folder and asked, "What the hell is the Guadalete Development Corps?"

Chapter 38

"Don't study history much, do you?" Adams chided her partner. They were at the El Paso Field Office going through several computer files that the techs decrypted from Ronald Mitchell's computer.

"Cut the crap."

"Guadalete is the site of a battle in Spain, very symbolic. Remember the Islamic group who wanted to build a mosque and community center near Ground Zero?"

"Yeah."

"Well, they were going to call it the Cordoba Center. Cordoba is the city where the Moors built the Grand Mosque in commemoration of their conquest of Spain, a real thumb in the eye to the vanquished. I think the people who wanted to build the community center were counting on American ignorance to miss the symbolism, but at least a couple of folks caught on and challenged the groups' motives. Guadalete is the site of the final battle in the conquest…"

"So you're saying an Islamic group has contacted Ronald Mitchell, whose only client is the Sinaloa Cartel, and given him a large sum of money?"

She nodded.

"What the hell for?"

Christa stared dumfounded at her partner. "Probably not a few bales of White Widow."

His eyes opened wide when he finally figured it out. "Oh my God. So where's the money?"

"Great question," she replied. "But I'm afraid the only one who can answer it was gunned down at a car wash."

Chapter 39

Besides the name of the organization, Sylvia Mora's team was coming up empty on the Guadalete Development Corps.

"It's a non-profit that has done modest fundraising, mostly from individuals in support of third world projects that stimulate economic growth," explained Sylvia. "They file all of their taxes and required reports on time and nothing seems out of order. Mitchell's files refer to an unspecified financial transaction, but we can't find anything else about it. Probably cash."

"Who runs the thing?" Paul asked.

"We've traced the Board of Directors, but so far they are just non-existent heads of Nevada Corporations. Each Director runs a business headquartered in Elko, Nevada, hundreds of businesses share the address."

"Must be one hell of a building," I observed.

"No," she replied. "Just a small three-bedroom house in a flea-bag desert town. For about five hundred bucks, you too can set up your world headquarters in fabulous Elko.

"Our source at the DE--" Paul shot her a look that cut her short, "--our source will let us know as soon as there's more."

It didn't take a genius to figure out she was going to say "DEA" and I was struck again by the feeling that Paul's reach was longer than you would expect for a tech mogul.

"There's something else."   She handed a second folder to Paul and tried not to look at me.

Chapter 40

Tuco watched the blips representing Martin and Olsen move across the laptop screen as they made their respective ways around town. The website updated the trackers' positions every thirty to forty-five seconds--not exactly real time, but close enough. The history painted a pretty clear picture: The girl spent the night at Martin's and shortly after she left he had made his way back to where he left his vehicle the night before. By the time Tuco picked up the live action, Martin had left a tech company called Trident and headed east. Towards the airport-- or his house.

Fifteen minutes later Tuco had his answer. The blip exited the highway and turned north towards the house on Louisville Ave. There were two more flights that would get Martin to Panama City, and it was critical that Tuco be on the same airplane. Once Martin was at the airport and no longer using his car, he would be impossible to track.

Just to be safe, Tuco booked two seats on each flight out of El Paso that afternoon, as well as all four flights the following day. The line on the cartel credit cards was more than enough to cover the ridiculously expensive, last-minute tickets.

As an added precaution, he gathered up Guero, left the dead girl's apartment, found a parking spot at the airport and settled in to wait. He considered a direct tail on Martin, but he didn't have the resources to do it correctly and the chance of being spotted was too great.

Catching up with Martin as he left for Florida was Tuco's only shot at ten million dollars and a life outside the cartel. He and Guero could settle someplace warm, maybe Costa Rica--or Thailand. The money would go a long ways towards buying a life of luxury on a tropical beach with a pretty, longhaired girl to mix his drinks and keep him warm at night. Katy would have been perfect for the job, but as they say, shit happens.

That had always been his mantra, or at least something to that effect, ever since the night he watched the broken kitten expire on his mother's living room floor. Shit happens, people die.

Most of the death around him, including that of his mother, elicited no emotion at all. Others, like Cordona and Cuchillo, brought him satisfaction. A few, Manny for example, and even Katy to some degree, elicited regret. Then there were those whose death brought him genuine sorrow. Tuco wept when his grandparents passed. They died while he was still a rookie in the *Policia Federal,* his grandfather from a heart attack while walking home from a *cantina,* and his grandmother less than a month later, peacefully in her sleep.

Guero's was a death he would not contemplate.

Then there was Alejandra. His skin prickled and the breath caught in his throat at the thought of her.

Movement on the computer screen saved him. Martin was mobile again, and his heart raced with anticipation as the electronic blip approached the turn to the airport. Forty-five seconds later the position updated on I-10 as expected, but Martin headed west. Away from the El Paso International Airport.

Chapter 41

I hardly remembered driving back to my father's house. The news in Sylvia's folder brought back another flood of painful memories. I'd been picking at the scab of Alex's memory for the past few days, but Sylvia ripped it off and the result was a bloody mess.

When Alex had left, it was like a part of me had been torn away. I pined away for weeks, consoling myself with the idea that she was pursuing something important and it was only temporary. When we started to lose touch, I realized that I might be clinging to a false hope.

We talked every now and then, but when she stopped answering, I got desperate. I called, texted, wrote, sent a couple of messages via carrier pigeon and tried to visit her in Glynco, Georgia, while she was exchange training with the U.S. Feds, but her reciprocal efforts were non-existent.

Then one day I got a long, hand-written letter explaining how much she loved me, and hoped that someday we would be together, but that she was doing something bigger than the both of us and she couldn't afford the distraction, blah, blah, blah. The paper smelled like her.

I never imagined that something bigger than us would amount to riding around dressed like a storm trooper and getting shot at by drug dealers, or screwing your fellow storm troopers.

The part about screwing her cop buddies was perhaps a bit of immature conjecture on my part, but it's been my experience that two plus two usually leads to four.

Turns out that Sylvia Mora and her team were pretty good at mining for information. They were so friggin' good, in fact, they managed to dig up the little tidbit that the rivalry between Tuco Medrano and the late Ramon Cordona, whose brains the former used to decorate a Juarez sidewalk, stemmed from more than a little professional envy. The two cops were in a cockfight for the favor of one Alejandra de la Rosa of the *Policia Federal*. Yep, my Alex was in the middle of Mexican love triangle. So much for the part about her hoping that "someday we'd be together."

Sylvia's team couldn't confirm which, if either, of the Latino studs was winning the war for her affection, but in my mind, guys didn't go around blowing each other's heads off unless there was some level of screwing going on. My mind raced through the possibilities and I wondered if she was with one of them when I had tried to see her in Georgia.

"SHIT!" I yelled as I banged on the steering wheel and bruised the heel of my palm.

Somehow I ended up back at my new house.

I knew something was wrong when Blu didn't greet me at the door.

Chapter 42

"Hi, Glynnis, this is Christa Adams, has anyone left a message for me?" She looked at John Reynolds and shook her head while pursing her lips crookedly. "Okay, thanks. Take care."

Katy Olsen's check-in call was over two hours late. The call to the office was a last hope--Olsen had both Adams' cell and office numbers, and the office voicemail was linked to her cell.

Katy had turned Confidential Informant nearly two months before, and had never missed an appointed check-in. She was nothing if not punctual, and with things heating up like they were, her tardiness made Adams' short hairs stand on end.

After the initial deception, and hours of anxiety over the late call, Adams decided it was time to let Reynolds in on the secret. If asked later why she ever kept it from him in the first place, Adams would be hard pressed for an answer.

Instinct?

He seemed to take it in stride. "Maybe she's screwing around with Martin and has lost track of time?"

"I don't think so. Unless she's going after the prize herself, there's no reason for her to be that daring." *At least I hope she's not that greedy.* "The team they gave us to tail her said her car is at her apartment building."

"Then why hasn't she called you?"

"Good question."

Chapter 43

For as long as I've had Blu around, the only time I've seen anything approaching aggression was on the rare occasion he perceived a threat to me. Alex once popped me playfully with a dishtowel and my less than masculine reaction made Blu think I was in trouble. He didn't move on her, but made it clear with bared teeth that a second swat with the towel was a foolish move.

Under any other circumstances, he was a complete push-over, and I'd always said he was the perfect watchdog; he would happily watch while someone robbed me blind, but on this day, his passive nature saved his life.

As I approached the front door and fumbled for the key, something about the muffled barking from the back of the house didn't seem right. Had I accidentally shut him in the bedroom?

Nobody jumped me when I opened the door and stepped into the entry. The living room was clear as far as I could tell so I breathed a little easier. With all of the crazy talk of drugs, money and murder, perhaps my imagination had run a little wild.

Then I wondered if Ronald Mitchell had the same feeling before his head fed on his own penis.

Everything seemed in order as I made my way back to my dad's bedroom where I spent the night with Katy. I opened the door cautiously. Blu stopped barking when I stepped in, but wasn't his ebullient self. He cocked his head, listening to things I couldn't hear and let out the occasional soft "woof." The room smelled faintly of sex, and something else. Cheap aftershave. It reminded me of a barbershop, the old-fashioned kind with a spinning striped pole, not Supercuts.

A Mexican barbershop.

Suddenly I heard muffled voices from the basement below my feet.

My heart beat like a jackhammer and I fought to keep panic in check. I was unarmed, cornered and didn't want to end up like my late attorney. Then I remembered why I was there in the first place.

On the floor at the back of the bedroom closet sat my father's army-surplus backpack that had been well past its prime when I was a kid. Half expecting the ratty old thing to disintegrate at the touch, I pulled it out of the closet and opened the rain flap. There, atop a rolled sleeping bag was a loaded Colt model 1911 .45 semi-automatic pistol and a box of cartridges.

The heavy pistol in my hand soothed my nerves better than a stiff drink. My thoughts cleared.

This thing could play out a couple of ways: I could be the hero and search the house for an unknown number of intruders with an unknown set of skills and weapons, or I could sit under cover in a defensible position and wait for them to leave. The odds favored option number two.

My dad's bed was a Japanese futon with a cotton mattress. It was uncomfortable as hell but might slow a bullet. Blu and I hunkered down behind the propped up mattress and waited quietly. Had they heard me?

Footsteps on the basement stairs sent my pulse back through the roof. Blu growled softly. I hoped they would simply leave, unaware of my presence, then I remembered my truck parked out front.

Turns out it didn't matter.

"Mira la puerta, esta abierto!"

Look, the door, it's open.

At least one Spanish-speaking male, and I assumed he wasn't talking to himself.

Creaky floorboards announced their slow progress down the hallway.

I often wondered what I'd do in a situation like this. Would I have the guts to pull the trigger on another human being? I had walked around Afghanistan everyday with an M-4 carbine and a sidearm, but counted myself lucky to have only been in one firefight. With twenty guys blazing away, you could never really be sure if your bullet was the one that took a life and there was psychological safety in numbers. That was war, but this was up-close and personal. In the end, these were men in my dead father's house, and I'm sure they weren't there to express their condolences.

I don't know what I expected from a drug dealer, but the guy wasn't trained for interior combat. He stayed close to the wall separating the bedroom from the hallway, and he didn't "slice the pie" to clear the doorway. Nope, he went the Hollywood route and I guess he was going to hop in the doorway with gun blazing before he acquired a target.

He never got the chance.

Some ill-advising experts suggest you announce that you have a gun and state your intent to use it. The theory assumes the home intruder would rather avoid armed conflict and flee the scene. In this case, however, I decided to go with the "surprise them with a bullet" technique.

When I saw his gun and a tattooed hand peek past the doorframe, I fired three shots through the sheetrock wall at the spot I figured was his center of mass. It wasn't the tightest three-shot group ever fired, but I chalked up my first kill.

My ears still hadn't fully recovered from the shock of the big .45 popping off in a small room so I didn't hear him fall, however from my position behind the futon I saw part of his arm and hand on the floor. The gun lay inches from his limp fingers.

I heard a shout from his partner, but couldn't make out the words. A door slammed and there was silence--well, not counting the ringing in my ears.

Blu shook his head vigorously in an effort to restore his own hearing, but otherwise seemed at ease.

After a few minutes of intense listening, I was confident the house was empty and left my shelter. The guy was dead, or doing a great job at pretending, so I stepped over his body and cleared the rest of the house.

Then I sat to consider what I'd done.

I had taken a man's life, but decided I wouldn't lose any sleep over it. He would have done the same for me.

Blu sniffed at the dead man, but kept his distance.

The body was dressed in gray Dickies trousers and a wife-beater t-shirt. He was well-built, bald, covered in prison tattoos, and definitely *not* Tuco Medrano.

Two bullet holes perforated his back: one between his shoulder blades, the second probably took out a kidney. The pool of blood forming under the lower wound meant it was a through-and-through; the high shot probably shattered when it hit his spine and stayed inside to wreak havoc on his organs. No, I'm not a coroner, but I *do* watch a lot of *CSI*--the original, not that Miami crap.

My head told me to call the cops, but my fingers dialed Paul instead. I told him what happened and asked his advice regarding the dead guy staining the wood floors.

"Any tattoos on the body?"

"Just a few…he might not have one on his dick."

"Probably does, but that's not important."

Good thing.

"Look on his upper back, any numbers?"

I didn't have to move his shirt to see the tat at the base of his neck. "A 'twenty-one.' Is he a Deion Sanders fan?"

"No, smart-ass, *Barrio Azteca*. They're a street gang affiliated with the Juarez Cartel. If you're feeling guilty about killing him, don't. You've done the world a favor. Now get the hell out of there before his friend grows his balls back and gets some buddies to come back for revenge."

"Shouldn't I call the cops?"

"Only if you want the most ruthless street gang in Texas to know you wasted one of their own. If you call the cops and even if this doesn't go public, the gang will know who you are. You said you never saw the other guy and he didn't see you, right?"

"Ninety-nine percent sure."

"Good. Just leave. Now. I'll get my people to take care of it. In the mean time, we should head to the mountains and get to the bottom of this mess."

There was that phrase again: "my people."

"Okay, I'll be there in fifteen minutes."

I ended the call and dumped the rest of my dad's old pack onto the bed. Besides the gun, there was the old sleeping bag, a two-man tent, some cooking utensils and his favorite cast-iron skillet. I repacked all of it and then put the .45 in the holster and strapped it on. "Why didn't you have this at the carwash?" I asked aloud.

Dad's ghost didn't answer.

Chapter 44

When I rolled into the parking lot of Trident Communications, Paul was standing next to a fully loaded Land Rover. I parked next to him and got out of the truck.

"You okay?"

"My ears are still ringing, but otherwise fine."

"That's not what I meant."

"I know what you meant," a little sharper than I intended. I continued in a softer tone. "Yeah, I'm okay."

I transferred Blu and my dad's pack to the Land Rover. It was full of more gear than I had ever seen.

"Wow. That's a lot of stuff."

"I like to be comfortable. Is that the gun you used?"

"Yeah, it was my Pa's," I drawled in my best *Deliverance* redneck. "Lucky for me it was in the pack, and loaded."

"How many rounds did you fire?"

"Three." He tapped something into his phone...I assumed it was a text message to "his people."

"I'm a little concerned about the dead guy in my dad's house."

"We can handle it."

"Yeah, about that. You mentioned something about paying for information when you dug up all that stuff on Medrano, but this is a helluva lot more than that. We're talking Harvey Keitel in *Pulp Fiction* kind of stuff here. What gives?"

He looked past me towards the mountains looming behind us. After a good twenty seconds, he let out a long breath. "I can't stress enough how sensitive this is…"

I raised my eyebrows.

"Telecommunications is a cutthroat business, and information is king. Business analysts call it 'uncanny intuition,' but the real key to my success is reliable intelligence. I got lucky with my first little invention, but luck can only take you so far.

"If I want to stay on top and keep those talented kids employed, I need to know my competitors' next moves, my customers' greatest need, and my investors' attitudes. I was fighting for multi-million dollar contracts, and I needed an edge, so I started with Sylvia and the whole thing kind of snowballed.

"She was former Naval Intelligence and was really good at digging for information--and I mean really good--but then one day she hit a brick wall, so we hired someone with a *different* skill set. The next thing you know, I had a team on my payroll consisting of former cops, feds, a former IRS auditor and even a convicted computer hacker.

"Their methods can be a little unorthodox, but they're undeniably effective and well-worth the investment."

It all seemed a little extreme to me, but then again, I wasn't running a billion dollar company. "That's all pretty impressive, but we're talking about getting rid of a *dead body*. That I killed! In my dad's house!" My pulse was racing again.

"Trust me, they are the best at what they do, and I pay them accordingly. That's about all I can tell you. I trust them to handle your little problem, you should too."

I digested that for a minute and despite the gross understatement about my "little problem," decided to trust him. He was right; my only alternative was life as a marked man. Those *Barrio Apache* assholes, or whatever they were called, wouldn't take too kindly to me killing one of their *vatos*, so the fewer people who know about it the better.

Paul must have felt like he needed to fill the silence. "Are we good?"

"Yes. It's just a lot to absorb. A week ago my biggest problem was a flight attendant who couldn't keep her legs shut. Have your people do what they need to do… and thank you."

It was strange to think of the man I'd always considered a tech-geek as a Machiavellian corporate puppet-master.

"Do you think our friend Medrano sent those guys?"

"No." He shook his head. "Odds are they were looking for him, not you, but just in case..."

He pointed to a pump shotgun and an assault rifle I didn't recognize slung old-school-style on a rack between the back seat and cargo compartment.

"There's also two Glocks in the console."

"Not bad." I liked the idea of the Glock. Besides the gang-banger in the hall, I hadn't shot for a while and I'd be all over the place at longer range with the big .45. The "plastic gun" was like the digital camera of the pistol world, just point and shoot for good results.

"An hour ago I would have thought this is overkill."

"It probably is. Once we head out west there's a slim chance in hell anyone will know where we are going and I have a plan to make sure we aren't tailed."

We climbed into the Land Rover when I remembered something important.

"I almost forgot Dad."

I walked back to the truck and retrieved the cardboard box filled with his ashes.

Chapter 45

Martin had stopped at the telecommunications offices again and there was no way that he would make it in time for the first of the two remaining flights out of El Paso. The last departure was not for another four hours, so Tuco cancelled the earlier reservation and settled in for the wait.

Guero sat in the back seat, biting his tongue in concentration, trying to survive a meaningless electronic battle. It amazed Tuco that his brother, who struggled when tying his own shoes, was so proficient at every video game he played.

Sensing his brother's scrutiny, Guero paused the game. "I have to go."

"So do I," replied Tuco. "Are you hungry?"

"Yeah! Can we have golden-crispy chicken McNuggets?"

Wary of the concentrated law enforcement at the airport, Tuco opted for a Burger King down the road. Nuggets were nuggets.

They ate their lunch in the restaurant and Guero had a hard time keeping his eyes off of the bright colored plastic and metal play gym outside. He knew better than to ask.

With their bladders empty and stomachs full, he drove back to the airport parking lot.

"Are we flying on the airplane now?" Guero asked.

"Soon, '*Manito*,"

"Where are we going?"

"Someplace warm, where we can live on the beach." He thought about Thailand and palm trees swaying in the wind. "We can go swimming every day, and lay on the beach like lazy goats."

Tuco pulled into the airport parking lot, logged onto his computer and absentmindedly continued his story. "We can eat fresh fish, and all the fruit we want. When we are thirsty, we can drink out of coconuts."

"What's a coconut?"

"Shit!"

During their late afternoon lunch with the king of burgers, Martin's blip had moved west into the desert. It suddenly dawned on Tuco where the *maricon* was heading and he had a fifty-mile head start.

"*Pinche madre,*" he swore as he started the SUV and pulled out of the parking lot.

Guero never got his answer.

Chapter 46

The land west of El Paso is a seemingly endless expanse dotted with mesquite, greasewood, yucca and the occasional lava flow. Sand has blown around the bases of the low, thorny mesquite, forcing the hardy bushes to grow higher and collect more sand. Over the ages the process results in sandy hillocks taller than a man and topped with scraggly brush. It's perfect habitat for the birds, snakes, lizards, rabbits and coyotes that call the desert home.

Several of my high-school classmates and I spent a lot of time running around the maze of sand hills, blasting any creature unfortunate enough to cross our path. That all ended with an agonized rabbit's scream and the realization that my actions had consequences.

Paul drove and I gazed out the window at the passing blur of telephone poles and low brush, lost in thoughts of Alex, Dad, dead Mexicans and what we might find in the mountains.

We sped down a graded dirt road that I had been on many times but hadn't seen in more than a dozen years. El Paso has changed noticeably, but this part of the desert was exactly as I remembered.

Paul's voice finally registered over the hypnosis of fence posts whizzing by at fifty miles per hour.

"You all right?"

"I'm just thinking about stuff. Amazing how the desert hasn't changed."

"It's changed. Remember how all that used to be out here was a bunch of ranch roads and rattlesnakes?" Paul asked.

"Yeah, pretty much what it looks like now."

"Maybe, but just to the south of us is a two-lane blacktop that runs all the way out to Columbus, and there's enough Border Patrol out here to conquer Cuba."

"Really? All I see are the rattlesnakes."

"Oh, they're here. They've got the fence, a blimp on a string and even Predator drones, but even with all of that they still can't stop the drugs or illegal immigrants.

"Last month they found a trailer load of dead illegals over by Kilbourne's hole... the *coyotes* were spooked and just ditched their cargo. Fourteen bodies were piled around a mostly dead eleven-year-old girl in an eight-foot U-haul with its doors padlocked on a hundred-degree day. They tore the flesh from their own fingers trying to claw their way out. That little girl will be fucked in the head for the rest of her life, and odds are they just shipped her back to Mexico or El Salvador or wherever she was from."

I'd heard several versions of the same story more than ten times since I was a kid. "I wonder if a life here is really worth the risk."

"Must be."

"Hey, if there's a paved road to Columbus, what the hell are we doing on this goat path?"

"For love of the old times, my friend. Besides, this is what the Land Rover was built for. Indulge me."

Just a rich boy with his toy car.

We crested a low rise, Paul pulled to the side of the road, and it dawned on me that he had another motive. We both got out and Paul scanned the horizon with a pair of binoculars that he really didn't need.

Blu hopped down from the SUV and ran around sniffing every branch and twig, pausing to lift his leg on a scrawny mesquite struggling to grow out of the dune formed at its base.

The desert was quiet except for the ticking of the cooling engine. What was a chilly start to the day had given way to comfortable warmth under a clear blue sky, and I knew from experience that my eyes would be struggling in the bright afternoon sunlight if I hadn't been wearing my trusty Ray-Bans.

Somewhere nearby a cicada, secure that the vehicle posed no threat, resumed its electronic-sounding buzz in an attempt to attract a mate. It seemed to me like mating season was long gone, but maybe he'd get lucky. Sad that the bug spent seven years of its life underground only to come to the party thirty days late.

As the dust behind us settled, it was clear that we were the only ones using this particular dirt road. A guy on a bicycle would kick up enough of a cloud to be seen for miles.

"Nobody following us."

"Really? All your technological genius and this was your plan?"

He flashed me the universal "You're number one" sign with his middle finger and reached into the truck to pull out the two Glocks. "Maybe we should shoot a few rounds, I haven't had the practice you have."

We grabbed a few empty beer cans out of the Rover and set them up as targets. Did I mention we'd had a beer or two on the drive out?

To calm my frazzled nerves.

After some really bad shooting, we knocked some of the rust off and actually started hitting the cans routinely. We finished with a flourish, recited a fake Latin prayer and double-tapped the last can execution-style.

Blu hid in the back seat of the SUV. Smart dog.

Chapter 47

Katy Olsen was dead, which was probably why she hadn't called, Jake Martin had fallen off the face of the Earth, and Tuco Medrano was on the run.

Bodies piled up, leads evaporated, and Christa Adams felt like she was wearing ankle weights in a marathon. They finally had the full resources of the El Paso Field Division at their disposal, even some help from Customs and Border Protection, but they paid dearly for the bureaucratic delays that plagued them throughout their investigation. To get back in the game, she pulled out all the stops and while *technically* not breaking any of the rules she twisted the hell out of them.

Adams had discovered Katy's cooling corpse after the crime scene analysts assigned to the surveillance team reported that she hadn't left her apartment building, and the only other traffic was a Hispanic man leaving with an extremely large and "apparently mentally challenged" companion.

The lab techs on loan from the El Paso branch office of the FBI were somehow unaware that those two men were precisely the subjects they were looking for. Had they been properly briefed, or paid any attention to the brief they had been given—a point of contention in Adam's after action report—they would have called it in and been instructed to follow Tuco Medrano and his brother. It wouldn't have made any difference to Katy Olsen, but at least they'd know the current whereabouts of her murderers.

At the scene, Adams' badge and some thinly veiled threats worked magic on the doorman. He revealed that Katy's well-dressed uncle and huge-but-friendly cousin had slipped him a hundred dollars to let them in the apartment.

So they could surprise her.

While not surprised that the good-looking young doorman had a key to Katy's home, Adams did find it ironic that he had let them in without question, but was suddenly reluctant to allow a DEA agent access to the apartment. He let her in after she threatened to crawl up his ass with a drug sniffing dog and a DEA-brand microscope.

Adams' subsequent After Action Report noted several key facts: Katy was dead from apparent cervical trauma, a review of surveillance footage provided for positive identification of Ricardo "Tuco" Medrano, and the doorman was terminated for gross negligence.

As she waited for the El Paso Police Department forensics team, her partner discovered a body of his own across town.

***

Now that a known cartel figure was spotted at the scene of a murder, they were cleared to raid a couple of houses known to be used by the Juarez Cartel and their U.S. affiliates, the *Barrio Azteca* street gang. In a coordinated effort with El Paso SWAT, they assaulted both homes simultaneously. After all, good news travels fast.

One of the houses yielded nothing more than a meth-fueled mid-afternoon threesome who hardly took notice of the black-clad cops with machine guns. None of the trio appeared particularly adept at the mechanics of a menage-a-trois and Reynolds was fairly certain that one of the two males would have ended up in an unintentional homosexual encounter.

The other assault team discovered the body of Rosario Diaz, aka *el Cuchillo,* an obscure sicario who worked for *La Linea.* A forensics team was on scene, but even without their expert opinion it was clear that something went dreadfully sideways between Tuco Medrano and his pit bull.

The dead man's blood type matched the evidence found in Ronald Mitchell's study, and the preliminary time of death would have allowed him to commit the atrocity in the hillside villa, but most compelling was the bag filled with the tools of his trade. He hadn't cleaned any of the medieval looking knives, scalpels or straight razors, and they were covered in dried blood matching that of the butchered lawyer.

Prints found in Mitchell's home belonged to the fingers holding a smelly pile of bloated purple intestines.

Chapter 48

Now that the adrenaline had worked its way out of my system, lack of sleep and too much alcohol caught up to me. I tried to get some sleep, but between the bumpy road, the thoughts swirling through my head and Paul's hair-band-greatest-hits-of-the-eighties CD, I gave up hope.

As we drove west the road deteriorated with the terrain. Sand and brush gave way to volcanic hills separated by deep arroyos. This was new territory for me.

Trips to the Floridas with my dad followed the much easier-on-the-kidneys I-10 to Deming, home of Irma's and the "almost internationally famous" Annual Duck Races. From Deming, another road covered in the great technological achievement known as asphalt led to a rough but blissfully short road to the mountain trailheads.

Paul did a great job of counter-surveillance, but I think he stayed on the goat path just to mess with me.

"Can we go find the paved road now? I'm running out of spare internal organs."

"Fine. You're such a girl."

"Lucky you're not a pilot. If I stayed in the bumps like this on a flight, the flight attendants would piss in my coffee."

All along the road I noticed intersecting trails and a lot of trash strewn in and about the bushes.

"What's with all the trash? This road doesn't seem so busy. Is it the wet… I mean *illegals*?" Old colloquialisms are hard to shake.

"Yep," Paul answered. "No way to stop it. Hell, if there were a line of Marines holding hands like schoolgirls from Brownsville to San Diego, they'd still find a way to make it through. It's all a numbers game… Border Patrol tries, but for every one they catch, ten make it through to the nearest Home Depot parking lot."

"What about the *narcos*? How much product you figure they get through here every night?"

"Who knows, but if I had to guess, I'd say not that much. It's easier to get it through the tunnels and border checkpoints back in El Paso where there's more cover.

"They can't search every car and truck coming across the border, so some are bound to make it through. They'll even stash big loads of drugs in Juan Q. Public's car. Imagine getting stopped for a random search on your way to an economics class at UTEP and having to explain the forty pounds of pot stuffed in your spare tire."

"I heard they are sticking magnetized bales of drugs under cars. Saves them the step of breaking in."

Paul nodded. "No end to their ingenuity."

Paul hit another bone-rattling bump that sent the box of Dad's ashes bouncing off of the seat and onto the floorboard.

"Do you think we can find that paved road before I crap out a kidney?"

Chapter 49

When the laptop battery died Tuco and Guero were speeding north on I-10 through Anthony, a small town bisected by the Texas-New Mexico state line. A large sign welcomed them to the 'Land of Enchantment.'

The computer warned Tuco that it was nearly out of juice and thirty seconds later went dead. Its power cord was plugged into the cigarette lighter, but apparently the little silhouette of an airplane stenciled on the adapter didn't lie. He cursed and slammed his palm into the steering wheel, startling Guero away from his game.

This was not good.

His only link to Martin was the GPS tracking site. He had tried to stop by Martin's house before they hit the highway, but it was a fruitless waste of fifteen minutes. When they had turned onto the street, Tuco saw a utility van parked at Martin's address and a couple of men in coveralls entering the house. They looked like any utility workers: cable installers, telephone men, carpet cleaners, but Tuco knew better. The van was unmarked and the men carried themselves with professional determination. It was all he needed to see to know it wasn't safe for him to stop, so Tuco passed the house and continued on his pursuit of Martin.

The van distracted Tuco and he hadn't seen the two tattooed men sitting in an early model Chevy Impala parked two houses up.

But they saw him.

***

Interstate-10 passed north through Las Cruces and curved west towards Deming and the Florida Mountains.

A couple years earlier, Tuco had tracked a pair of drug mules who decided that stealing their load would lead to a bigger payday than simply delivering the narcotics as planned. They thought they could hide out in the isolated Floridas, but it didn't work out so well for them.

Tuco hoped that Martin's late start meant he was planning to stay the night in or near the mountains. If he didn't stay he would have to backtrack to get out and that would buy some time for Tuco to intercept him. Considering that not much had gone according to plan so far, catching up was a long shot at best, but a long shot is always better than no shot at all. Now that the computer was dead, the odds were that much longer.

It's in God's hands now. Tuco remembered his grandmother's favorite expression, and shook his head at the idea. He hadn't thought of God since the day he and Guero stood at the side of his grandmother's grave, when her rough hewn coffin was lowered into the rocky soil of the *colonia's* hillside cemetery.

She had ensured they never missed weekly Mass, but aside from going through the motions for her sake, Tuco never opened himself to the concept of God. It wasn't that he didn't believe in Him--in fact was pretty sure that he had earned himself a prime spot in Hell. He just couldn't reconcile himself to a deity who had so forsaken his brother and him. When the dirt shoveled onto the pine box containing her body, Tuco's last thought of God was a hope that his grandmother was finally in the presence of her precious *Dios*.

Whether it was God, luck or the Man-in-the-Moon, Tuco knew he needed a little help from someone and it was out of his hands for the time being. The realization calmed him and he settled down to the sound of the tires humming on the pavement and the soft electronic noises coming from Guero's game.

He replayed the last few days that had started with the ambush, Cordona's execution and a moment of weakness while he stood transfixed by Alejandra de la Rosa's emerald eyes. Tuco realized it was that brief instant of self-doubt, more than the mistake of lifting his mask for Cordona that had set the gears in motion for his attempted escape from the cartel.

He recognized the irony that his desire to free himself from senseless violence resulted in the deaths of three people, and in all probability, more would die. How did the saying go? *If you want to make an omelet, you might have to kill a few chickens?*

Tuco smirked at the absurdity. His brother looked up from the game he was playing, smiling with a mouthful of crooked teeth. Despite his intellectual shortcomings, Guero made up for them with an uncanny sense of empathy and unconditional loyalty. Tuco owed him a better life and any means were justified to that end.

His thoughts turned back to the escape plan--or lack thereof. He had been so focused on the money that he had no idea what to do once he had it. Surely the police were on to him and it isn't exactly easy to keep a low profile with a giant like Guero stapled to your hip. Finding a tropical paradise beyond the reach of the cartel was easy. Getting there from the U.S. might present a problem. His mind churned through the options while they pushed westward into New Mexico.

The desert sun hung low in the sky making it difficult to see the road ahead. Tuco drove the car into the blinding glare and reached carelessly over the seat, searching for his jacket. He really needed a smoke.

In the brief instant he took his eyes off the road grabbing for his cigarillos, the car drifted onto the shoulder and its tires whined loudly on the warning strip like a poorly played tuba. He looked up in time to see the twisted piece of metal that was once part of a passing tractor-trailer, but not in time to avoid it.

Chapter 50

We'd been on pavement for twenty minutes. Blu finally mustered the courage to move off of the floorboard. He curled himself in a tight ball on the Land Rover's supple leather seat, next to the box-full-o-Dad that I had lifted off the floor.

"This is my favorite time of day in the desert."

"Yeah," Paul replied. "It doesn't look quite as desolate in the late afternoon light. Somehow the greens look… greener. Are you sure you can find this place?"

"Absolutely," I lied. It's been a good twenty years since I camped out here with my dad, but how much could it have changed?

It was over an hour since our marksmanship demonstration, and we felt pretty confident that Tuco Medrano, the *Barrio Aztecas* or Guido the Killer Pimp weren't on our tail and we had plenty of time.

We moved west towards the town of Columbus, where we'd turn north towards Deming. Somewhere between the two towns is a turnoff marked by a tall tower of rocks held together by loose concrete mortar. It is a construction technique common in the Southwest, but what makes it memorable is that some smart-ass with metalworking skill set a weathervane at the top of the twenty-foot cairn. I say smart-ass because what from a distance looks vaguely like your standard rooster is actually the clever silhouette of two dogs in coitus. I christened the place the TDF Ranch. You can do the math.

We rolled into Columbus as the sun settled onto the distant peaks.

"You know this is the only place in the continental United States invaded by a foreign army since the war of 1812?"

"No shit?" Paul replied.

"No shit. Pancho Villa and his band of merry men crossed the border, shot up the town, killed 16 people and stole some weapons and horses."

"Where'd you learn that obscure bit of trivia?"

"My dad told me that story." A wave of …nostalgia? …regret? …loss? …guilt? washed over me. I looked back at the cardboard box on the seat next to my sleeping dog and realized it was a bit of all the above.

I shook off the feeling. No way I would soften on him now. We were here to fulfill his last wish and see where this goose chase ends. If I want to face my lost childhood and abandonment issues, I'll book a spot on Dr. Phil.

As if he read my mind Paul chimed in. "You know your father was alright in my book. I think you have been pretty hard on him.

"Of all our friends, he was one of the only dads who seemed to give a damn. He always asked how things were going and he took the time to listen to my answer. After my dad died, he really went out of his way to help. I'll never forget that."

Paul's father had died when we were eleven. He had owned a small convenience store in El Paso's Upper Valley. On a night like every other, he called Paul's mom and let her know he'd be home after he closed up and prepped the store for the next day's business. When he hadn't arrived home nearly two hours later, she started to worry.

After two and a half hours, she looked in on Paul and his young sister asleep in their beds, threw on her shoes and drove to the store to check on her husband. She found him sprawled unconscious in a puddle of Coca Cola, bleeding from an open gash that exposed the creamy white of his skull. The stepladder and broken soda bottle lying next to him completed the tale.

He had lingered in a coma for two weeks before leaving his wife to raise their two children.

From then on, my dad made it a point to take Paul on most of our camping trips. Now that I thought about it, I realized he never had the pleasure of a trip to the Florida Mountains and the beautiful TDF Ranch.

"You always used to bitch and moan when you went on those camping trips. I never understood that," he said.

"Hey, I thought I was missing out on Swisher Sweets, Mad Dog 20/20 and the chance to get laid."

"No one was getting laid when we were twelve."

"Yeah, but there was always the chance!" I protested.

"Bulllshiiit. You didn't even get to second base 'til you were fifteen."

"Fourteen and three quarters." *He doth protest too much.* We both laughed.

"Okay, Casanova, didn't mean to sully your reputation as a master cocksman."

"No worries."

"My point is your dad wasn't as bad a guy as you have him painted up in your mind. Maybe now that he's gone you should give him a break."

"Maybe so."

Needing a change of subject, I looked at my phone. The battery was dead.

"Don't suppose you have an iPhone charger?"

"You expecting a call?"

"No, just wanted to pull up a map to cover my ass. I forgot about GPS."

"Here."

Paul handed me his phone with full signal and I studied the map.

"Looks like our turn is eighteen miles ahead, assuming I picked the right road."

By the time we reached the turnoff, the purple shadow of the western mountains covered all but the highest peaks of the Floridas, which glowed orange against the twilight sky like jagged, tobacco-stained teeth. We pulled over to stretch our legs and give me a chance to make sure this was the right road.

Surprisingly little had changed over the years since I was there with Dad. The rock tower was half crumbled, and while Blu raised his leg on what remained, I poked around in the rubble looking for the fine example of cutting-torch art. It was nowhere to be found, more than likely pilfered and proudly displayed in a mobile home living room as one of the finest examples of silhouette dog-on-dog action ever created.

Gone forever was the perfect metaphor for my trips to the Floridas. Ever the persecuted pre-teen, I felt like I was the one being screwed every time my dad brought me out here.

Even though the signpost I remembered so fondly was missing, I was positive this was the right road to the campsite. The beer can justified my confidence.

Resting at the base of the ruined spire was a nearly pristine Schlitz beer can. Glad that I'd impressed on Blu from an early age to NEVER pee on a can of suds, I picked up the vessel.

"Damn, I didn't know they were still brewing that swill!" Paul said.

"I think they stopped for a while, but lucky for us, it's back." Dad left it as a message to me. Filled with sand so it wouldn't blow away, the can was marked with a Sharpie. Three black letters obscured the back label, "T-D-F."

Chapter 51

"Can you fix it, Tuco?" Guero asked as the interstate traffic whizzed by.

"Yes, Guero."

"Can I help, Tuco?"

"Yes." His answer was nearly drowned in the blast of wind from a passing semi.

The gust sent sparks flying from the cigarillo Tuco puffed as he surveyed the damage. His last second correction had saved the rear tire, but was too late to prevent the metal road debris from slicing through the right front. The tread separated quickly--the tire was gone before he could brake and the expensive chrome alloy rim was ruined.

He handed the tire changing tools to Guero one by one, exaggerating the action like a nurse handing instruments to a surgeon. They were in a hurry, but Tuco knew it made his brother feel important.

The sun was down, but it was still light enough to complete the change. He found the lift point and told Guero to pump the jack handle.

"I can pick up the truck!"

"Yes you can, 'mano." *Probably without the jack*, he thought. "Two more... last one... good job, Guero!"

His brother beamed with pride.

Tuco removed the lug nuts and handed them to his eager assistant. "Don't lose these, Guero."

"I won't losed them. I'll be veeery careful."

As Tuco lifted the spare into place, a car pulled up behind the stricken SUV. Tuco couldn't see much beyond the glare of the headlights, but the black steel push bars on the front of the car told him it was a police car. He was grateful he still wore the sport coat that he'd put on against the chilly desert air. It concealed the semi-automatic tucked in his waistband.

The holes on the spare rim aligned with the lugs and settled into place on the axle just as the lawman, wearing a felt Stetson, stepped from behind the SUV. Fortune was on Tuco's side. The blown tire was on the passenger side, out of view of the traffic lanes.

"Looks like a pretty good blowout ya had there!" observed the overweight deputy with a mixed accent, part Hispanic and part Southwestern drawl.

Tuco stood to face him, ready to draw. "Yes, it got my attention, officer."

"Good job keepin' it under control. That rim's gonna to cost you a pretty penny." The cop stood back and out of reach, but didn't seem particularly wary.

"I know, not very happy about that."

"Need any help?"

Before Tuco could answer, Guero interjected, "I'm helping Tuco. I didn't losed the nug luts…see?" He held out his huge hand and one of the chrome nuts fell to the ground and rolled under the truck.

Tuco cringed at the use of his name and picked his aim points. Deputy Nuñez, according to his name badge, wore a vest under his beige uniform shirt. Tuco visualized three in his face and forehead.

Nuñez cackled good-naturedly, misreading Tuco's tense reaction to his helper's mistake. "Well, it looks like y'all have things under control. Sorry 'bout that rim. Have a good night and drive safe."

"Thank you, officer."

It can't be this easy, Tuco thought as the deputy smiled and waved at Guero. "Don't losed your nuts," he jokingly mimicked before walking back to his car in a fit of belly laughter.

Tuco fought the urge to put two slugs in the back of his head for insulting his brother. The deputy posed no immediate threat but instinct and old habits are hard to overcome. He knew that the man meant no offense and it was best to let it pass.

When the policeman shut his car door, Tuco reached under the car to retrieve the lost lug nut. His view was blocked but he heard the crunch of tires on the rough shoulder and assumed it was the cruiser pulling away. He found the chrome nut and wormed his way up to see that the police car hadn't moved.

The deputy sat in the driver's seat with his head down, concentrating on something in his lap. Movement at the front of the car caught his eye and he looked up with a perplexed expression.

The last thing Deputy Nuñez saw was Tuco reaching for the holstered pistol tucked into his waistband.

Chapter 52

Paul and I sat next to a pitiful excuse for a campfire while Blu licked paws unaccustomed to the rocky desert ground.

After turning off the highway, we had followed a decently groomed gravel road past what once was destined to be the Florida Estates, "A Desert Community in Paradise." No one with any sense or money had bought that line of BS, so now it was nothing more than a crumbled stone tower marking a lattice of sand-blown dirt lots. The straight road gave way to a winding, bumpy path into the foothills where we found the TDF "ranch house," a sorry, roofless shack. We spent the last of the fading light gathering anything that would burn--no easy task in a barren friggin' desert.

When Paul started picking up dried cow pies, I put my foot down.

"Hey, they cook with this stuff in India," he protested.

"Maybe so, but it's still dried feces, and I don't want that smoke in my lungs." Besides, with the high-tech-thintex-goreulated-Antarctic-Expedition sleeping bags that Paul brought, I figured we'd be okay.

I sat on a low wall eating a surprisingly good chicken parmigiana backpack meal from Paul's stash. I'd have much rather stopped at Irma's to enjoy another variation of chilé, meat and tortillas, but we would have ended up setting camp in full darkness.

The package said the meal was prepared to the same standards as Meals-Ready-to-Eat enjoyed by the U.S. Military, but I had eaten hundreds of MREs in Afghanistan, and they were road kill compared to this stuff. I could warm a government-issue MRE faster by putting it under my arm than using the chemical heater that came in the package, but this baby's heat pack had the chicken piping hot in under ten minutes. Guess this company wasn't the lowest bidder for the military contract.

Paul's "fire" made more smoke than flame or heat and he was on all fours blowing on its base with all his might.

"Blow much harder and you're going to bust a nut."

He looked up, red faced. "This looks a hell-of-a-lot easier on *Man vs. Wild*."

"That's 'cause producers build it for him. Face it, you're just a city boy n' can't start no fire…but you are a pretty good cook." I saluted him with a plastic fork full of tomato-sauce-covered breaded chicken.

He continued the effort for a few minutes before giving up. "Okay, Mr. Grylls, show the Mexican Telephone Man how it's done."

"Observe," I said smugly, and set down my cup of amaretto-mocha pudding.

A quick rearrangement of his smoldering disaster yielded the optimal fuel, air and heat mix, just as my dad taught me back in the day. Paul shook his head as the fire sprang to life.

When I stood from my Boy Scout demonstration, the light of my expertly crafted fire revealed something that we missed in the darkness. Painted on a rock low in one corner of the dilapidated shack, and lost in a sea of alcohol-inspired graffiti, were three familiar letters scrawled in charcoal from a dead campfire.

I was eager to get back to my pudding and figured it was just another signpost from my dad letting us know we were in the right spot. Paul, however, was intrigued and discovered it was more than just a "Dad was here" marker.

Under the rock was a Ziploc bag containing ten thousand dollars, two triple-A batteries and the last recorded confession of the man whose ashes we were about to scatter in these godforsaken mountains.

Chapter 53

Doña Ana County Sheriff's Deputy Rick Nuñez should have run the plate on the SUV when he first stopped to see if they needed help, but he had chosen to follow his instinct. The man changing the blowout and his retarded assistant seemed nice enough, so he skirted procedure a second time when he didn't run the plate after returning to his cruiser.

His shift was nearly over, so he sat in his car killing a few minutes by sling-shotting cartoon birds at fortified pigs. The game monopolized his attention. He didn't notice the Chevy Impala pulling up behind him with its lights off, but he did catch the movement of the man in front of the cruiser.

The tire changer was drawing a gun.

By the time Nuñez understood what his eyes saw, two bullets tore through his skull and broke the synaptic connection.

***

The *Aztecas'* unprofessionalism cost them their lives.

Tuco hardly registered the bright blooms of blood and clotty matter that splashed across the deputy's windshield. He concentrated instead on the gunmen pumping bullets into the car.

His reaction was automatic and his first shots fired before he had finished warning his brother. "Guero, GET DOWN!"

He engaged the best shooter first, not that the order mattered to the final outcome. Four shots in just under three seconds took both men out cleanly.

The short one in the checkered shirt and chinos might have had a chance if he had shot at Tuco instead of the seated deputy with his back to them. Before Tuco's rounds caught him in the face, his shooting form was solid and it was his rounds that hit Officer Nuñez. His partner, on the other hand, chose the sideways gangland–style grip and put three jagged holes in the trunk lid before eating Tuco's bullets.

Pendejos. *Always take out the most capable threat first,* Tuco thought as he quickly dragged the bodies out of sight of the highway. Fortunately traffic was light on the interstate highway, and no one had seen the brief shoot-out. He turned his attention to Guero.

"Are you okay?"

"Yeah I'm okay, Tuco. They shooted that policeman Tuco. Why did you shoot them?" Guero was confused by the role reversal.

"They were going to shoot us next, *'mano.* I'll explain later. Go sit in the truck."

Once Guero was safe, Tuco turned his attention back to the dead *Aztecas* and loaded them into the back seat of the Impala. He destroyed their cell phones in case they had tracking features. Then he finished changing the tire and positioned the vehicles so it looked like the deputy had stopped to investigate an abandoned vehicle. He hoped the glare of the cruiser's flashing lights would prevent passing drivers from seeing the bloody mess in the front seat. Satisfied the arrangement would buy him some time, Tuco got in the SUV and continued west.

He admonished himself for not detecting the tail and realized they probably picked him up when he had passed Martin's place. It was a rookie mistake and now that the cartel knew where he was, he'd have to be more careful.

Nobody said this was going to be easy.

Chapter 54

The pocket-sized Flip Cam had a tiny screen, so Paul and I huddled like a couple of kids looking at a Playboy and watched the video. My old man's face filled the LCD. His hair was grayer and longer than I remembered, but he still looked pretty good for a guy who'd made it his life's work to keep Schlitz Brewing Company in business.

From the background, it looked like he had recorded the video here at the campsite. He wiped his face with his hand in a gesture that revealed his age and took a deep breath before starting.

"Well hello, son. I hope you're doing well. What's it been, ten... twelve years?" His deep voice had a slight western drawl.

He took another deep breath. "If you're watching this, then I'm probably dead and odds are it's that fat prick Mitchell that did it. Either that or you and I are drinking a couple of Schlitz and laughing about this, but I'm guessing that ain't the case."

A thought occurred to him and he paused. "If you're not Jake Martin, then this ain't none of your business and you can screw off, you nosy fuck."

He laughed before returning to business.

"I don't know where to start and don't want to bore you with a bunch of unimportant crap, but I owe you an explanation for everything that's going on. You've probably guessed that it ain't my business acumen that's led me to be a car wash tycoon. Hell, son, you and I both know I couldn't turn a profit selling fuzzy dice at a low-rider convention. Nope, it was dumb luck and a case of doin' the wrong thing at the right time.

"It might surprise you that I have a bit of a booze problem," he stretched out "booze." "Well, not much of a surprise, but at any rate, I got outta hand one night and wound up in the pokey for a fuckin' 'public intox.'

"So I'm settling in for a long night in the drunk tank with a puke-covered college kid and two Mexicans who smelled like a hooker's armpit when this fat lawyer who I don't know from Adam posts my bond, gives me two hundred bucks, a cab ride home and a business card with '2 p.m. tomorrow' written on the back.

"Even at two, my head was still pounding pretty good, but not so much that I didn't notice the nice set of tits sittin' behind his reception desk. If you haven't met Katy yet son, I highly recommend it."

Paul looked at me. "Apple didn't fall far from the tree."

My dad continued, "Anyway, I'm blabbing and need to get serious. Point is, that's how I came to meet Ronald Mitchell, and that's how he lured me into laundering money for the Sinaloa Drug Cartel."

He paused for a few seconds, looked off-camera, took a swig of Schlitz and grinned. "I guess that's not a completely accurate statement, he just presented an opportunity that I jumped at like a bum on a half-smoked cigarette.

"All in all it's pretty simple. I walk out of Mitchell's office the proud new owner of a coin-op car wash. It's a pure cash business, with most of the cash coming straight from the cartel. Inside of three months I have six locations that turn over a million a year in legitimate income, triple that in reported, and ten times that in untraceable cash flow. It may not seem like much when you consider *they're* doing thirty to forty billion a year, but I'm just one of many doing the same thing. If it's coin-operated in El Paso, you can bet the cartel owns it.

"Since the Mexican Government made it hard to spend U.S. currency in Mexico, most of the money is used to buy goods and merchandise that's shipped south over the border and sold at a comfy profit.   They learned that neat little trick from the Colombians.   It's pure genius.   Some big outfit in El Paso handles all of that, but it's way above my pay-grade.

"Anyway, enough Cartel Finance 101.   In retrospect I'm not proud of it but it more than paid the bills and the way I see it, if I can make some money off of the idiots who want to screw themselves up with drugs, then why the fuck not?   Hell, if our government gave half a shit about the heartache that the drug business causes, they'd legalize the junk and take the money out of the equation.   Thousands of dead Mexicans in Juarez would probably agree with me.

"Here I am, digressing again."   He took a deep breath and rubbed his face with both hands.

"The reason I'm dead and you're watching this is that greedy ass-hat, Mitchell.   We had a sweet deal going, he and I.   Easy money.   Hell, his deal was even sweeter because I think he was running at least two or three others like me… but he fucked it all up, the traitorous bastard.

"One day he comes to me and says he wants me to help with a special deal.   Something that *he* set up, and… hold onto your socks… it's for ten million dollars with a *ten* percent fee!   All I have to do is take delivery, hide the money, then transfer it to the 'real' money-laundering outfit I mentioned earlier.   Presto, we split the fee.

"Seemed simple enough and by that time I was pretty cocky, so I agreed to do the transfer."

Dad paused to take another swig of beer.   "Coupla' days later the cash is delivered to one of my car washes hidden in some cases of liquid soap, complete with instructions to keep it safe and wait for more instructions.   So I store ten million bucks in my little secret room.   By the way, I figured you'd like the new basement.   That AV setup cost me over a hundred grand… and I'm sure you found the secret room.   I left lots of clues."

If it hadn't been for the randomly dropped bottle of beer, I don't think I'd have ever discovered his discreet storage facility. I wonder what else I had missed.

"Hope you got to eat at Irma's. Irma died a few years ago, but they still make the best damn *rellenos* in the western hemisphere." As he rambled on about her food, I took an exaggerated bite of a Clif bar that tasted like peanut shells mixed with Elmer's paste and glared at Paul.

"Anyways, here's where it gets interesting. Ronnie Boy shows up at my front door dressed in a trench coat and asks me if the money is safe. I tell him of course it is, 'cept for the million I used to buy a solid-gold vibrator for his secretary. He didn't appreciate my little joke, and he starts gettin' real edgy.

"The bastard starts to lecture me on how this is a 'big fucking deal'... as if the Sinaloas are nothing more than schoolyard bullies... and if we screw with the "Guadateca' or 'Guacamole' or whatever-the-fuck these assholes call themselves, then our lives could get real shitty, real fast.

"Then he drops the bomb and lets it slip that these jackwads aren't Mexicans at all, but get this, they're fucking terrorists! I can't believe what I'm fuckin' hearing!

"So I ask him, 'Terrorists?' and he just nods."

Blu nudged between Paul and I, curious to see what had us so entranced. I paused the video and rewound to watch that last part again.

Paul broke the silence, "Well, I guess we know what Guadalete is."

"Holy crap," was all I could manage.

"Must be a Muslim conquest thing, like the Cordoba Society...those jack-offs who wanted to build a mosque near Ground Zero."

"Holy crap."

I restarted the video.

"'What the fuck, Ron?'

"'It's just this once,' he says, 'and we get to split a million dollars. All you have to do is deliver the money.'

"Before he could give me the address, I told him to go fuck himself. Like I said, I got no problem with cleaning a little dope money, but I ain't gonna help a bunch of fucking ragheads commit murder in the U S of A. Fuck that bullshit!"

I could tell he was pretty worked up, and despite the low light and bad camera, I could see the redness in his face.

He slowed the pace of his monologue. "I should have played it cooler, maybe gotten the damn address, but my temper got the best of me. Mitchell didn't take it too well. He ranted on about this and that, questioned my loyalty…if you can believe THAT…and told me I'd be sorry.

"That was two nights ago, so here I am at the Two Dogs Ranch with ten million dollars and wondering what the hell to do next. At least the money is safe, which should buy me some time, but one way or the other, I'm gonna have to go to the cops with this. Maybe the terrorism angle will be enough to keep me out of jail for the laundering gig, assuming I don't wake up with my throat cut.

"Hopefully he's full of shit and I'm overreacting, but I don't think so. Guess tomorrow I'll update my will."

Dad trailed off, lost in thought for a few moments before standing up and turning off the camera. A split second later he was back on screen. The background was a bit darker and he'd clearly had a few more Schlitz in the interim.

"Who'm I fuckin' kiddin'? I'm a fuckin' dead man.

"I'm so sorry." He went quiet for a few drawn out seconds, struggling with intoxication and emotion. "I'm sorry for all I've done and haven't done, Jake. I'll try to fix this mess, but I think you're gonna have to clean it up, son. There's two duffle bags up at the mine with redneck car alarms and five million each." He thrust out five splayed fingers for emphasis.

"I ain't gonna tell you what to do son, just be careful and don't trust Mitchell farther than you can throw him.

"Good luck. I love you, boy."

He reached up to turn off the camera when for a brief moment his eyes cleared. "Oh yeah, the key is your birthday."

The screen went blank.

"Pretty ballsy of your dad to put his foot down."

It was tough to speak around the lump in my throat. "Yeah, despite all of his bullshit, I guess I'm not surprised that this is where he'd make a stand. He always loved his country."

I took a few minutes to process what we just watched. Looks like I stepped into something pretty deep. Money laundering, drug cartels, terrorism. Oh my.

"Well, I guess we know why we're here. No wonder Medrano is after me."

"Ten million is a lot of money."

"Do you figure the terrorists are on to this?"

"Not likely." Paul thought it out. "They probably don't even know anything is in the air yet. Based on Mitchell's timeline with you, it seems like he had 'til the end of this week or early next."

"What about the guys expecting the money? The 'big operation' he was talking about."

"Same deal." Paul started to fidget.

"Something to add?"

An awkward silence settled over us, broken only by the crackling fire and the sound of Blu working the sore pads of his feet.

He stared into the flickering campfire and mumbled, "I have some bad news."

"Bad news? My father's dead because he was laundering money for the narcos, I killed a guy in his house, and a cartel enforcer who happened to be screwing the only woman I ever loved wants the ten million in terrorist cash. How much worse can it get?" My voice was a little shrill.

"Alex was one of the *federales* in the ambushed convoy."

Chapter 55

Tuco and Guero pulled into Deming as the last vestige of daylight faded to black on the western horizon. The highway incident took close to thirty minutes, so they'd been out of contact with Martin for over an hour and counting.

That was more than enough time to grab the money and disappear. It would be nearly impossible to intercept Martin and take the money once he was back on the road to El Paso. Tuco really needed some luck.

The first order of business was to get the laptop up and running. He hoped for one of the big box electronic stores like a Best Buy, but when he saw that Deming isn't much more than a travel stop in the middle of nowhere, he was thrilled to find a Wal-Mart.

Even more thrilling was the fact they carried an AC adapter for the Apple machine. They also picked out some snacks, drinks, pillows, blankets and batteries for Guero's game. He anticipated a long uncomfortable night in the Escalade listening to Guero's snores and smelling his gas.

Tuco made his contribution to the Jobs and Walton empires using a cartel credit card.

With the supplies loaded into the truck it was time to eat. He drove around the town for a few minutes, to make sure they weren't tailed. Once satisfied, they pulled into a throwback diner popular in the gentrified big cities, except it was the real deal. Built in the fifties, the diner had apparently been remodeled sometime during the style-challenged seventies and hadn't been touched since.

The grimy, vinyl-upholstered booth sighed like a tired old lady when they slid into it. Guero bounced up and down a few times, fascinated by the whoopee-cushion effect of air rushing through the cracked seat.

A plump Hispanic waitress, wearing a hairnet and an apron stained by two week's worth of spillage, sloshed a couple of kiddie-size cups of ice water and menus on the formica table. She mumbled something about being right back before waddling off.

She returned as Tuco crawled out from under the table, successful in his search for an electrical outlet. He pre-empted her drive-by, drinks-only request and sent her huffing back to the kitchen with an order for a Mexican combo plate and a grilled cheese sandwich with an extra large plate of chili-cheese fries for Guero.

By the time the computer blinked to life and Tuco logged onto the GPS tracker site, the waitress, Lupe according to her nametag, returned with their food. Her thumb was slightly inserted in the open end of one of Tuco's enchiladas. She dropped off the plates without so much as an "enjoy" or much less a "can I get you anything else?" Tuco knew exactly why she waited tables in a run-down diner in the middle of nowhere.

Much to his surprise the food was pretty good, made better by the fact Martin's tracker had been at the same spot in the Florida Mountains for nearly an hour and a half. The dwindling pile of fries on Guero's plate indicated he too thought the food at Irma's Diner was pretty good.

Tuco breathed easier and took the time to savor his dinner knowing that Martin was not moving and well within reach.

"Guero, do you want some ice cream for dessert?"

Wide eyes and a chili-rimmed smile was all the answer he needed.

Chapter 56

"What did you say?" I barely whispered even though I heard what he said about Alex and understood completely. Paul knew better than to repeat it. He just looked at his feet and let it sink in.

I had a hard time remembering how to breathe.

It took a few minutes to recover from the physical shock of the blow he delivered to my psychological solar plexus. My vision narrowed and everything around me took on an otherworldly quality. The snap and pop of the campfire grew louder and more acute, competing with the liquid beat of the blood coursing through my body.

Images of Alex snapped through my subconscious like graffiti past a subway train window: A pony tail bouncing in the light of a distant streetlamp, green eyes blinking awake on a soft down pillow, long tan legs wrapped around a corrupt *federale* wearing tactical black.

Nervous fingers twirling silky brown hair on our first date, a soft lip chewed in concentration over a second cup of coffee and a half-finished Friday crossword, blood flowing like tears past wide-open lifeless green eyes.

Egyptian cotton draped provocatively over feline curves in the dim light of pre-dawn, delicate fingers peeking out from under a coarse cotton sheet on grimy asphalt.

The images flashed through my mind, like a macabre slideshow of Alex and me, then Alex and Medrano in various states of sex and murder. I wanted to make him bleed, to reach into his chest and crush his heart like he had crushed mine.

I realized it wasn't exactly rational.

Paul must have noticed the seed of insanity blooming on my face. "Are you going to be okay?"

"Yeah, I think so. I just raced through the seven stages of grief and settled on pissed off."

"I'm really sorry man," he offered. "Sylvia showed me this morning after you left the office and I needed some time to figure out how to tell you."

"Are you sure?"

"Pretty much. Sylvia's source confirmed that she was part of Cordona… the guy on the sidewalk's… team." And the other guy who might have been screwing Alex, he didn't add. "All reports indicate no one survived the attack. Sylvia is working on finding out more, but--" I looked up at him, "--I wouldn't put a lot of stock in miracles."

"I want to kill him."

"Well, you will probably get your chance. I kind of expected him to be on our tail today and was surprised when he wasn't. Something doesn't add up."

"Dad's lawyer couldn't put two and two together with the Florida thing, what makes you think a cartel thug could figure it out?" I asked.

"Don't underestimate this guy. He did well as a cop and has survived in a pretty tough crowd. Takes more than brute force to do that."

"Bullshit. No way he knows where we are." And in a colossal display of poor judgment I asked, "Do you have any booze?"

Paul just stared at me for a moment and then reached into his pack and withdrew a bottle of tequila that would have set me back a week's pay. I'm sure it was handcrafted by distillers who were paid pennies a day, and then sold for five hundred bucks a bottle, but all social injustice aside, it's some of the best stuff that's ever passed my lips.

We had passed the hand-blown crystal bottle a couple of times when Paul said, "Maybe that's enough for now." The bottle disappeared back into his pack.

My mood darkened and I fed twigs to the fire while Blu doctored tender feet before turning to his crotch. It reminded me of an old joke that ends, "You'd better pet him first."

Paul tried his best to divert my thoughts from Alex by asking subtle questions about Katy.

"What did she look like naked?" Well, not too subtle.

I didn't bite so he gave up on the light banter.

We sat and watched the fire eat up more of our precious fuel while I fiddled with Dad's pistol.

Paul sensed the insanity coming back. "What's the closest you've come to killing someone...before today?"

That was easy.

"It was in Afghanistan when I was out buying hearts and minds. One of the Humvees in our little caravan breaks down and since I don't know diddly about Hummer engines, I pull perimeter guard duty while a couple of Nebraska farm boys stick bubble gum in the flux capacitor, or whatever. While they work on the truck, a local pulls up behind us in an old beater Russian car, gets out and starts gesticulating like we killed his cat and screwed his daughter...all on account of he can't get past us on this goat-path of a highway."

I really wanted another swig of tequila.

"As he walks up to the convoy, I level my rifle at the guy and tell him to stop in Urdu, Pashtu, English, Sign Language and Swahili for good measure, but despite my raised hand and an M-16 pointed at his chest, the numb-nuts just keeps coming, waving his arms like he's got a high pressure inflator stuck up his ass. I'm yelling 'STOP' at the top of my lungs and he just keeps getting closer to my ten-yard limit.

"I click off the safety, sight in on his chest and am just about to pull the trigger when Allah slaps some sense into the dumb son-of-a-bitch. He stops his wailing, turns around and climbs back into his Russian piece of crap to wait patiently for us to fix our American piece of crap and clear the road."

"Wow."

"Yep, one more step and I would have capped the guy. Same thing happened to a buddy of mine a week or so later but he pulled his trigger. Turns out, the guy was wearing an explosive vest but it still messed with my friend's mind for a while."

"Wild. So is the *Azteca* messing with your mind?"

I stared into the flames. "With all the good news you've given me do you think I give a rat's ass about a dead gang-banger? He had it coming. With any luck, Tuco Medrano is next."

And with that happy thought, the conversation ended and the *Alex and Medrano* mental slideshow returned for a second engagement.

Chapter 57

With all of the thoughts swirling through my head, the cold desert air, and a thin piece of foam between my back and the rocky ground, I didn't think I'd get much sleep, but I can tell you that I slept like a truck driver at a Sylvia Plath poetry reading.

But despite Paul cutting me off, I felt a bit groggy for the second day running. In some circles, that might be considered a sign of alcoholism, but in my circle that's just a good start to the week.

My back hurt. Maybe I'm too old to sleep on the ground, or maybe it was the fist-sized rock under my left shoulder blade. I couldn't believe I missed that sucker in the dark after a couple shots of tequila, but even more incredible was that I was able to sleep with the small boulder wedged between my ribs and scapula.

The fire was a cold pile of white ash, the air chilly on my face and the sky grey in the predawn. Paul was an amorphous blob of nylon and Thermo-fil on the far side of the fire. It brought to mind a body bag except for the slow, rhythmic movement of his breathing. I could see the vapor of my own breath, but just barely. Blu lay curled up in a ball at my feet.

Funny how our bodies are programmed by memory; I could almost smell the bacon frying.

I thought of my dad. He would always be up at the first hint of light on the horizon, laying out greasy slices of pork fat he called bacon on a massive cast iron skillet that was one of his most prized possessions. The thing weighed a ton and I'm pretty sure it was the first iron implement created by man.

I'd usually wake up as he was finishing his first beer of the morning, putting on a pot of coffee and starting the "mountain eggs." Mountain eggs are nothing more than over-easy eggs cooked in the sea of grease rendered from the discount bacon, seasoned with a hint of ash from the campfire or his Camel cigarette. Sopped up with white bread toasted on the open fire and washed down with boiling hot coffee, mountain eggs are the best breakfast on the planet.

I slipped off my sleeping bag like a used condom, made sure there were no creepy-crawlies in my shoes, and walked down to the Land Rover to see what I could find for breakfast.

"Son of a bitch!" Nestled behind the massive ice chest was a case of Dura-Flame fireplace logs. Clearly Paul hadn't packed his own truck, but at least one of his hipster employees knew something about camping in style.

The closest thing I found to Dad's cast-iron skillet was a compressed-gas camp stove that looked more like a camera tripod than a cooking tool. The Space Shuttle kitchen was overkill for the protein bars but it would work well for the French press coffee maker. Yep, a French press. The Dura-Flames were a nice touch, but forget anything else I said about the geek in skinny jeans knowing anything about camping.

I hauled the loot back to our cozy campsite and sparked up a fire-log according to the manufacturer's instructions and munched on a protein bar. The two were interchangeable in their saw-dusty goodness. As I sat water to boil on the Buck Rogers stove, the magnitude of the situation dawned on me.

I had been so wrapped up in the thing that affected me, namely Alex, that I missed the most important part: my father gave his life to stop a group of terrorists. It was a ballsy move.

The thought of terrorism reminded me that I should probably check in with my friends at the DEA. I pulled my phone out of my pocket and the battery was still dead. Imagine that.

Paul was up and around; guess he couldn't sleep through me prodding him with my toe and Blu licking his face, so I asked him if his phone had a signal.

He pursed his lips and shook his head.

"More bars in more places my ass."

"Shoulda' brought a sat-phone."

"You have a freakin' sat-phone and you didn't bring it?"

He shrugged.

I tossed him a protein bar. "After you finish your breakfast we'd better get started. Once we get a little higher we might get a signal and I can call the DEA people and warn them about the terrorists."

"Where is the mine?"

"Just below that peak." I pointed at a tall promontory that loomed behind Paul.

He looked up and grimaced.

"It's not much more than a test shaft that some dude carved into the back of an existing cavern. Shouldn't take more than an hour or so to get there."

"Don't suppose there's a tram or anything?"

"Quit being a pussy."

"Hey, your dad said something about the money that I didn't understand--what the heck is a redneck car alarm?"

Chapter 58

By the time we started out the sun had emerged over the peaks to the east. The trail to the old test shaft was only a mile or two long, give or take, but wound over some pretty rough terrain and gained nearly fifteen hundred feet in elevation.

Our crumbling stone hut perched on the bank of an *arroyo*, and one of its corners sat just a few feet from the unstable vertical edge of the shallow gulley. The sandy bottom of the wash was drier than a British joke, but after a good thunderstorm in the mountains, it would fill bank to bank with frothy brown water and tumbling rocks. One or two flash floods would wipe out what's left of the shelter, but in the desert that probably wouldn't happen in my lifetime. Probably.

Paul and I eased down the three-foot earthen cliff into the *arroyo* bottom, outfitted with packs filled with a few more protein bars, a first aid kit, knife, space blankets and some extra layers of clothing just in case it cooled off. The packs had built-in Camelbak water bags and I considered filling mine with a couple of beers, but changed my mind. I put the beers in the pack and filled the bag with water.

We strapped pistols to our hips like a couple of doomsday preppers; I considered taking the Glock, but having my father's old Colt on my hip somehow felt better. We left the rifles in the Rover. They would give us better range and firepower, but would be tough to carry over the rocky terrain. As we started out, I was nagged by the feeling that I forgot something very important.

***

The wash narrowed considerably as it rose into the mountains and the sandy bottom gave way to rock and hardpan. Mesquite and the occasional juniper dotted the hillsides mostly covered by *ocotillo*, *cholla* and Spanish dagger--cute little desert plants that had more pricks than a Philadelphia Eagles home game. When we were kids, we called the *chollas* the "jumping cacti," because no matter how careful you were when passing one, the little bastards seemed to jump out and stab you with hundreds of bright yellow needles.

Blu ran ahead, not knowing where he was going but funneled in the right direction by the steepening walls of the *arroyo*. He'd stop every now and then to sniff a territorial marker left by the local wildlife and claim it for his own with a squirt of urine.

Eventually he came to a four-foot wall of rock that during a rainstorm would be a waterfall. He sat and waited for us to catch up.

With a wave and an "Up!" he was at the top of the rocks in an instant. Paul and I weren't so nimble.

"This isn't going to be easy, is it?" Paul complained more than asked.

"Just a couple more like this and the rest is an easy climb." Well, easy for a twelve-year-old kid, but it would probably kick our asses. "We'll follow this canyon for awhile and then climb a low saddle that will get us to the ridgeline. Are you afraid of heights?"

"Not so much the height, just the sudden stop at the end of a fall. Why?"

"There are a couple of tight spots along a ledge that might make your ass pucker a bit."

"Lovely."

The hike brought back some vivid memories, and I came to appreciate the place I thought I hated so much as a kid. As desolate and abandoned as the place seems, people have been in these mountains for centuries.

Dad had showed me pottery shards and petroglyphs left by pre-Columbian cultures when the climate was much different. The Spanish left their own mark--an elaborate sandstone inscription in their language praising God and King Philip dated 1582. By then they figured out that the cities of gold were a myth and their diseases had decimated the native populations responsible for the other art in the mountains.

Apache raiders hid from the Mexican and American cavalries in the steep canyons of the Floridas, eking out a miserable subsistence on the desert's limited resources. I had found a couple of arrowheads to prove they'd been here. Then, of course, there were the prospectors, ranchers and land speculators crazy enough to think they could scratch a living out of the granite, sand and prickly plants in these inhospitable mountains.

As a young kid worrying about the good time I was missing back in El Paso, I wasn't impressed with all of the knowledge and education that my father had tried to impart. Now that I was older and *much* wiser, his message finally started to sink in. Floating at the periphery of my thoughts was the idea that maybe life was bigger than a bottle of Mad Dog in a paper sack.

It took us half an hour to reach the spot where we would leave the canyon floor and climb to the low saddle between two peaks on the main ridgeline. The canyon walls were shaded from the morning sun and the air was still cool, but the effort had both of us in a good sweat.

Two sets of footprints along the way, one coming and one going, somehow drew me closer to the father I hadn't seen in years.

Chapter 59

The night wasn't nearly as long or uncomfortable as Tuco had expected. With the rear seats removed, the Escalade's cargo compartment was more than adequate for the two of them to stretch out. It was the longest night of sleep for Tuco in over a week. As he stumbled awake, the smell of bad breath, stale farts and body odor gently assaulted him.

The cool morning air outside the truck rushed in when he opened the rear door and did more to restore his senses than coffee ever could.

He shook Guero's meaty leg. "Wake up, '*mano*, it's a beautiful morning."

His brother issued a phlegmy protest and rolled away, pulling the Wal-Mart blanket tighter around his shoulders.

Tuco crawled out of the SUV, stretched and relieved himself on the sandy ground. He surveyed the terrain he hadn't been able to see when they had pulled off of the highway seven hours before. The Caddy was parked six or seven hundred yards east of the highway on a gravel trail that led to the mountains a few miles farther on. The land sloped gently up to the base of the rocky buttes, and in the morning light he saw that the dirt road followed a ridge along the high side of a broad wash.

The GPS locator showed that Martin had stopped in the mountains less than three miles from where Tuco stood pissing in the dust.

From his vantage point Tuco saw... nothing... and he was pleased. The dirt track had one set of recent tire marks, presumably Martin's, and there wasn't so much as a shack within eye or pistol shot.

As he tucked himself back into his pants, Tuco smiled and felt for the first time like he might be able to pull the whole thing off. Then he remembered there was something he had to do.

He pulled out his cell phone and hefted it in his hand, considering the ramifications of turning the device on and placing a call. There were no guarantees that he would make it out of the mountains alive, and this might be his last chance to pass some very important information.

There was a good chance that the cartel could geo-locate his phone; he knew this because he had set up the protocols on other lieutenants' devices. His was somehow left out of the process, but that didn't mean his phone hadn't been modified later. Trust was a foreign concept to the cartel.

He could have easily avoided the problem by purchasing a throw away mobile device, but it just didn't enter his mind when they stopped at the Deming Wal-Mart. *Another opportunity lost*, he thought. He sighed, pressed the power button and dialed an old friend's number.

Tuco finished the call, turned off the phone, reached into the back of the truck and shook his brother's leg more vigorously. "C'mon, Guero, wake up!"

Acrid smoke rose from his first cigarillo and Tuco jonesed for a hot cup of coffee as Guero sat up, rubbed his eyes with hammy fists and let out a cavernous yawn.

"I'm hungry."

Tuco handed him a handful of breakfast bars and marveled that his brother's first words weren't "where the fuck are we?" But it was always about the simplest needs and basic observations with Guero: "This road is bumpy," "those plants look stickery," and "look, a little house!" All preceded "what place is this, Tuco?" as they drove slowly up the road towards Martin's last position.

"Whose car is that?" Guero asked, pointing to the Land Rover parked next to the dilapidated stone shack.

"I don't know, '*mano*," Tuco answered absentmindedly while scanning the camp. "Wait here and I'll see if anyone is home."

Light smoke rose straight into the still air from inside the roofless shack, but there was no movement or indication that anyone was inside. Tuco figured that the best approach was direct--odds were they had no idea who he was, and if they did, he had lost the element of surprise long before he pulled into the campsite.

The Rover appeared to be full of camping gear--more than he would expect for one man. That could complicate things.

The fear that Martin waited in ambush was put to rest when he saw the interior of the building. The smoke came from a burned out fire and the camp had been cleaned up—clearly they left before Tuco's arrival.

He motioned for Guero to join him.

"Who builded—built--the fire?" asked Guero, proud he caught his own grammatical error.

"A man I want to talk to," Tuco replied while looking at the footprints in the *arroyo*. They headed into the mountains, seemingly unconcerned about being tracked.

"Guero, listen, I want you to wait here. Stay close to the truck and if anyone comes, honk the horn over and over. Understand?"

"Yes, Tuco. If someone comes, I'll honk the horn."

The faint sound of a dog barking echoed down the canyon and made Tuco reconsider his plan.

Chapter 60

Blu trotted along about a hundred feet ahead of us and I caught occasional glimpses of his head and tail through the sagebrush growing in the *arroyo* bottom. Paul kept up pretty well, but I could tell by the way he negotiated the sand and gravel path that hiking wasn't high on his list of favorite activities.

I was about to suggest he choose the packed gravel patches instead of the sand and unstable rocks when Blu started barking. It wasn't his usual "pay attention to me 'cause I'm awesome" bark, but one that seemed a little more urgent.

Paul got to him first. "Holy shit!"

When I reached them, both were frozen in place in the middle of the trail, staring at the base of a large boulder. Tucked in a small depression washed out by the last thunderstorm was a fat green rattlesnake.

I know, rattlesnakes aren't green, and with a barking dog and two hikers gawking at it, a rattlesnake should be making lots of noise with his tail thingy. But this snake *was* green, well, greenish, and it didn't seem to give two shits that we had invaded its space.

"That's a big snake," Paul said. "Why isn't it rattling its ass off? Is it dead?"

I'd seen it once or twice as a kid. The cold-blooded little bastards hibernate in the winter and are active in summer, but during the transition months they are at the mercy of the weather. They hunt after the sun goes down while their bodies are still warm, but as the temperature drops they get sluggish, find a spot to hunker down and wait for the sun to warm them in the morning.

"No, just cold. It got pretty chilly last night and he's just waiting for it to warm up. I'm kinda' surprised he's not hibernating."

"Are you a herpetologist now?"

"No, I watch a lot of the Discovery Channel."

I found a four-foot greasewood branch and reached under the boulder overhang.

"Dude, please don't mess with the freakin' snake!" Paul pleaded as he took a couple of large steps backward. Blu went with him but stopped his yapping.

"Don't be such a puss." My bravado suddenly felt foolish. I gently probed the coiled-up critter with the stick and lifted him out of the depression. It draped over the end of the stick and moved its head listlessly from side to side, like it was swaying to a Lawrence Welk polka. The body was a good four feet long and as thick as my forearm--fat for the coming winter.

Blu moved back a couple more feet and let out a soft "woof," probably the smartest among us.

"Let's just kill the thing and be on our way."

"No, today's his lucky day." Even though I didn't care much for snakes, I wanted to save my anger for Medrano. I moved the rattler to the side of the trail next to a small sage, where it slowly slithered back into a tight coil without so much as an expression of gratitude.

"We still have a couple of clicks to go, better start humpin'."

Paul took an exasperated breath and started off with a mock salute and a parodied march. He was paying more attention to the snake than to his path, and on his third step his right foot came down awkwardly on a loose, basketball-sized rock in the *arroyo* bed. The stone rolled and pinned his foot to a larger boulder and his exaggerated stride threw him off balance.

The sound of his tibia and fibula snapping as he tumbled ass over teakettle sounded like a rifle shot and echoed off of the canyon walls.

His scream reminded me of the rabbit I shot years before.

Chapter 61

The jagged bone was sticking out of Paul's leg and we were hours from any real medical facility. The best chance of saving his foot was setting the bone and that was going to be nasty. The worst part was the squishy, crackling sound when I straightened out the grotesquely angled leg.

Paul passed out.

I nearly lost my breakfast.

For the first time since my return from Afghanistan, I was grateful for the first aid training and experience of watching medics work on kids in the field.

Other than the antibiotic cream, the first aid kit was relatively useless, so I used the snake-charmer stick, some straps from Paul's pack and a spare t-shirt to fashion a combination splint-bandage. I gave him the beer from my pack and wished it were the tequila we had left at the camp.

Besides the short loss of consciousness, he bore it like a trooper. He used every profanity known to man in English, Spanish, Italian and maybe Russian, but he never screamed. Once the splint was in place I made sure he didn't fall into shock.

"We need to get you some help. I'm gonna climb to higher ground and see if I can get a cell signal."

"Bullllshiiit," he replied. "You're not leaving me here." He turned his head in the direction of the snake still coiled in the sandy washout. "I don't want to wait around here for that thing to wake up."

Neither of us was thinking rationally; otherwise I would have walked over and removed the snake's head with a .45 caliber bullet.

"Okay, I'll take you back to that wide spot in the canyon a ways back and then climb the saddle with your phone. I'm bound to get a signal up there and they'll have a chopper out here in no time. If any critters show up, you have your gun."

"Okay." I think he started to settle into mild shock.

There was no way his leg would bear any weight, but once I had him up and draped over my shoulder, I realized we wouldn't make it very far. We struggled back through the sand and gravel the way we'd come. Each step emphasized the stupidity of trying to move a man in his condition, but he wouldn't let me stop until we were well away from that snake. Funny what your mind fixes on in an emergency.

Blu traipsed along the trail ahead of us, stopping occasionally to piss on bushes that he'd already marked. As we neared a bend that obscured the view down the canyon, Blu stopped and stared with his ears up and let out a single bark. I was wrapped up in the thought that I should just go back and kill the snake and completely ignored his warning. When I limped around the curve, I found myself staring at the handsome face of a smartly-dressed, armed Latino.

He smiled and waved.

Chapter 62

I was so busy trying to manage Paul's mostly dead weight that I missed Blu's warning and there I was--face-to-gun with Mr. Ricardo, aka Tuco, Medrano.

He didn't really smile.

Or wave.

"Slowly pull the pistol out of the holster and set it down. His too."

"My hands are kind of full," I replied. He raised the aim point of his large-bore gun from my chest to my face.

"Okay, okay. No reason to get testy." I slowly pulled my gun, let it drop softly to the sand and reached around awkwardly to do the same with Paul's.

For all he knew, I detached his pecker and dropped it in the dirt. Pain had finally overcome him and he was on another planet. It worried me.

I released the straps on my backpack and let it fall to the ground--Paul's was back at the site of my impromptu medical clinic.

Standing a few feet behind Medrano was one of the biggest men I'd ever seen. He tried his hardest to look mean, but his eyes kept drifting to Blu, and I could tell he wanted to smile. Something in Tuco Medrano's dossier about a retarded brother flashed through my memory, but it hadn't said anything about the man's size. He was bigger than a rhinoceros.

I turned my attention back to Medrano. "My friend is hurt badly and needs help."

"Step back from the weapons." He was all business. "Over there, against the rock. Sit. Slowly."

I helped Paul backwards toward the granite wall of the canyon. Medrano moved in, retrieved the guns and went through our packs with one hand. He removed the protein bars and Camelbak bladder from my pack replaced them with our pistols.

"*'Mano*!" he barked. The large man was bent at the knees, smiling and motioning for Blu to come. The dog just looked at the hulk and put his ears back.

"*Hermano*!" Medrano snapped again and then softened considerably. "Please take this to them."

The big man lumbered over and brought us the bladders and bars. He set them gently at my feet.

"What's this?" he asked while fumbling with the Camelbak hose.

"Water," I answered.

"Oh. I'm Guero." He backed away sheepishly and was still clearly baffled by the drinking tube.

"What happened to him?" Medrano asked.

"Fell. Compound fracture. That means…"

"I know what it means," he snapped. "Is that it?"

"Yes, I think so," I answered too quickly and felt like I had missed an opportunity. I picked up the water bladder and offered it to Paul. Now that we were seated he seemed to be coming back to himself.

"This really hurts," he croaked.

"I know, buddy. We'll get you out of here soon," knowing that wasn't very likely. I looked back at Medrano and repeated, "He needs medical attention, soon."

He actually seemed torn, but only for a fleeting second. "He will get it, but you are going to help me first."

"What do you want?"

"Don't fuck with me, Mr. Martin. You can make my life simple and help me find what your father has stolen, or I can kill both of you now and take my chances." It was the most matter-of-fact statement I think I've ever heard. Not an inch of room for negotiation.

"How do I know you won't just kill us anyway?" Better now than after a long hike.

"You don't, but I am a man of my word. Besides, what better offer do you have?"

I thought about it for a few seconds. "Reasonable enough."

Reasonable indeed, but he underestimated that I could use this mountain to my advantage. He also didn't realize that I really, really wanted him dead.

Chapter 63

I made Paul as comfortable as possible, sheltered by the granite cliff face and shaded by a small cottonwood. He was fairly lucid and we had a private moment while Medrano was busy instructing his Sasquatch-looking companion. They talked quietly several yards away, and every once in awhile the big guy's head bounced up and down like it was on a spring.

"You doing all right?" I asked Paul.

"Better now that we've stopped moving. Guess that was a bad idea." Blood soaked through the t-shirt I had used for his splint, but from what I could see it didn't appear that he was still bleeding. Or much, anyway. His toes were pink and it looked like he had good circulation in the foot.

My greatest concerns were shock and infection, but he seemed coherent so the immediate danger had passed. Still, I knew he was in a great deal of pain and I wanted to get him help as soon as possible. I fed him the last four ibuprofen tablets from the first aid kit.

"Looks like we're up to our ass in this now," Paul observed.

"Yep, sorry about this, *amigo*. Any suggestions?"

"Yeah, take him to the money and let's get the hell outta here."

"I don't know. If I do that, I think we are both dead men. You saw what he did to his best friend and to…" I trailed off and didn't finish the statement.

"Yeah. So what should we do?"

"I'm starting to get an idea. We'll probably split up here and he'll leave you here with that big bastard. I think it's his brother and he'll have instructions to kill you if we don't get back within a certain time. Figure you can handle him?"

We looked at the two men. If it weren't for his enormity, you'd think Medrano was instructing a five-year-old child.

"He's the retarded one from Sylvia's report. I can deal with him, you just be careful with Medrano."

"I got it." But I didn't sound as confident as I intended.

Medrano finished with his brother and walked back towards us.

"How is your leg, Mr…?" Medrano asked.

He had no idea who Paul was. That was good.

"Paul. You can call me Paul, and I'm just peachy."

Chapter 64

What started out as a routine laundering investigation had ballooned into a bloody trail littered with bodies, and Christa Adams' best lead had decided to take a walkabout. While she and Reynolds were picking over the murder scenes and hitting more dead ends, Martin had left a message on her office line letting her know that he was heading out to the desert to camp and "clear his mind." Who the heck camps in the desert?

Her calls to his cell phone went straight to voicemail. She figured that he was out after the money and once they caught up to him, he would have lots of explaining to do. Assuming, of course, that Medrano didn't get to him first. Hopefully, if he lived *and* found the money, he would do the right thing and turn it in. Despite his smart-ass attitude, she kind of liked Jake and would hate to have to haul him off to federal prison.

Things were starting to unravel, and for the first time, Christa felt like she was in over her head. She and her partner sat in the DEA field office at a conference table haphazardly strewn with crime scene photos, folders, loose papers and notepads. She looked intently at the pile of miscellaneous crap and willed it to tell her a story. Her inexperienced partner sensed her desperation but was wise enough to keep his mouth shut.

A white board on the wall behind her covered in a cobweb of marker lines joining events and players in her little drama served as a visual reminder of all they didn't know. She turned to the board, drawn to the word "GUADALETE" neatly printed with a red dry erase marker. Just the sight of the word increased her anxiety.

All throughout the investigation, she kept the connection tight to her vest, partly because she didn't want to lose face if she was wrong, but mostly because she wanted the credit if she turned out to be right. Problem was, if her suspicions were correct, she should have turned this case over to the FBI and their superior resources. She'd still get credit, but not nearly the glory she'd reap from breaking the case as the lead investigator.

On the other hand, pride has led many down the wrong road.

Whispers in the hallway said the Bureau was already sniffing around the case, and apparently it was getting some high level attention.

It had been a good run, but now that the lead pool was drying up, Christa considered throwing in the towel and handing everything over to the FBI while she still had any hope of plausible deniability. Better late than never, and she could avoid career suicide by claiming ignorance on the Guadalete connection until the last minute. She was fairly confident that Reynolds would back her.

Running on four hours of sleep and out of ideas, Christa leaned back in her chair and sighed. Reynolds said what she was thinking before she could: "Maybe we should pass this over to the Bureau."

She pursed her lips and nodded slowly, but before she could answer, a lanky kid with a laptop stumbled into the conference room.

"Hey Christa, I've been looking all over for you. Check this out." He set the computer in front of her and opened the screen.

The man looked vaguely familiar. He was some kind of analyst that she'd seen around the office, and it irked her that he used her first name. The irritation nearly caused her to miss the point of what he showed her. He rambled on about "emulation" and "decryption" before he pointed at a pulsing dot labeled "DM" on a map in southern New Mexico. "Does that mean anything to you?"

"Yep." She looked at her partner and smiled for the first time in days. "It means we can tell the FBI to kiss our ass."

Chapter 65

Tuco Medrano sat on a small boulder and dismantled our guns. He removed the trigger mechanisms, smashed them with a rock, and chucked the recoil springs into a cactus field across the arroyo. That pretty much turned our pistols into paperweights.

During a pat down search that flirted with molestation, he found our phones and a nice folding knife that had served me well on deployment. One of my best friends, a college classmate and Navy SEAL, had given me the knife as a gift two months before he died a hero in Afghanistan.

Tuco took the battery out of Paul's phone and slipped it into his pocket but crushed my already dead iPhone with the rock he used to destroy the triggers--apparently he was not a Steve Jobs fan. The bastard pocketed my knife.

I used the quiet moment to size up Mr. Tuco Medrano, Drug Lord extraordinaire.

Our boogeymen are bigger than life and I had expected a taller man, but Tuco was just shy of six feet. His chiseled good looks were consistent with the photos in his dossier, but his hair had grayed along the sides, not common for a Latino. Maybe too much stress at work.

His unusually light, almost grey eyes conveyed the cold intelligence that undoubtedly kept him alive in his unpredictable world.

He moved like an athlete and even through his khaki pants and button-down shirt his physique exuded power.

As for yours truly, I wasn't in the best shape of my life and the late nights and hard drinking over the past few days had taken a toll. So, unless I was lucky and got in a quick shot to his balls or a thumb in his eye, I'd come up short in a hand-to-hand bout with Tuco. Yes, I know my limitations.

So in summary, a gunfight was out, a knife fight was a non-starter, and assuming he was dumb enough to lay down his knife and gun, a good old-fashioned ass whoopin' was an iffy proposition at best. The only things left were my wits and charming personality.

In other words I was screwed.

Navy Survival School had taught me that a hostage should try to build a rapport with his captors. You know, so it's harder for them to cut his throat or put a bullet in his head when the demands aren't met.

"So Tuco… do you mind if I call you that? Come to these parts often?" I asked. Paul cringed.

He looked up, expressionless. "Just once. To kill some mules." He went back to stuffing our divided gear into two backpacks.

I assumed by "mules" he didn't mean the four-legged, obstinate variety.

So much for rapport. Guess I'd have to kill him after all.

He set one of the packs at Paul's feet and slung the other over his shoulder. "I'm leaving you most of the supplies and instructed my associate to keep you comfortable. If Mr. Martin cooperates, you will get help soon."

"You can call me Jake." Still building rapport. "And if I just tell you where to find the money, we can be out of your hair that much sooner."

He didn't jump on my offer, but I was relieved that he still didn't seem to recognize Paul. A near billionaire in the hands of someone like Tuco Medrano could be a game changer.

"Are you waiting for an invitation… Jake?" But he didn't say my name in a friendly, rapport-building kind of way. My lethargy had perturbed him.

Good.

I stood and looked back at Paul. He nodded.

"Stay here, Blu." I could tell that was the last thing in the world that he wanted to do, but he would stay nonetheless.

I turned to start back up the trail towards the millions of dollars my father had left unattended in the desert.

Chapter 66

Guero watched his brother and Jake disappear around the bend. Tuco left him with instructions to take care of the hurt man and make sure he didn't try to get away. He was also supposed to look mean and keep quiet, but all Guero wanted to do was pet the dog that was watching the two men walk away. Once they were out of sight, Guero walked over to the injured man and sat cross-legged in the sand just a few feet away from the dog. Blu's ears went back as the big man approached, but when he held out a linty piece of beef jerky that he pulled from his pocket, the dog forgot his nervousness and took the treat gingerly after an inquisitive sniff.

Guero stroked the heeler's back as he gnawed on the jerky.

"Good dog." He looked over to Paul. "He's soft. I like the way he feels. My name is Guero, what's your name?"

Paul, reclining against a sand berm that Jake piled up, tried to smile. "Nice to meet you, Guero. My name is Paul."

"Paul… what was your friend's name again?"

"Jake."

"Jake, oh yeah! I thought it was Jack, but I knowed I was wrong. I have some gum, you want some gum? It's Juicy Fruits, my favorite kind. It's a lot better than Mexico *chicle*."

"Yes, please."

Guero fished through his pocket and produced a barely wrapped, lint-covered stick of chewing gum. He dug for another, better wrapped piece that he handed to Paul.

"Thank you."

"*De nada*," he replied. "That's Spanish for 'you're welcome.' Do you know Spanish?"

"Yes."

"Me, too." Although, besides "you're welcome," he could only count to six and say "goodbye." He smiled, showing his crooked teeth and popped the first stick in his mouth smacking his lips loudly.

"Mmmm, I like Juicy Fruits." His brows furrowed and his eyes shifted conspiratorially. "Uh oh, I'm not supposed to talk to you. You won't tell Tuco, will you?"

"No, I won't tell him."

Guero's face softened immediately and he went back to noisily chewing his gum and petting the dog. Blu sniffed at the big man's pockets, looking for more jerky.

"Is Tuco your brother?" Paul asked.

"Yeah. We take care of each other. We're going to the beach to drink coconuts and get away from the bad cartoon men."

"Cartoon men?" As soon as the question left his lips, Paul realized Guero was talking about the cartel.

"Yeah. They maked Tuco do bad stuff. Like Cuchillo. He tied me up and made Tuco sick so he sleeped a long time, but when he woke up we played a trick on Cuchillo and Tuco cut open his tummy with a knife. Cuchillo was bad and his breath stinked. Now we can go to the beach and drink coconuts and watch the nekkid girls swim in the water." He lowered his head and giggled at the thought.

"I'm s'posed to take care of you. How's your gum? Do you want some water?"

Paul shook his head. "No water, thank you... the gum is delicious. What beach are you going to?"

Guero shrugged. "The one with coconuts and nekkid girls," he replied as if it were the most natural answer in the world.

"Yeah, that's one of my favorites."

A thought occurred to Guero. "Is Jack, I mean Jake, a bad man?"

"No, Jake is a good man. One of the best…" he trailed off.

"Good…"

Guero leaned back against the cliff face and gently ran his hand up and down the length of Blu's back. The dog gave up on finding more jerky, and lay in the sand with his head between his forelegs content with the petting.

The desert was still and the morning chill gave way to pleasant warmth. Paul's leg throbbed painfully, but he tried to ignore it as best he could. He sat in the makeshift sand-lounger and listened to Guero chew his gum. The reddish grey canyon walls stood out in stark contrast against the clear, brilliant blue sky. The sun hid behind the sheer wall at their back but within the hour the canyon would be awash in its bright light.

Paul noticed that the silence was not as complete as it first seemed. The desert buzzed with life and he picked out individual sounds that made the white noise. He heard the tweets, chirps and whistles of birds he couldn't identify, and the occasional flight of an insect that reminded him of baseball cards in bicycle spokes. Another late season cicada droned on in the distance. When he stopped concentrating on the individual sounds, the noise of the desert morphed into a low, electric hum and it calmed him as he watched a black turkey buzzard circle lazily on a thermal high above.

The three sat lost in their wide range of thoughts. Guero sat happy with his gum and a new friend to pet; Paul did his best to ignore the pain; and Blu contemplated the merits of Particle Theory.

His keen ears heard it first and he stood, looking up the canyon. Paul wondered if they were on their way back, but it was way too soon. Then he heard the echoing report of a pistol shot followed seconds later by another, but he didn't hear the scream that caused Blu to bolt up the canyon at a full run.

Chapter 67

I led the way up the canyon, retracing our steps back to the site of Paul's mishap, towards the abandoned mine. Tuco followed several steps behind with his weapon holstered. I found that curious, but was grateful that a misstep wouldn't result in a bullet between my kidneys. My friend, the Navy SEAL, once told me that a trained man with a knife would beat most men with a holstered gun inside of twenty feet, but I didn't have a knife and I figured Tuco Medrano was faster than most.

There's a fine line between building rapport and being a pain in the ass, and I wanted to cross it. If I kept him on edge, the next part of my clever little plan might just succeed.

"Nice boots."

Tuco grunted an unintelligible response. They *were* nice boots, obviously handmade and lacking the gaudy attributes of most Mexican footwear. The only bling on the otherwise conservative design were understated silver toe-guards accenting the hand-rubbed black leather.

"I hope they don't get all scuffed up out here in the desert. That would be a shame." The hard leather soles and pronounced heels would be a liability if he had to move quickly in this terrain--for example, if he had to chase someone.

"My shoes will be fine. Keep moving."

I sped up for a few strides and then eased off the pace, trying to close the gap between us. It didn't work so I went back to targeted small talk, hoping to get under his skin and keep him on edge.

"So, what is your brother's name?"

"What?" an edgy reply.

"The big man--he's your brother, right? I saw the family resemblance." They looked nothing alike.

"He's not…" He cut the denial short, realizing that I knew more than I let on, then he changed tactics. "He's called Guero."

"I thought that meant 'blonde'?"

He didn't reply.

"Ahhh…" I was surprised that I made the connection so quickly. "You're Tuco, the Ugly."

Really building rapport now.

I found it ironic that the hoodlum walking behind me took his name from one of my favorite movies. But then again, I remembered that we grew up in virtually the same neighborhood. It was time to reveal more of my hand and hopefully bore deeper under his skin.

"You know, this might not be the first time we've met."

"I doubt that," he replied.

"No, it's possible. You went to Morehead, right? We're about the same age, and if you played football…"

"That's enough, Mr. Martin!"

Good rapport is such a delicate thing.

"Just tryin' to be friendly."

"We don't need to be friends."

"Good point. I saw the video of you killing that cop. *He* was your friend, right?" I prodded him and it hit a nerve.

"Cordona got what he fucking deserved," Tuco almost hissed. "Now shut up and keep walking."

"Yeah? What about the rest of the cops you massacred?"

"They knew what they signed up for."

"Even Alejandra de la Rosa?"

He stopped in his tracks near the spot where Paul broke his leg. "I didn't... She..."

The sun had warmed the small canyon considerably since our morning visit, and the unmistakable threat response of an angry western diamondback cut Tuco's reply short. Television just doesn't capture the unnerving effect of a rattlesnake doing its thing--the modified keratinous scales at the end of the snake's tail make a hell of a racket and can scare your hair straight. I expected the display, but when the snake started rattling and the canyon walls amplified the sound it startled me. My plan depended on the same reaction from Tuco and I wasn't disappointed.

When Tuco turned towards the canyon wall, looking for the rattler, I used the distraction as cover for my escape. I turned and ran towards a small fissure in the opposite wall. Just a few feet away, the opening led to an open gallery that branched into two narrow slot canyons. I explored them many times as a kid and knew they wound their way up opposite sides of the mountain.

It wasn't the perfect plan, but it gave me the only chance for escape. I promised myself that if it worked, I'd never kill another snake.

I almost made a clean getaway, but Tuco had something else in mind. Three steps from the fissure I heard the first shot and the rattling stopped. As I ducked into the gallery, I heard the second shot and something that felt like a red-hot poker attached to a baseball bat whacked me in the upper arm.

Startled and pissed-off more than hurt, I screamed a bad word and squeezed through the small crack in the canyon wall.

Chapter 68

Jake Martin had grated on Tuco's last nerve. He was a smart ass and the last thing that Tuco needed at the moment.

The man varied his pace, walked through sand instead of staying on the hard packed surfaces, but Tuco had seen right through it. He thought he was stalling the march to his own execution. Tuco couldn't blame him, but really wasn't planning to kill him. Unless, of course, he didn't cooperate.

Martin's banter evolved from small talk to personal details about Guero that bothered Tuco and set off alarms. Was Martin more than he appeared? How did he know so much? Was this a set-up?

Even the cartel didn't know about his middle school days in El Paso… And now Cordona.

Who was this man?

The accusation about Alejandra had thrown him for a complete loss. He was fumbling for a reply when the rattlesnake let loose his warning. Though he'd never heard it before, he knew exactly what the sound meant and he reacted instinctively. The last thing he needed was an unhealthy dose of injected hemotoxin.

He turned to the threat, drew his pistol and searched for the noisy snake, vaguely aware that Martin had jumped back out of his peripheral vision.

It took a couple of seconds for Tuco to find the rattler, coiled angrily next to the purple sage. The head hung above the sand at the end of an s-shaped body, the tail a black and white blur. Tuco leveled the Sig and fired a single shot. The snake's head disappeared in a puff and the body writhed--its back and belly flashing alternate shades of dark and light like a helical wind ornament at a craft fair. The unnerving rattling stopped.

Tuco turned just in time to see Martin disappear into a narrow crack in the far canyon wall. Without thinking he raised his weapon and fired.

Tuco approached the fissure cautiously. He couldn't see into the darkness and knew that a cornered man can be unpredictable and dangerous. The small spaces and limited sightlines negated the advantage afforded by his pistol.

Hanging a few feet outside the opening and moving from side to side to view as much as possible of the interior, he took a deep breath and eased into the constricted gallery. He was ready for an attack, but it never came and the small natural room was empty.

The narrow entrance wasn't much wider than a man's shoulders, but opened into a sand floored room large enough to accommodate a small car. Above his head, the walls converged to a narrow ribbon of clear blue. His breathing slowed and as his eyes adjusted to the relative darkness, Tuco saw that his shot had connected.

The bullet left a scar on the crumbly granite and blood specks surrounding the impact site told him it passed through flesh along the way. Probably a superficial wound or there would have been more blood, and seriously-hurt men don't usually scream intelligible obscenities.

Further into the chamber, the floor transitioned from sand to rock, and Tuco couldn't tell which of two small passageways Martin chose. He didn't want to round a bend in a narrow canyon and get bashed in the head with a rock. He retreated back to the arroyo and surveyed the scene.

It had been a mistake to underestimate Martin.

Tuco wanted to play this clean, but was not going to let this man stand in the way of his ultimate goal. Martin had chosen not to trust, but it was the wrong choice.

Chapter 69

A tour each in Iraq and Afghanistan, and I have to go to New Mexico to get shot. Priceless.

I sat on a ledge overlooking the narrow head of the slot canyon I used to escape Tuco Medrano. If he followed me, he would die here. I wouldn't think twice before crushing his head with a fist-sized granite rock.

He shuffled around in the main gallery, the sounds channeled by the ravine like a speaker wire, but I guess he was smart enough to stay put.

As my adrenaline level ebbed, my arm throbbed with every heartbeat. The slightest muscle movement set off a barrage of excruciating pain. I eased out of my bloody zippered sweatshirt expecting to see a gaping wound with extruded muscle and torn flesh, but the bullet had merely grazed my arm above the elbow, cauterizing a shallow gash as it went. The bleeding slowed to a seeping ooze, the flesh on either side of the crease started to swell, and it looked like I would live.

Tuco didn't seem to be following me, but I wasn't going to hang around to make sure. I stood and started along a thin ledge below the ridgeline that separated me from the main canyon. It was a faster but more precarious route to the abandoned mine.

As I inched along one of the narrowest ledges, face to the wall and arms spread like a kid hugging an elephant, Tuco's voice echoed off the rocks and I nearly lost my footing.

"That was a foolish move, Martin!"

I thought it was brilliant, except for the getting shot part.

"You should have trusted me. Now I'm going back to wait for you to bring me my money. Your friend Paul Castañeda can keep me company. You remember him, don't you? Paul Castañeda? You have one hour… Jake."

Now we were back to first names, but I still didn't trust him.

Chapter 70

Tuco discovered his brother sitting cross-legged next to Paul on the makeshift lounger having clearly forgotten the instructions to keep his distance. Everything in the temporary base camp looked like he left it, but there was something missing and he couldn't put a finger on it.

"Where's Jake?" Paul asked.

"Hopefully doing as he was told."

"I heard two gunshots."

"Yes. I winged your friend as he slipped away… where's the dog?"

"He runded away," Guero answered with a disappointed shrug.

"He bolted up the canyon when he heard the shots. What do you mean you 'winged' my friend?" Paul pressed the subject as forcefully as he could under the circumstances.

"I didn't see the dog."

"Answer me!" He tried to cover the exasperation with authority, but it didn't work.

Tuco ignored the question.

Paul gave up and changed tactics. "So… what now?"

"We wait. I gave him an hour to bring me the money." He looked at his watch. "If he doesn't come through, I have to decide where I can get the best price for you. What's your life worth, Mr. Castañeda?"

Paul sat up higher, wincing with the effort. "The question is, 'How much am I worth to Vincente Carillo?'"

What does he know of Carillo? Tuco thought. As he mentally sifted through the ramifications of the statement the silence stretched on.

Paul let him think about it.

"Your friend knows a lot about me, and I can only assume that you have something to do with that."

Tuco waited for confirmation, but it was Paul's turn to remain silent.

"Of course you do, so I guess you know that if I go back to Mexico, I am a dead man. A fucking video camera made sure of that."

"I'd say you did that to yourself."

Tuco shot a dark look at Paul that faded nearly as quickly as it appeared.

"It was worth it."

"They say he was your friend."

"He was my best friend, but turned out to be a treacherous *maricon*. He destroyed me and in the end it was all for nothing."

"Was it the girl?"

The dark look returned to Tuco's face. This man had a great source.

"What girl?"

"Don't be coy, Mr. Medrano, I know about de la Rosa."

Tuco started to tell him to go fuck himself, but instead fished out a cigarillo, fumbled with his lighter and looked at his watch. There was at least forty-five minutes left until Martin's deadline, so he lit the rough cigar and took a deep drag before starting his story. "They said she was just a rich kid with something to prove, that her daddy bought her way into the *Grupo Especial*, but it wasn't true. She pulled her weight and could hang with the best of us."

He exhaled a cloud of the acrid smoke and was lost in the memory of her. "You've never seen a more beautiful woman. She could look right through you with those eyes… like green fire." He took another slow drag before continuing.

"She didn't want anything to do with either one of us, but Ramon… Cordona… just couldn't accept that. He figured since he and I were the best and she wasn't sleeping with him, she must have been screwing me. I was in his way and had to go, so the hypocrite set me up.

"It's common among the *federales* to pick up some odd jobs here and there, and I was no exception. Nothing that crossed the line *too* far, but enough to get me in trouble if I got caught."

Disquieted by Paul's benign look, Tuco added to his explanation. "I have a brother who needs me, Mr. Castañeda, and did what I had to do. The bastard thought I was fucking a girl who wasn't interested in either one of us, so he made sure I got caught. He ruined my career and everything I had worked to build for my brother and me."

"So you chose to kill eight innocent cops just to get back at the guy who screwed you over?"

"Innocent?!" Tuco flared. "They were heading out to raid one of our meth labs, take everything they could find, and sell it to Sinaloa. No one is innocent. It was just business and we killed them to send a message."

"And what message did you send by killing the girl? 'If I can't have her, no one can'? You're no better than your friend."

The girl. Again.

"What is your obsession with her?" Tuco hissed. "You and Martin?" The answer dawned on Tuco before Paul could reply. "You? Alejandra?"

Paul shook his head slowly. "No, not me. And if I know *my* friend, you'll never see that money."

Tuco snuffed out the cigarillo and rubbed his face with both hands wearily. "You are wrong, my friend. One way or another, I will get the money… and by the way the girl is not dead. She was wounded, but I left her alive. I could never hurt Alejandra."

Chapter 71

"Blu! Come here, boy!" I said unnecessarily as he loped quickly up the trail with ears back and tail wagging.

I knelt to greet him and he bumbled into me, forepaws on my thighs and tongue swabbing my face. He hadn't brought the cavalry like Rin Tin Tin, but I was still glad to see him.

The cactus that clogged the trail and left some spines in my leather boots wasn't as kind to Blu. He yelped when I pulled one of the more deeply imbedded thorns from his shoulder, but otherwise he seemed no worse for wear.

I was tired, thirsty, and my arm hurt like hell, but buoyed by Blu's arrival, I picked up the pace to the mine less than a quarter mile up the trail. I only had forty minutes left.

The mine's entrance was well hidden, and if Tuco figured he could just get rid of us and follow the arroyo to riches, it would be a sad result for him. He'd search for days and be lucky to ever find it--but I knew what I was looking for and from this approach, the opening in the side of the mountain looked like a beauty mark on alabaster skin.

My dad had once told me the natural cave formed when a bubble of gas trapped in the Earth's rocky crust was exposed by tectonic lift and erosion. A hopeful prospector wielding a pick, shovel and a box of dynamite completed the work. He either died or gave up without finding the mother lode, but not before adding a few hundred feet of winding exploration shaft to the twenty feet of gas-bubble cave formed by mother nature.

Blu balked at the entrance and I didn't blame him. It was dark and smelled like bat droppings. Guano might make good fertilizer, but the ammoniac, moldy-sponge odor waters your eyes.

The bats live in a hidden chamber, probably another unexposed bubble in the granite that joined the main chamber via a crack in the ceiling. At dusk one evening long ago, my father and I had watched thousands of the twittering creatures pour out of the crack to fly away in a long undulating formation. My dad told me that the diminutive creatures could clear a ton or two of insects from the sky in a single night. We slept there through the night as the bats hunted by sound, returning unnoticed. The smell of all those digested insects triggered another not-so-bad memory of my father.

When Tuco had confiscated my tools of destruction he had also taken my damn flashlight, which would prove useful in a dark cave full of scorpions, black widows, rabid squirrels and relatives of the presumably dead snake in the arroyo.

I stepped into the antechamber and let my eyes adjust to the darkness. As features took shape out of the gloom, so did the memory of my father sitting across a small campfire. We had watched the bats crawl from their crack as he told me stories about Coronado, Goyathlay, William H. McCarty and Doroteo Arrango. That he knew the birth names of Geronimo, Billy the Kid and Pancho Villa always impressed me. I liked to imagine that any one of them might have used this spot at one time or another to take shelter from a cold night or his pursuers. He had a lot of good stories and I didn't realize how much I missed the way he told them with firelight dancing in his eyes. I suddenly felt small and contemptibly unforgiving. Unfortunately, I didn't have time for that touchy-feely, Oprah Winfrey bullshit so I shook it off, checked my watch and turned back to the task at hand.

Thirty minutes left.

Blu watched from the entrance while I surveyed the cave. The spherical chamber, slightly smaller than a single-car garage, was partially filled with tailings from the five by two foot exploratory shaft. Most of the rubble from the excavation lay a hundred feet below in a semi-conical pile reaching its way up the steep mountainside, but I guess the miner got lazy towards the end. The bat crack was where I remembered it, nearly obscured by soot covering the ceiling ten feet above my head.

I shouted into the entrance of the shaft to let anything with teeth know that I was coming and avoid an unpleasant encounter. No response, so I ducked into the tight passage and immediately felt the walls closing in around me.

Forget everything you think you know about mines. There're no tracks with cute little ore carts or big timbers holding the mountain at bay, just a roughly carved tunnel with barely enough room for a stooped miner carrying a bucket. I have no idea how he swung his pick in this claustrophobic space.

I opened my eyes wide to help me see into the gloom, but it didn't help. Shuffling along with my bad arm extended and my good arm over my head to keep from knocking my skull on the jagged ceiling, I felt my way down.

I've got to hand it to the old man, he chose a pretty good hiding place, maybe too good for someone without a flashlight. I had barely finished the thought when I tripped and brushed my wounded arm on the jagged rock wall.

"Ahhh! SHIT!"

Blu barked. Concerned, but not brave enough come in to help. Good dog.

Thankfully the ten million dollars broke my fall.

True to Dad's word, the money was split between two large canvas bags--military-style duffels from the feel of them. Any hope of hauling both of them out at once evaporated when I yanked on the handle of a bag and nearly gave myself a five-million-dollar hernia. My left arm was still on fire from the fall, but I somehow managed to pull one bag out of the mine and into the sun.

As suspected, the bag was an olive-green canvas Navy sea-bag. The poorly conceived bags are long and skinny, with backpack straps and an opening at one end. Perfectly designed to prevent access to your belongings and ensure that all of your uniforms got wrinkled like an old man's scrotum, sea-bags have been tormenting U.S. Sailors and Marines since 1775, but are pretty good for stashing a bunch of cash. Dad had bought them at the same army surplus store where he got the backpack I found in his closet.

As described in his video, the bag was secured with a combination cable-lock. It ran through four metal eyelets and a sturdy metal loop that held the bag closed. I rolled in my birthday, 7-2-1, opened the lock and folded back the flaps to reveal a flashlight, a tiny .380 semi-automatic pistol and a redneck car alarm protecting a vulgar pile of neatly-bundled twenty-dollar bills.

I've never seen that much money in one place, and there was another stash in the cave.

With flashlight in hand, I boldly returned to the second bag. With the exception of the gun and flashlight it was identical to the first. I thought the car alarm might come in handy, so I took it and left the bag in the dark tunnel.

I sat outside the entrance and considered my situation: I was tired and hurt, and was up against a trained killer. Fatigue got the best of me, and my mind wandered as I watched an airliner cut a swath across the clear blue sky.

I shook myself out of the trance and realized I was on a deadline. Only twenty minutes or so to get back to Paul. Unless I sprouted wings or grew a rocket nozzle out of my ass, there was little chance I'd make it in less than thirty. I hoped Paul still had all of his toes when I arrived.

I pocketed the gun and flashlight and quickly fashioned a bag out of my sweatshirt for the car alarms. Did I forget to explain the redneck car alarm?

Dad loved James Bond movies. Every time Albert Broccoli released a new 007 masterpiece, we were the first in line at the theater.   The spy gadgets in Q's lab fascinated my father; personally I liked the silhouettes of naked girls bouncing around the opening credits.

One of the movies featured an Aston Martin that exploded when a bad guy beat on its window with a rifle butt. Tap, tap, BLAMMO!--dead henchman. Of course the car was toasted in the blast so I'm not sure it was very practical, but it made for good cinema.

Dad fiddled for weeks with explosive experiments that would make today's ATF have a conniption. He mixed flash powder from firecrackers, black powder from shotgun shells and anything else he thought might burn quickly. I'm glad he didn't know about ammonium nitrate or somebody might have lost an eye.

When my mom's brother heard about the experiment, he laughed out loud and called it a redneck car alarm. Dad was offended, but the name stuck.

He never developed much of a working prototype, but he did come up with some pretty cool and innovative little explosive packages with cable-lock-and-stopwatch triggers. They look like something out of a Roadrunner cartoon but were perfect for booby-trapping a bag full of cash--or throwing like a grenade.

Thank you, James Bond.

Armed with two bombs, a gun and a flashlight, I felt like I had a fighting chance.

Chapter 72

Christa Adams sat next to her partner, wedged between two FBI Quick Response Team agents in full battle gear. She closed her eyes, took a deep breath and said a short prayer as the powerful Customs and Border Protection helicopter lifted off the tarmac at the El Paso Air Operations Center. Christa hated flying, and after her words with God she put most of her energy into keeping breakfast in her stomach.

The pilot came over the intercom: "We're forty minutes out from target's last known position." As far as Christa knew, the "target" might already be dead.

Jake still wasn't answering his phone.

A roadside party, attended by a county sheriff's deputy and two *Barrio Azteca* heavies, had been discovered late the previous night. Unless Jake had gone totally rogue, it was clear to Christa that Medrano was the host, and apparently he had the same GPS info that she did. It was also apparent that the *narcos* were on Medrano's tail, which could make the desert pretty crowded. That's why the guys in black were riding along in the helicopter-- they should have been airborne hours before, but the wheels of bureaucracy turn slowly.

Local and state law enforcement stood ready to assist, and had blocked all egress points, but they wouldn't be allowed on scene until the feds called for them.

Medrano would be a huge boon to the DEA and Christa's career. Never before had there been an opportunity to catch a high-ranking cartel member on American soil. His capture could tip the scales in the war on drugs.

As the primary investigating agent, Christa was technically in charge of the operation but knew that in the minds of the FBI Quick Response Team, she was just along for the ride. It wasn't in the testosterone jockeys' culture to take orders from a DEA money-chaser, but that wasn't going to stop her from asserting herself. This was her operation and she wasn't going to let anyone steal it from her.

She worked up the courage to look out the window. The helicopter sped west at a thousand feet, and as the ground rushed by, the dark spots of vegetation on the flesh-colored ground reminded her of razor stubble.

The helicopter lurched violently and she managed to hold down the *huevos rancheros*, but not before getting a chunky throat-full that tasted of eggs, cheese and bile.

Chapter 73

When the *Aztecas* had failed to capture the rogue enforcer and the trail went cold, Jose Luis Fratello knew that his own fate was sealed. He sat on a leather couch in his expansive living room, spinning the loaded cylinder of a nickel-plated Colt .45 revolver given to him by a shady gun dealer in Texas. It was a thank you gift for a large, illegal purchase of rifles he later learned was central to the scandal that brought down a U.S. Attorney General.

His decision was simple: tell *Don* Vicente about the failure and hope his death would be quick, or remove all doubt and end it immediately with the big .45. He had decided suicide was a coward's choice and picked up his telephone to call the *Don* when one of his lieutenants interrupted him.

A discreet, well-placed information leak to a cartel informant in the *Policia Federal* made its way quickly to the top of the Juarez Cartel. Passed from elements within the U.S. Justice Department who wanted to keep the status quo, the message breathed life into a search for Medrano that had been left for dead on a desert highway. Contrary to Tuco's fear, the cartel could not geo-track his cell phone.

"*Patron,* the *Americanos* have told us where to find Tuco."

Gracias a Dios, he thought.

***

Fratello, with a new lease on life and the prospect of suicide fading, laid out his new plan to the *Don*.

Narco operations on American soil were risky, but letting Medrano fall to the Americans would be devastating. The *Aztecas* had already demonstrated their ineptitude, so after brief consideration and with a wordless nod of his head, Vincente Carillo Fuentes, boss of the Juarez Cartel, authorized a mission to kill his former enforcer.

Fratello dialed a cell phone and issued instructions to his men waiting at a coffee shop in tiny Columbus, New Mexico.

Chapter 74

Tuco looked at his watch and it told him exactly what it had thirty seconds earlier; Jake was five minutes from the deadline and nowhere in sight.

After spilling his guts to Paul, a complete stranger, he settled into a dark, brooding silence that even Guero acknowledged by sitting against the cliff with his knees tucked into his chest like an asylum inmate in a padded room.

Despite his own bravado, Tuco knew that his future lay in the hands of Jake Martin. Under other circumstances Paul Castañeda might bring a nice ransom, but as it stood, Tuco's life expectancy in Mexico could be measured in milliseconds. Even if he presented Paul to the Sinaloas, the best he could hope for would be a death that didn't involve the slow removal of vital organs.

Jake was really his only hope. He looked at his watch again.

"Time's almost up."

"He's coming. That's pretty rough terrain, and you said you wounded him. Besides, both of us know you don't have a choice but to wait for him."

The truth of the statement angered Tuco.

Paul sensed it but pushed him anyway. "You have two problems, Mr. Medrano... you don't have the money and even if you did, you can't disappear with it. Do you think the cartel will let you get away with their money?"

"*Their* money? Carillo doesn't even know it exists! They want me dead because of Cordona. Nothing more. If you knew what that money was for, your friend would bring it to me on a silver platter."

"Guadalete?"

Tuco blanched. "What do you know of Guadalete?"

"Enough," Paul lied. "Why don't you fill it in for me?"

Tuco once again found himself in the uncomfortable position of explaining himself to this man. "Guadalete is a front organization for Al Qaeda in the Arabian Peninsula."

Paul nodded as though the information wasn't news to him.

"The ten million dollars is payment to the Sinaloa Cartel to transport ten operatives across the border from Juarez to El Paso."

"Sinaloa? But you work for the Juarez Cartel."

"Yes. I captured a Sinaloa accountant, and he volunteered the information." Paul raised his eyebrows at the word "volunteered," but Tuco ignored him and continued. "The terrorists boarded a freighter in the African port of Djibouti and sailed to Veracruz. They then made their way to Juarez where they are waiting to be smuggled across the border." He smirked derisively. "The idiots could have paid any *coyote* ten thousand pesos to get them across, but I guess they have more money than sense."

"So what happens when the money isn't paid?"

"Sinaloa has them in a safe house, and if the agreed-to sum isn't transferred, I would imagine they will be... eliminated."

"Are you sure?"

"No, but I've seen to it."

"You've *seen to it?*" Paul asked insistently.

"I've seen to it, Mr. Castañeda, and that's all you need to know. I don't condone terrorism." He looked at his watch. "Three minutes."

Paul thought about the revelation and how it filled in the blanks. Was this a *narco* with a conscience? He made a decision.

"The way I see it, Mr. Medrano, you need help to get out of this alive and with the money. I have an idea.

"Jake believes you killed Alex and you'll probably kill us, too. You need to do what he says. If you don't, he'll have a plan to make sure you don't see a penny of that cash. Follow his instructions and I can help with the rest."

"How?" Tuco played along, curious where this offer from a man *in extremis* would lead. He'd heard the same offer from countless victims of the cartel.

"I'm thirsty. May I have some more water?"

The man was stalling. "By all means. Guero, please get him some water."

Puzzlement crossed the large man's face until he remembered the bottles in the backpack. He retrieved one for Paul and squatted on his haunches to hand it to the injured man. Not particularly coordinated on a level surface, Guero lost his balance on the unstable sand and steadied himself with his free hand. On Paul's broken leg.

Paul screamed involuntarily as his leg shifted and the ragged ends of his tibia grated against each other.

Chapter 75

Tuco's imposed deadline loomed but I still needed ten minutes to put my plan in action and confront him on my own terms. I made up about five minutes, which wasn't too bad for a guy with a bum arm toting a hundred pounds worth of twenties across some pretty rough terrain. That my dad did it going uphill, twice, was really quite impressive.

I chose the longer route back because I couldn't have possibly negotiated the narrow ledge with the bulky sea-bag. At a couple of the steeper sections I just let gravity do its work on the bag and prayed it didn't burst, giving me a twenty-dollar-bill confetti shower.

Approaching the spot where I so masterfully escaped, oh yeah, and got shot, I heard Paul's scream echo up the canyon.

"You motherfucker!" I yelled in rage.

I wasn't even a minute late. The sound of my friend in obvious pain gave me the energy I needed to make the final push. I shimmied back into the crack and took the branch of the slot canyon that I bypassed during my getaway. The alternate path wasn't more than a hundred yards or so to the top, but the hundred feet of elevation gain was a real bitch. I made it to the top in five minutes and puked what was left of the protein bars into a patch of scrubby sagebrush.

Standing just below the flat top of the peak, I saw part of the dilapidated stone shack we used for our base camp. The Land Rover was hidden from sight by a rocky hill. I could see the jacked up four-wheel-drive pickup that I assumed belonged to my friend, the Mexican drug lord. I was half right.

Blu waited obediently with the money while I belly crawled the rest of the way up the peak and peered over the edge of a sheer drop to the canyon below. Less than fifty yards across the arroyo sat Tuco and his brother with their backs to me. Paul lay on his improvised lounger just where I left him. He looked calm and seemed to be talking with the brothers. Not the scene his scream led me to expect.

It was time to execute my plan.

I kept low and yelled down to the rendezvous point. "Paul! Are you alright?"

He flashed the OK sign and a thumbs-up, not what I'd expect from a torture victim. That was good for my plan.

"You're late!" Tuco yelled. "Where's the money?"

"Close by. It's not that I don't trust you, but I saw what you do to your friends, so let's just say I don't trust you." He didn't respond. "Just listen to me and we'll all get what we want."

He stood, the gun in his hand.

I continued, "Look to your right... just before that bend. There's a small side canyon that will lead you to where I'm standing now. You can't miss it.

"I'm going to take another route down while you come up. Your brother waits with Paul. Clear so far?"

"Why should I trust you?"

Paul said something I couldn't hear. It must have had an effect on Tuco. "Go on," he said.

"I'm going to leave with Paul. Your money is here in a locked bag... wait with it until you hear me blow the car's horn. The bag's rigged. If you try to open it without the combination, it'll detonate and if you're lucky enough to live through the explosion, there won't be much left for you to spend. *Capice?*" I always wanted to say that when it mattered.

"Yes."

"Before we leave, I'll leave the combo for you where you can find it."

My plan was weaker than Hitler's attack on Russia. A monkey could figure out that all he had to do was cut open the bag to bypass the device. If Tuco was lying about letting us go, we were screwed, but if he played along at least long enough to get to the money, it might be the head start we needed to get away.

He holstered his gun and started walking towards the bend. I thought about asking him to leave the weapon, but I was sure he had more than one, and probably wouldn't have agreed anyway.

Blu and I doubled back down the hill and through the slot canyon. When we finally reached Paul, he sat up and seemed okay. Guero sat off to the side and seemed more interested in Blu than anything else.

"Glad you made it back," Paul said, "I was starting to worry."

"You and me both. I heard you scream, what happened?"

"Guero over there lost his balance and used my leg to steady himself. Thought I was going to pass out again. Now it's kind of numb."

I checked his splint. The leg had swollen and cut off the circulation, which explained the numbness. He needed medical attention, and soon.

"I'm going to need to loosen your splint. It might hurt a little."

He nodded, but the look on his face told me how he really felt.

"Did you really find the money?" he asked as I hurriedly worked.

"Yes, but I only brought half. It was all I could manage, and even that was a bitch. Kinda' surprised he went for it. It's gonna take him a while to pick his way through the cactus patch between here and the top of that hill, so if we can get a move on we should have a pretty good head start."

"Nice plan. Come up with that all by yourself?"

"No, saw it on *The A-Team.*"

"Nice. What happened to your arm?"

"Bastard shot me, but it's just a crease." It still hurt, but I wasn't going to bitch about it to a man with a shattered leg.

"What's his story?" I nodded over towards Guero. Blu enjoyed a good rub behind the ears and they were both oblivious to us.

"He's harmless. Got the mind of a little kid and thinks they are going to the beach. Medrano might be giving us the straight scoop."

"Well if he's not, the odds are a little more even." I showed him the gun and little bomb. He winced as I retied the splint; I took it as remorse for his comment about my plan.

"Listen... Medrano told me he didn't kill Alex... she was alive when he left the ambush."

"What? You believe him?"

"Pretty much, yes. He seemed genuinely surprised when I asked him why he killed her... and he really doesn't have a reason to lie. He followed your instructions when all he had to do was kill us and take the money. You don't really think someone like him would be scared off by your little booby trap, do you?"

He had a good point, but I didn't dare to hope.

I turned to help Paul to his feet and had a clear view across the arroyo. Tuco emerged as he approached the sea-bag at the top of the hill. He was looking to the east with his back to us. so he couldn't see the man slinking up the canyon floor.

This newest arrival to our little party, now staring intently at Tuco, looked like he was on his way to a *quinciñera*. He was dressed in a pale yellow *guyabera* with dark polyester pants and pointy boots that they only sell in Mexico. If it weren't for the scoped M-4 rifle pointed at Tuco, I would have laughed my ass off.

Chapter 76

Christa's stomach finally settled down and she was relieved that she hadn't carpeted the helicopter with her breakfast. The pilot descended closer to the ground as they approached the Florida Mountains.

They had agreed on an insertion plan prior to takeoff. After a low approach from the east, they would scan the area with the aircraft's infrared detection system and set down at a designated landing zone. Topographic maps and satellite imagery showed a good, flat spot near Jake's last known position. If they found Jake any distance away from the landing zone, members of the QRT could drop out of the helo on fast ropes to secure the target.

"Two minutes. Ground units are rolling." The pilot's voice had a warble in it that matched the thumping rotor blades.

Each member of the team rechecked their weapons and gear, and gave the thumbs up.

The chopper lurched like an amusement park ride and a new wave of nausea washed over Christa as the aircraft climbed up into the foothills. It seemed like they were only a few inches off of the ground, following a wide ravine that would take them over a low saddle and straight to the landing zone.

She didn't notice that John Reynolds held a long barreled rifle with the confidence of an experienced sniper.

"One Minute."

Chapter 77

Things started to happen pretty quickly, and as a pilot, that's generally when I tend to excel. But, unfortunately, as a gunfighter my skills were lacking. I sat Paul back out of sight near Guero and kneeled behind a dense clump of bushes, watching the new arrival.

Tuco continued looking eastward, oblivious to the man with a rifle crouched behind a large boulder. All I could see of the guy dressed in the pastel yellow waiter's shirt was his rifle barrel pointed towards Tuco at the top of the cliff. I suddenly realized what Tuco was looking at when I heard the familiar sound of air beaten into submission by rotating blades. It was a military helicopter and probably not some bumpkin out for a ride in his really expensive toy. I hoped it was the cavalry coming to the rescue.

Either way, the most imminent threat was fifty yards away wearing an embroidered shirt. Maybe it was Stockholm Syndrome flaring up again, Paul's news about Alex, or maybe he just had a bigger gun and better chance of hitting the interloper in our little drama. But for whatever reason, I felt a strange, tenuous allegiance to Tuco. The scene reminded me of the end of Tuco's favorite movie, except we weren't in a graveyard and I'm not quite as cool as Clint Eastwood. But still, I could almost hear the iconic wail of Ennio Morricone music playing in the background.

Shooting at the new guy with the weak and inaccurate Ruger was a sure way to get shot, so I thought of something better: stand, throw the bomb, hide behind a rock and wait for the bomb to go "boom." If I were lucky, the bomb would hurt the bad guy. Otherwise, the loud noise would alert Tuco, who would shoot the distracted bad guy while I drew a bead on him with the Ruger.

Unfortunately, the plan fell apart when I threw the bomb. Blu, who lives to play fetch, caught sight of it and set out like a rocket. Time slowed as the options played out in my mind's eye: stay hidden and let my dog blow himself up, or save my dog and expose myself to the bad guy. Easy choice.

I stood and yelled "Blu, WAIT!" at the top of my lungs. "Wait" is his stop-dead command, and he froze on a dime.

The bomb continued its graceful arc and landed six feet short of the *narco*, who, alerted by my shout, leveled his rifle in our direction.

I shouted, "Blu, COME!" as the bomb exploded like a drunk New Yorker--loud and obnoxious, but with little bite.

Then, the son of a bitch shot my dog.

Chapter 78

At the crest of the hill, Tuco detected a faint, intermittent beat that broke through the wind and drone of buzzing insects. He recognized the deep bass staccato of a helicopter but the acoustics of the canyon prevented him from seeing it. They would stay low and use the mountains for concealment, so he kept his eyes on the sky to the east. The sound of the rotors grew louder and he expected to see the aircraft at any moment.

Tuco knew that the helicopter was coming for him and he was exposed on a coverless hilltop. He turned to grab the bag and duck out of sight when he saw the drama unfold in the canyon below.

Jake Martin stood and shouted something at his dog just as a flash-bang exploded. He saw the flower of light, smoke and dirt a second before the sound reached him. The pistol was in his hand in an instant and he reflexively fired three rounds at the man shooting what looked like an M-4 at Martin. The rifleman's pastel *guyabera* bloomed red with the hits, Tuco kept his gun trained on the threat and scanned the terrain for another *narco*. They never worked alone.

Guero stood behind Martin, and waved to Tuco. *Guero, get down!* Martin held something in his hand. *Is that a gun?*

He was vaguely aware of the large black helicopter looming over his shoulder, when the sniper's bullet pierced his heart.

Chapter 79

The tiny beads of condensate coalesce into a weighty drop and slide down the side of the brown bottle, cutting a swath through the crushed coral granules that coat the glass like crystal sugar on a donut. As I take a sip of the cold beer, a chunk of wet sand falls off the bottom of the bottle and lands with a plop on my sunburned chest.

"Shit," I say after swallowing the deliciously bitter IPA. I hate sand on sweaty skin.

"Don't be such a baby."

Alejandra lies on a beach lounger next to mine, sporting a rose-yellow bikini and a tan I can never hope to duplicate. She turns her head to face me and arches her brows from behind the dark glasses hiding her beautiful eyes. Her smile is mockingly sympathetic.

As has become my habit, I run my eyes over the graceful creature laying next to me, taking in the swell of her chest, flat plain of her belly and long stretch of toned legs. Her olive skin glows with the combination of sun, dewy perspiration and tanning oil; the only flaws are too much swimsuit, the angry scar of the bullet wound in her left shoulder and some barely visible powder burns on the left side of her face. The surgeons did a great job on the facial damage caused by Tuco's intentionally-missed, but far from harmless, pistol shot--the red striations have nearly faded away.

My little scratch pales in comparison to her battle trophies.

We're sitting on the beach in Key West, watching cloud shadows alter the blue shades of the Atlantic--or is it the Gulf of Mexico? I guess it doesn't really matter.

I'm done ogling Alex and look out over the water. Six months have passed since my little adventure in the desert west of El Paso.

In an ironic twist, Tuco Medrano saved my life and got killed for his effort.

***

All hell broke loose after I threw Dad's sorry excuse for a bomb. The fashion-challenged *narco* turned towards me and fired wildly. He missed me, but shot Blu in the leg. Tuco, alerted by my impotent explosion, put three bullets in the *quinciñera*-bound henchman, ruining a classic shirt and obliterating half of his face. I was grateful for the intervention, because with Blu down and yelping pitifully, I'm certain I was next. Tuco's shots were the best I've seen, more so considering the rapid delivery, fifty-yard distance and elevation difference.

While the drama unfolded, Christa Adams and her band of DEA/FBI party-boys arrived on the scene in a big black helicopter. In the ensuing confusion, someone in the chopper put a round through Tuco's chest, killing him instantly. Christa watched the best potential lead in DEA history die, sprawled across a blood-soaked green Navy sea-bag.

Within minutes the place was crawling with local cops who found another *narco* lurking around with a rifle, but that one wasn't wearing a snazzy shirt.

When Adams and her sprightly young partner found me, a couple of paramedics had hauled Paul off to the helicopter, and I was doing my best to keep Blu from bleeding out in the sand. The high-powered .223 round missed his body and any vital organs, but his rear leg was a tortured, bloody mess and he whimpered as I tried to stanch the flow. I thought he was a goner.

"Your friend is stable and we have him in the chopper. It's time to go," Adams said.

"I'm not leaving my dog," I glared at her.

"I don't expect you to. There's a kit in the helicopter, bring him and let's go!"

Paul lay on the floor of the aircraft, strapped to a stretcher and clearly under the influence of some pretty strong drugs. He smiled dreamily and gave me a half-assed thumbs-up. A burly man with a kind face dressed in black fatigues gently took Blu from my arms and went to work on his bleeding leg. All I could do was pray and hope he knew a little bit about veterinary medicine.

Guero Medrano sat handcuffed and hunched over on a jump seat more suited for a man half his size. He looked fearful and alone, more like a child than a man. The sight of my injured dog seemed to deflate the big man further.

I realized that he had very little concept of what was going on and felt bad for him.

As we lifted off and pulled away, I saw some FBI guys—based on the big yellow letters on their backs--making their way to the top of the small hill where Tuco was still sprawled face-up on top of the sea-bag full of cash that had cost him his life. His arms were spread in a gesture that looked like supplication. I glanced at his brother, grateful that the scene wasn't visible from his side of the helicopter.

I turned to Christa and shouted across the noisy cabin, "Seven-twenty-one!"

She cocked her head.

"The combo that disarms the bag!" I yelled and pointed out the open door. "You might want to let those guys know before they lose a few fingers!"

She shouted into her radio as I leaned back against the bulkhead and closed my eyes. Relief washed over me like melted butter.

***

My beer is empty and I'm watching a three-legged Blue Heeler stand knee deep in the foamy water, snapping at the incoming waves like a joyful, blithering idiot. His jumping days are over, but he can still track down and catch a Frisbee with the best of them.

***

Paul and Blu eventually recovered, but sadly each donated a leg to the cause. Blu's was shattered beyond repair by the bullet, and Paul's was lost to an infection two months into the ordeal. The doctors couldn't explain it, but sometimes the unthinkable happens, even to guys with lots of money.

For my part, I survived the seemingly endless interrogation, but thanks to Christa Adams, came out of the inquisition smelling like the perfume section of an airport duty-free shop. I got to keep my father's assets and was awarded a ten percent finder's fee for the terrorist money.

With the cash and a robust carwash business to keep me stuffed with beer and Pop-tarts, I turned my back on the dream and resigned my position at Tex-Mex Air. I really miss flying those puking-drunk college kids.

It was Paul's intelligence director who had confirmed the news about Alex. During a visit to Paul's in-house recovery suite, Sylvia Mora handed me a blue folder labeled "Alejandra de la Rosa." It was filled with pictures of the ambush scene, including a very alive Alex being loaded into an ambulance. The folder also had an info sheet on the hospital where she recovered under heavy security. Elated, I kissed Sylvia right on the lips.

Sylvia, with the help of Christa Adams, helped me get the credentials I needed to enter the *Hospital Angeles*. It is the most modern and advanced hospital in Juarez, and if I had to guess, probably not the default choice for public servants. Alex's family connections certainly played a part in the special care she received.

With all of the action over the preceding days, I was never more anxious than when I stood in front of the door to her hospital room. She was asleep when I arrived, and despite the best efforts of the medical staff to get rid of me, I sat for two hours and waited for her to wake. Every imaginable scenario danced through my head while I sat watching her nap, but they all boiled down to one simple question: Would she even care that I was there?

When her eyes opened and found me through the fog of sleep, she smiled and said, "I dreamt you were here."

I couldn't speak past the lump in my throat.

***

After Paul and Blu were stabilized and I had a good night's sleep, Christa Adams and her partner Bill or Tom or whatever his name was drove me back to the Florida Mountains to help me lay my father to rest. On the way, we stopped at Wal-Mart to buy an urn, because he deserved better than a cardboard box.

Okay, it wasn't Wal-Mart.

Dad was right where I forgot him before starting out on our trek up the canyon, sitting on the front seat of Paul's Land Rover.

Christa graciously transferred his remains to the urn, which she placed gently in a backpack.

"Jake, look at this." It was John--his name was John--and he held up the empty box.

"It's how we, and Tuco, found you," said Christa pointing to a small black plastic square taped to the interior wall of the box.

"Ronald Mitchell must have placed it there to track you to the money and I'm quite sure he sent Katy after you for good measure," she explained.

"You mean it wasn't my charm?"

She ignored the comment and dropped a bomb, "Katy was murdered the day you headed out here. Two men matching the Medranos' descriptions were seen at her apartment building. She worked for me. Actually, she's the one who turned me onto your dad."

I let that sink in and we started the walk up the canyon to scatter my dad's ashes. John stayed behind.

"There's a couple of things I wanted to talk to you about," she started hesitantly.

"Yeah? What's up?"

"Did you let anyone else know where you were going?"

"No, just Paul and I."

"That's what I thought. How well do you know Paul?"

"We grew up together. He's helped me through some tough times. I consider him one of my best friends. What are you suggesting?" I said it with a conviction I really didn't feel.

"Nothing, just curious. Someone leaked your location to the cartel… that's the only explanation for your party crashers. I have to explore all possibilities, including some within my own organization. Just between you and me, there are a lot of folks out there, and not just the *narcos,* who wanted Tuco dead."

I thought about that for a minute, "You know, I don't think he was going to kill us, in fact, he saved my life. Maybe you should start with the guy who shot him."

She pursed her lips in a strained expression and looked over her shoulder, back down the canyon at John. "I know."

That involuntary turn of her head said it all.

In case you were wondering, I was a team player and told her about the second sea-bag. It just wasn't worth hauling that frigging thing down the mountain. Yeah, I don't buy that line of crap either, and as it turned out they knew it was ten million. Not that I didn't think about it, but life would be too complicated if I was always looking over my shoulder.

Speaking of looking over my shoulder, the terrorists were never found. Paul told the Feds about what Tuco revealed to him in the desert, and according to his sources, the authorities were able to verify some of the details, but the trail went cold in Juarez.

The idea that terrorists might be at large just across the border has cost me more than a few sleepless nights.

***

It was much warmer than the day Paul and I had set out to find Dad's treasure, and we were sweat soaked when we reached the summit above the old mine. This was Dad's favorite spot. From the summit you could see Texas to the East, Mexico south, Arizona west and the Black Range of the Gila Wilderness to the north. An Indian summer thunderstorm billowed white and majestic over the Juarez Mountains.

He loved the stark beauty of the desert and the history that it held, and despite my best effort, I loved it too.

Christa stayed behind a respectable distance and I stood alone with my father, a steady wind moaning quietly as it passed over the rocky peak. I gently unscrewed the urn's lid, said a short prayer and set my father on the wind. As his ashes poured out in an expanding, swirling cloud, with them flowed the last of the animosity that I had harbored for years. In that moment, I forgave my dad and only wished that I had done it sooner.

As the last of him disappeared on the breeze, a peace settled on me and I knew that he knew.

***

After she was released from the hospital, Alex took a leave of absence from the *Policia Federal*. We had a lot of emotional, and, uh, physical catching up to do, so I hired a man to run my car washes. Paul recommended him, and rumors abound that his assistant is a large Hispanic man of limited intelligence who has an affinity for dogs and an unlikely benefactor in the form of the richest man in El Paso.

We left El Paso and the three of us made our way around the country, convalescing. Well, Blu and Alex convalesced. Once the scab fell off of my arm, I was pretty much good to go.

And yes, I felt a little emasculated by that.

Alex was still driven by the need to make a difference in Mexico, and the more I tried to talk her out of that and into a life of luxury, lived half-naked on a beach, the more she resisted. Fortunately, her notoriety as the only survivor of the "*Avenida Norzagaray* Massacre" gave her all the credibility she needed to move out of the kinetic and into the political war on Mexican corruption.

She set my mind at ease about what that means for our relationship during a romantic dinner overlooking Monterey Bay. She looked across the candle lit table with the flames dancing in her green eyes and said, "No matter where I fight my battle, I won't do it without you again."

That's good enough for me.

***

The corruption has always been and will always be there, so for now, her battle can wait. For a while, at least, we are going to sit on this beach, drink our sweaty beers, and I'll do my best not to think too much about what we are going to do later.

Epilogue

Sergeant Jorge Montoya of the *Policia Federal Grupo Especial* owed his daughter's life to Tuco Medrano.

On a cold winter night, Sinaloa *narcos* had taken her from their home. The best Montoya could hope for was a life of sexual slavery for the pretty sixteen-year-old, the worst was a gruesome death sent as a message to any policemen audacious enough to do their job against the cartel. Tuco had saved her from both.

The former *federale*, after an impassioned plea from Montoya, used his network of informers to locate the girl. His *La Linea* death squad left the three Sinaloa kidnappers swimming in pools of their own blood. The girl had been raped, but was otherwise unhurt. As a favor to Montoya, Tuco made sure the leader died slowly and that he knew how it felt to be violated before he breathed his last.

Tuco had been a good cop and Montoya hated to see him brought down by Cordona's treachery, but when he delivered Cordona to Tuco in repayment for saving his daughter, he wasn't expecting the loss of the others in the convoy ambush. Montoya was despondent over the death of his team members, many of whom he'd known as rookies. As he neared the bottom and considered suicide, Tuco threw him a lifeline, a chance to atone.

Two nights after Tuco's last telephone call from the desert, and just one night after Tuco met his own end in New Mexico's

Florida Mountains, Montoya sat geared up in the lead vehicle. It was his first field mission in over three years, but he felt confident, and wouldn't have missed it for the world.

The target was weak and unfortified, and the plan to take it uncomplicated. Two unmarked SUVs stopped a half block from the address Tuco specified in his call, and disgorged ten heavily armed *federales* from the *Grupo Especial*. They continued on foot, concealed by the darkness of early morning, and surrounded the single-story cinder block structure.

Montoya crossed himself, praying that Tuco's intel was solid. On his signal, they cut power to the house and detonated small explosive charges placed on the front and back doors. They breached the two-room house with guns blazing. There would be no prisoners.

When the shooting stopped, ten young men of Middle Eastern descent lay dead with multiple gunshots to the head and chest. Most were hit before they knew what was happening, and not one shot was fired in self-defense. Amongst their belongings was a single handgun and over four hundred pounds of military-grade plastic explosives.

The cops loaded themselves, their gear and the C-4 into the SUVs and returned to the station. They dropped Montoya at his house along the way. With his debt to Tuco Medrano paid in full, curled close to his plump wife, he slept like a baby for the first time in years.

The ten dead terrorists, who looked Mexican enough, were written off as just another death- squad atrocity in a city numb to the violence.

THE END

Acknowledgments

Borderland, at various stages, has been seen by many and improved by all. Deck Deckert kept me honest and my writing is better for it. Alison Dasho was the first to objectively view my effort, and the hardest on my ego. After much lamenting and gnashing of teeth, tequila was indeed the answer and I eventually took her recommendations to heart, and believe the flow is more intense and my characters stronger for it. I look forward to working with both of them on future projects.

To all of my first readers--my brother Ryan, Darrell & Teri Davis, and Brenda Harbison--thank you for the sharp eyes and great suggestions. I am grateful for the kind words and encouragement, and apologize if the book dominated any conversations.

It takes commitment to read a work in progress, but sheer determination to read it more than once. Especially when the fate of your favorite character doesn't change. Sorry, Stacy, but he had to go. I appreciate your thoughtful comments and wise counsel. Your compassion and perspective have helped shape the story.

Sean Murphy also read *Borderland* more than once, and at a level of detail that would rival any professional editor. His command of grammar is second to none, and he kept me from looking like an illiterate monkey. Thank you for your dedication, dependable friendship, and sage guidance.

And of course there's Mom--my tireless champion and biggest fan--who's loved every crayon-and-paste-glob creation I've ever brought home; and Dad for putting up with both of us.

No one has borne the burden of a new writer's schizophrenic ramblings with more grace and class than my optimistic wife and partner, Jodi. She is my sounding board, coach, cheerleader, marketing guru and creative advisor, and has invested as much time, effort and emotion in this work as I. Could never have done it without you, Hon.

About the Author

Raised in El Paso, Texas, Scott Feuille (pronounced "fuel") uses pen name Anson Scott. An international pilot for a major U.S. airline and a 20-year Reserve Naval Aviator, he recently returned from a year in the Horn of Africa, serving the Global War on Terror. Both of his grandfathers, (one was the President and Publisher of the El Paso Times newspaper and the other was one of the first television news anchormen in El Paso) were published authors. Scott is a former Board Chairman of the Boys & Girls Clubs of North Central Texas and an avid supporter of the Wounded Warrior Project. When he is not writing, he enjoys scuba diving, playing hockey, making furniture and fine jewelry, collecting wine and traveling with his wife, Jodi. His debut novel, Borderland, is the first in a planned series of Jake Martin adventures.

You can find him on Facebook.com/BorderlandNovel, and at his web site, www.borderlandnovel.com